THE ELF KING'S LADY
QUEENMAKERS SAGA V

BY
BERNADETTE ROWLEY

ACKNOWLEDGEMENTS

To Louise Cusack for her inspiration and advice
over the last ten years.

To my street team who are always there to support me.

To my husband, Michael, and my sons for their unending love and
support and for sharing in the disappointments and triumphs
of a writing life.

TITLES BY
BERNADETTE ROWLEY

(in suggested reading order)

DEDICATION

Dedicated to my husband, Michael.

TABLE OF CONTENTS

CHAPTER 1

LADY Alique Zorba ground the dried leaves into powder with more than her usual enthusiasm, her hands clammy despite the early spring day.

"Stupid man," she said, "perfectly suitable woman right under his nose and he chooses some vagabond from the wilds!" Of course, that vagabond was easily the most beautiful creature Alique had ever seen. Even she would admit that, though not to the woman in question.

She paused in the grinding, shaking her head. How was she to convince Nikolas Cosara he had made a mistake? That Merielle "no-name" wasn't the woman for him? That only Alique could make him happy? He was probably with Merielle right now. Her gut burned to think of Nikolas with *her*. She returned to the mortar and pestle, adding another herb to the mix.

A sharp knock sounded at the door to the chambers.

"Doctor Mosard," a deep voice enquired, "I wonder if you could spare a moment of your time?"

Alique closed her eyes, barely suppressing a groan. She knew that voice. It belonged to one of her least favored acquaintances, General Kain Jazara, leader of the Wildecoast Army and thorn in her side.

She composed her features and turned to the door. "The doctor is in the herb garden, General."

Jazara bowed. He looked good, fit and strong, his charcoal gray uniform molding the hard muscles of his shoulders and thighs, his dark hair just long enough to cover the tops of his ears. A pretty picture he might make, but his arrogance made Alique grind her teeth.

"Lady Alique, I'm sorry to disturb you. I'll leave you to your work."

"A minute, General." She must act as soon as possible and Kain was Nikolas's best friend.

The general stopped before the open door and turned back to her. "Lady?" he said, eyebrow raised.

Oh, he really doesn't want to be in my company any longer than necessary.

"I'm loath to mention this, but I'd never forgive myself if I didn't and something was to happen."

"Go on." His impatience was palpable.

"I speak of Lord Cosara and his liaison with that redhead. She's not suitable for him and I fear he's making a terrible mistake that he and the kingdom will regret. What do any of us know of her?"

Kain had gone very still. "I admit I'm concerned about Niko, but he's a big boy and can make his own decisions."

"But she's a nobody. We don't even know her last name!"

Kain closed the door and entered further into the room. "I'm sure the queen will have her say in the matter. Lady Merielle will be investigated and if she is found wanting, Her Majesty will step in."

"If," Alique muttered. "The woman is clearly hiding something; anyone can see it."

"This means a lot to you, My Lady."

Alique frowned, discomforted at revealing so much of herself. "I had long thought Nikolas and I were suited, but he has never looked twice at me."

"That must sting," Kain said.

"I know what you think of me," she said, "but Nikolas needs a wife and I happen to believe I am more suitable than a beautiful tramp with no background."

"Calm yourself, Lady Alique," Kain said. "I agree this union is a concern and that you would be eminently suitable. I've even expressed that to Niko."

Alique gasped, never expecting the general would have spoken up for her. "Really? What was his response?"

"He told me to butt out, or words to that effect."

Alique lowered her eyes, lest Kain see how desperate she had become, how disappointed she was. "Oh."

His fingers lifted her chin gently so he could look into her eyes. "Never fear. I'll talk to him and see if I can convince him he's making a huge mistake."

"You will?" She should have been offended that Kain Jazara's fingers still rested on her skin, but she couldn't think straight.

"I will." He released her chin, bowed and walked to the door. "I'll let you know how I go."

And he was gone, just like that! Alique placed her fingers where Kain's had been and shivered. She took a deep breath to quiet her hammering heart and restore some composure. It was just the shock of being touched by a commoner. It had nothing to do with the handsome and virile man who had left her work chamber seconds before.

* * *

Kain's steps took him away from Lady Alique in more of a hurry than usual. She got under his skin far too easily.

But she was right - Lady Merielle wasn't a suitable wife for Nikolas, the queen's cousin and admiral of the King's Navy. The woman, who had turned up on Niko's doorstep and taken advantage of his protection, worried Kain. He wanted to know more about her but there appeared to be no more to know. He huffed out a breath. As if he didn't have enough to ponder over with dark elves threatening.

Little was known of the *Lenweri*. The last uprising had been almost twenty years before when the king's brother, Jiseve, had pushed them back into their mountain stronghold. Now Jiseve was dead and the *Lenweri* were pushing closer and closer to the towns and cities of Thorius.

If that weren't enough, Prince Jiseve's death, and the disappearance of his daughter Alecia, had thrown the succession into question. And

King Beniel wasn't coping with the loss of his brother, heaping added responsibility onto the queen and onto Kain.

Kain was a fighting man and didn't relish these political intrigues the nobility concerned themselves with. It was one of the reasons he loved Nikolas. He was a man of the people and not your usual lord. But a marriage to Alique would have strengthened the queen's side of the throne. It didn't make sense for Niko to disregard the kingdom in his choice of a wife. Kain would tell him that, but whether Niko would listen was another matter.

* * *

Lady Alique strolled the drafty hallways of the castle on her way to attend Queen Adriana. Today she would have to mention her medical studies and her need to have more time with Doctor Mosard. She was falling behind in her learning, staying up half the night to read the tomes the doctor kept sending her.

A week had gone by and she hadn't seen or heard anything from Kain Jazara. She knew he was absent and hoped he had been to visit Nikolas. Alique had been on tenterhooks all week, waiting to hear from her unlikely ally. She tried not to get her hopes up, but an alliance with Nikolas would make many things easier. It would keep the queen and her parents happy; after all, the monarch had agreed that Nikolas would be lucky to attract such a wife. Alique had everything going for her: youth, intelligence, beauty, and breeding.

She was so engrossed in her thoughts of a royal marriage, she failed to see the man coming toward her.

"Lady Alique," General Jazara said, bowing and stopping in front of her.

"General." Alique swallowed sudden nerves. "Do you have news?"

Kain looked to the side. "I suggest we find somewhere more private to talk. Any suggestions?"

Alique nodded and led the way down the hall into a small sitting room used for visiting guests. Kain followed, closing the door. His dark eyes ran over her body and she shivered.

"Your news, General?"

"I've just returned from the Cosara estates. It was good to see Niko, although his lady was in residence."

"They're living together already?"

Kain snorted. "She has nowhere else to go." He strode across the room, his hand rubbing the back of his neck.

Alique's heart warmed further that Kain worried so for his friend. "You discussed the lady in question with him?"

"I did." He spun to face her. "Damn it, he's so smitten. I never thought to see it. Niko has never been like this in all the years I've known him."

Alique's stomach tightened and tears threatened. *So much riding on this and all for nothing.* But she couldn't let Kain see her pain. She cleared her throat and took a deep breath.

"Thank you for trying, General. It was a hopeless cause from the start. I should have seen that."

His eyes snapped to hers. "You've accepted this news better than I could have hoped."

Alique's chin came up. "I know when I'm beaten."

He frowned. "So, you're giving up?"

"What do you advise I should do? Go to his estate and plead with him to reconsider?" Alique sat in a nearby chair and smoothed her skirts. "Do you think that would have any effect?" If she concentrated on her breathing, perhaps she would get through this meeting without embarrassing herself.

"No, it would only annoy him," Kain Jazara said. "He's under her spell and there's no reasoning with him."

"Then I must move on and forget I ever had any desire to join my life with his."

"You can do that? Just *decide* to move on?"

"There is nothing easy about this, General, but I try not to waste my time on hopeless causes. Thank you for your help. That will be all."

Kain stared at her as if he couldn't believe his ears, then bowed and left, his back stiff and hands clenched.

What did he expect? That she'd throw herself on the ground and weep? Or ride out and plead her case directly to Nikolas? Alique had her pride, and if Nikolas was too stupid to see that Merielle was unsuitable, then she would sit back and watch him reap the consequences. And be smug when disaster followed. The trouble was, smugness wouldn't comfort her on the lonely nights.

* * *

Kain didn't know what to make of Alique Zorba. She never acted as he anticipated. He had expected her to be distraught, vocal, angry… but not that quiet acceptance of her failure. It was a pity there was no hope for the union. Nikolas needed a decent wife, one who was used to court life. Alique Zorba was the perfect combination of beauty and breeding - a woman who understood the demands placed on those close to the throne. Instead he appeared to have chosen Merielle, a beautiful woman sure enough, but one who would never make the grade.

He felt a pang of guilt at the thought. He should be supporting Nikolas, not waiting for him to fail. Merielle had been good for him so far, bringing him back to a normal life, but Kain still didn't trust her. She had no past and it made him suspicious. All Kain could do was keep an eye on the mysterious redhead and be there to pick up the pieces when she made her move.

CHAPTER 2

THE next day after luncheon, Alique attended Queen Adriana, along with a handful of ladies, in the royal sitting room. She set to mending one of her gowns, but her mind was only half on the task. Just as well it was all she needed to complete the fine crimson stitches in the hem.

Try as she might, she couldn't get Nikolas Cosara out of her head. It didn't help that some of the ladies wouldn't stop gossiping about Merielle.

Alique ground her teeth as another lady speculated about where Merielle had come from. Wildecoast castle was rife with gossip at the best of times, but when one of its most eligible bachelors succumbed to a mysterious woman with no past, it was bound to be one of the favorite topics.

"What news of Princess Benae and your brother, Ramón, the new stewards of Brightcastle, Alique?" Lady Emmella asked. Alique could have hugged her. Emmella was her closest friend amongst the queen's ladies, and the question was clearly designed to take the topic away from Nikolas.

She smiled at her friend. "Thank you for asking, Emmella. I heard only yesterday that Ramón is recovering from the chest wound he sustained defending the king and Princess Benae from the assassins at Prince Jiseve's funeral. Benae nursed him herself. She's quite gifted in that regard."

"The rumor is Princess Benae is pregnant," Lady Diseta said. Diseta was the oldest of the queen's ladies and it was thought she'd never marry. She trained the ladies and Alique believed her fair, if very strict.

"And the prince died in the marital bed, in the act." The youngest lady, a blonde called Krina, fixed her wide blue gaze on Alique. "How appallingly embarrassing!"

Alique ground her teeth. "It is tragic, Krina, and I would thank you to remember a man is dead." She turned to Diseta. "Benae is indeed with child. If it's a son, he'll be next in line to the throne of Thorius. Ramón and Benae will administer Brightcastle until the babe comes of age."

"How cozy," Krina said. "I remember rumors of impropriety between those two when they visited. Now they will run the principality. It seems Sir Ramón and Princess Benae have benefited handsomely from Prince Zialni's death."

Alique glared at the young lady and opened her mouth to deny the charge but was cut off by the queen.

"That is gossip I will not allow, Krina!" Queen Adriana snapped. "Honestly girl, sometimes I wonder about your mouth. Go and supervise the servants dusting my room, and when they are finished, I will have another chore for you."

Krina looked horrified as she stood, curtsied and left the room.

"I apologize," Adriana said, turning to Alique.

Diseta spoke before Alique could. "Your Majesty, I'm sorry my latest charge cannot guard her tongue. I'll take her aside for special training."

"I trust it will not happen again," the queen said. "Now, let us have some of the special tea my dear husband brought back from Brightcastle town."

Adriana rang the bell for the servant and Alique went back to her hem, trying to dispel nerves that made her hand tremble. She didn't know what upset her most – the shock of Krina's veiled accusation or remembering how close her brother had come to death without her knowing. If she had lost Ramón... Well, she didn't even want to think of it. Their last words had been less than adequate: her teasing him about his feelings for Benae and him snapping back in defense. It had been poor behavior on her part, and she regretted it.

Thinking that those words might have been the last they ever exchanged made her reflect on her status in the court of Wildecoast. She didn't wish to be an idle lady, manufacturing gossip to keep herself amused. Even if Ramón and Benae had… It didn't matter what they had done. The king had blessed Ramón's stewardship of Brightcastle and even knighted him. Her brother would help Benae with the day to day running of the principality for as long as he was needed.

She came back to the moment to find a messenger whispering to Adriana. The queen's eyes widened, and she blanched, glancing over at Alique.

What now?

"You are excused," the queen said to the messenger. She turned to Alique. "I have just been brought news that your family farm has been seized by bandits."

Alique sprang to her feet. "My mother and father?"

"It is unknown who is at risk, but I assure you help is being assembled as we speak. The messenger came to me from General Jazara."

Alique curtsied to the queen. "I must go, Your Majesty. Please excuse me." Without waiting for permission, Alique hurried from the room.

* * *

Kain Jazara strapped his bed roll to the back of the saddle and stowed his provisions in the saddle bags. After a quick check of his sword and knives, he turned his attention to his men. Fifty should be enough. He had no information about the force that held the Zorba estates, but he could send for reinforcements if needed.

Kain's eye fell on a striking blonde woman in a dark green velvet riding habit, and he groaned. *Alique Zorba, the last person I need.*

He bowed to her as she stalked up to him.

"Is it true, General? My family? Held hostage?"

"I can't confirm anything until I investigate, Lady Alique," Kain said, "but that's the word I have. One of your workers was released in order that he could let the king know of the hostage situation. I have questioned him and believe he tells the truth."

"Who was it?"

"A laborer called Dolf."

"He is trustworthy and solid." Alique clutched her upper arms, nails white. Her blue eyes pierced him. "Did he say who was there? My parents? Goddess! My sister takes the boys out to visit this time every week. She is heavy with child…"

"Lady Alique," Kain said, "I know this must be distressing news but I'm sure the situation can be resolved. I'll get word to you as soon as I know what has occurred."

"Don't try to reassure me, General. We both know how this could end."

"I'm not underestimating the situation, if you're concerned about my judgement." Kain clenched his teeth to stop the angry words spilling out. Of all people to be involved in this, Alique was the last he wished to deal with.

"I'm coming with you," she said.

"Out of the question, My Lady." The thought of Alique amid negotiations with armed bandits was almost enough to send a shiver up his spine. *Almost.* Thank the Goddess he wasn't that easily troubled.

She gathered herself and stood to full height, which was average at best, but those eyes could cut stone at fifty paces. "This is my family, and I won't sit here safe while they're under threat. Make me promise whatever you like, but I *am* going with you."

Kain stared at her but she met his gaze unflinching, something not many could do. He raised and discarded several arguments in his head, but in the end came up with nothing.

"What does the queen say to this?"

"I doubt she knows, but I also doubt she could stop me, short of a royal decree. Adriana understands how I feel about my family."

"You'll only get in the way," he said.

"Then I'll try to stay *out* of the way," Alique said. "I have healing skills which might be of use."

Kain examined the stubborn set of her delectable mouth and knew he was wasting precious time. "You may accompany us but stay back. I'll detail a guard to watch over you and you must stay with them. We'll be out overnight." He turned to a nearby soldier and ordered the man to pack a tent and a few other items he thought Alique might need. "Do you have a medical kit, My Lady?"

"Packed on my horse, General. I'm ready to leave when you are."

Alique's black mare was brought from the stable and held for her to mount. Kain almost groaned out loud when he realized she'd be riding side saddle. No chance of pushing the pace then. Perhaps he could take a group ahead and allow her to follow with her guard. Already the woman was giving him a gut ache.

He let out a long sigh. "Mount up and move out. Darin, take nine men and guard the lady." With those orders he trotted his horse across the stable yard and through the palace gates.

* * *

Alique and her guard were one hundred paces behind Kain and his men. From her position amongst the soldiers, she could just make out the general's gray uniform atop his prancing black stallion. At least he had impeccable taste in horses, but the man was an arrogant ass. To think he had tried to stop her checking on her own family. And now he refused to ride with her?

Each time Alique tried to pick up the pace, the soldiers with her crowded her mare, Ebony, and she had to pull back. None of them seemed to respond to her glares. They had their orders.

As the afternoon wore on, the wind freshened and Alique pulled her cloak around her – a serviceable cloak she had used when checking stock on the family farm. It was a deep forest green and unlikely to draw attention. She couldn't be faulted there.

Two hours into the ride, Kain called a halt and Alique's party caught up. Kain had dismounted and talked in hushed tones with his second in command, a nondescript, stocky sergeant called Jer Blas.

Alique pushed her way into their conversation. Kain glared at her but held his tongue.

"What do you plan?" she asked.

Kain cleared his throat. "We need to be closer yet before we decide on tactics. How far would you say we are from the estate now, My Lady?"

Alique looked around at the countryside. "An hour or a little more, perhaps," she said. "Forest borders the northern edge of the farmland. It's a possible vantage point from where we can formulate a plan."

Kain studied her, his eyes narrowed. "Yes, that would work, as long as the bandits aren't holed up in those very woods."

"It's a risk we must take, General," Sergeant Blas said.

"I don't like this," Kain said, as if talking to himself. "I wish I knew who they are and where they came from."

"And what they want!" Alique's nerves were raw. What if she lost them all?

"We'll know soon enough, My Lady." Blas turned to Kain. "Mount up, General?"

"Mount up," Kain ordered.

Alique hurried to Ebony and mounted, kicking her out from the pack of soldiers and joining Kain. She would not be left behind again.

* * *

Kain tried to ignore Alique as they trotted toward the Zorba estate; a difficult task with her riding right beside him. After the first few miles, he gave up trying to convince her to drop back and detailed a dozen men to ride in front of them. She scowled at that, but said nothing. She'd soon find out she couldn't have her way in all things. Unfortunately, she was getting her way far too often.

Lady Alique Zorba wasn't a woman who had been said "no" to often enough. Kain knew the type, having two younger sisters who were very similar and equally as spoilt. His sisters, however, had not the advantage of being beautiful blonde noblewomen. Alique was used to being the center of attention, and her months spent as lady-in-waiting, and with Doctor Mosard, had done nothing to change her high opinion of herself.

Not that she didn't deserve to hold herself in high regard… *Goddess!* Why was he talking like this in his head? He had important matters to deal with, and the least of his concerns should be the alluring young woman who rode beside him.

Kain turned his attention to the countryside they were riding through. It was open farmland, the lifeblood of Wildecoast, along with the fishing industry. They passed all types of farms, from dairy through to beef and pork, cereal crops and fruit trees. Most farms had a mixture to spread their earnings and risk, and consisted of several small holdings under one local lord who oversaw the entire operation.

He noticed Alique's knuckles white on her reins. "What sort of farms make up your estate, My Lady?" Perhaps that would distract her.

She frowned. "Similar to the other mixed farms, but larger," she said. "Also, we breed horses for the army, which you would already know. And we have a sizable lumber business, leasing the woods I spoke of earlier."

"Ah, yes, my father uses timber from your farm. He says it's the equal of any in the kingdom."

Alique smiled. "Not as good as that from further north and west, I think. I didn't know your papa was a carpenter."

"He's a master carpenter. His business is in the town and thriving, so much so that he's too busy, and wanting myself and my brother to help him out."

"But you don't wish to?"

"It's not that, so much. I'd do almost anything for Father, but giving up my whole life? It's too much to ask."

"The army is that important to you? You don't seem that content, if you don't mind me commenting."

Kain flicked his gaze across to Alique, stunned at her perception when she knew him so little and seemed to like him even less. "The army is a compromise, a way I can work with horses."

"Ah, so that's what you love, what *stirs* you?"

He'd achieved his goal, to distract her from the job ahead, but at what cost? Kain unclenched his jaw with difficulty. He didn't wish to expose too much of himself, especially to Alique, who was merely an acquaintance.

"Never mind, General," she said. "If you don't wish to tell me of your dreams and desires, you need not."

The way she said *desires* stirred him. She was just being flirty, but the reaction of his body was disturbing and unexpected. Perhaps if he treated her as he would his youngest sister, it would put everything between them on a safer footing?

Before he could reply though, Alique changed the subject. "The stallion you ride is beautiful. I know he's not one of ours. From where did he come?"

Kain cleared his throat. "A horse trader from up north sold him to me last year. Snow was a mean one when I first acquired him, but he's coming around with a lot of patience. Still likes to get a nip in if I'm not careful."

"Snow?" Alique's azure eyes were puzzled. "That's his name?"

Kain shrugged. "I thought it was original at the time. He's almost been more trouble than he's worth, but I saw something in him that day, and he has pulled me out of the fire on more than one occasion. Fearless he is."

Alique ran an appraising eye over the coal-black horse. "Deep of chest and strong of leg," she said. "Looks like he'd have endurance and speed. A good prospect for breeding."

Kain opened his mouth and snapped it shut. Oh, she was good, this woman. Worming in under his guard with her observations and questions. It'd be difficult to stay one step ahead of her. "You should know."

"Ah," she said, "non-committal. Let me know if you ever decide you want Snow to become a daddy. I'm sure Papa would jump at the chance to have him at stud for a season." Her eyes clouded and she looked ahead and pointed. "That smudge there is the forest to the north of the Zorba estates. Another half hour and we'll be there."

CHAPTER 3

ALIQUE, Kain and the soldiers reached the Zorba estate in less than half an hour. They gathered under the trees after ascertaining no bandits lurked there. Alique led them to a small clearing she and her brother and sisters had played in as children. It was large enough for a dozen soldiers and their horses, and the rest of the men spread out through the trees to keep watch for the enemy.

Alique dismounted, trying to peer through the trees to the estate house, but seeing nothing. Kain squatted to draw in the dirt with a stick, and she looked over his left shoulder.

"We're here," he said, scribbling in the dirt. "The manor house is here, the stables behind the house, the staff quarters here." He looked up at Alique. "Correct?"

She nodded, impressed. It appeared he had done his research.

Kain looked back at his dirt map. "Dolf told me there is a lane that runs south of the house and winds its way past thirteen other estate properties." Kain drew the road in and handed the stick to Alique. "Can you sketch in the properties, My Lady?"

She frowned as she completed the task, including the locations of the buildings on each farm. It wasn't easy to remember it all but when she had finished, she was happy with her dirt map.

Kain raised one dark brow. "Very good, My Lady, most comprehensive." He gathered his men. "Have a look at this map. This is the area of our search. As you can see, the task is a large one, or potentially so. We'll work methodically through all these buildings, beginning with the manor house."

A thought occurred to Alique. "Why didn't Dolf come back with you?"

Kain's eyes dropped. "He was in no fit state. The bandits beat him before they sent him off. I think they wished to give us the message they were serious. They certainly did that."

Alique's heart lurched at his words. That her family could be exposed to barbarians who would harm a gentle man like Dolf! "Will he heal?"

Kain stood, still not meeting her gaze. "He was badly shaken, his fingers broken, and his face so misshapen he could only see from one eye. He passed out soon after bearing his message."

"Will he be well?" she said, teeth clenched.

"Honestly, I don't know."

He barked out a few orders and the soldiers broke into five groups of ten men so they could search all the buildings of the home farm simultaneously.

"Where do you want me?" Alique asked.

"You stay with me. I wouldn't like to have to explain to the queen if you were injured."

"Perhaps I can take care of myself?"

"How? I don't see any weapons." His hard gaze ran over her and Alique felt summarily dismissed.

How dare he? Well, he didn't have to know about the five knives hidden about her person. She could defend herself if any bandit was stupid enough to lay hands on her. She wasn't bad at knife throwing either. Perhaps not a skill most ladies possessed but her father had insisted his children all learned basic self-defense. And they had practiced it on each other growing up. Many were the nights one or the other of them had lain with cuts and bruises, or worse. Mama had patched them up and said not a word. Oh yes, Alique could defend herself if needed.

"Let's see what we're dealing with," she said, and pushed her horse toward the trail that led to the homestead. Behind her, Kain growled. Let him! He'd discover she wasn't just a fine lady who sat at home and allowed others to do the dirty work. She didn't examine the reason she needed to prove herself to Kain. He was insufferable and had to be put in his place, that was all.

A trio of soldiers passed her, and she found herself beside Kain again, with the remainder behind. Two groups had been sent into the homestead via the front entrance, and the other two would beat their way through the forest and come at the buildings from the back. Her group would enter the clearing after the first two groups had approached the homestead and completed an initial inspection. That way if there was immediate hostility, not all the force would be engaged.

They reached the edge of the sheltering forest and drew up within the cover of the trees, waiting. Alique's horse fidgeted, sensing her impatience to get moving; to discover the fate of her family. She calmed her features, hoping her heart would follow suit, and glanced across to Kain.

Alique had heard great things of Kain Jazara and so far, she couldn't fault his tactics. The men respected him, and he was obviously a supreme horseman. He was rumored to be a master swordsman and almost as good with a horse bow. It was even said he had an uncanny knack of anticipating the enemy. But now, as he sat his horse, he seemed focused inward, as though he were listening. His preoccupation unsettled her. What was wrong with the man?

The thought only served to make her tense and so she practiced deep breathing to steady her nerves. All would be well; she would make it so. The Zorbas had already borne more than their fair share of grief, with her older sister Elinor, Ramón's twin, dying in childbirth four years past. And they had gone so close to losing Ramón himself just a matter of weeks ago. Alique still felt a pang of dread that she might never have seen her big brother again. When they were reunited, she would set about healing the hurts she had inflicted by being self-centered and mischievous. Ramón had always been her best friend and she had never recognized it until she almost lost him.

The twenty soldiers appeared under the leadership of Sergeant Blas and formed up in front of the homestead in ranks of five abreast, with the sergeant in the center of the front row. Alique could see the other two units circling around the back through the outbuildings. It appeared they had broken up into bands of five men and were conducting a quick check to ascertain if anyone was present.

Sergeant Blas dismounted and drew his sword, four men following his lead. They approached the front door, some of the other fifteen soldiers leading their horses around the sides of the mansion and peering into windows. Blas sent three men through the front door, but all was quiet inside. Alique tried not to dwell on what it might mean.

"Let's go," Kain said, and pushed his horse forward. She followed, happy to be moving at last.

They pulled up at the house and Kain dismounted. "Stay here."

Alique didn't think her jaw could be any tighter and despite her urgency to see her folks, she nodded.

He wasn't long. "They've been in the house. Furniture is tipped over and breakfast interrupted. No blood, but signs of a struggle." He mounted his horse and they turned their attention to the outbuildings.

Alique nodded. "I knew it couldn't be that simple."

The twenty men who had searched the outbuildings were now strung out amongst the stables, cottages and plow sheds, keeping watch on the paddocks.

Corporal Darin approached. "No one inside the stable from what we can see, General, but we need to enter to be sure. The worker cottage has been checked."

Kain turned to Alique. "Stay here," he said.

He dismounted and walked toward the stable entrance as if his word would be followed. She dismounted and followed him, with some of the soldiers. He was still distracted, for he didn't notice her dogging his steps.

The odor of the stable assailed her and calm descended. This had been her favorite place when she lived on the farm, and she had spent many a day in her troubled teens up in the loft, breathing in the soft scent of the hay and listening to the gentle snorts of the horses.

All was quiet today, too quiet. There were no sounds of horses, and at least some of the breeding stallions, and the work and riding horses, should have been stabled here. The hairs stood up on Alique's neck. She hurried forward to mention the horses to Kain, but he had already placed his hand on the ladder that led to the loft.

Alique heard a soft click followed by a sharp cracking and hurled herself forward against Kain, shoving him aside as the loft and dozens of bales of hay came crashing down. Alique grunted, the air knocked out of her chest, but soon she was coughing, her eyes smarting at the dust. The soldiers made quick work of shifting the avalanche of hay and pulling her to her feet.

"Thank you, soldier," she said, dusting her dress off. Her face and hair must look a mess, but better that than Kain buried under the loft timbers. She looked for him and saw him unmoving, his face white.

"Something is amiss!" Alique felt underneath his head and her hand came away red with blood. "He must have smacked his head as he fell," she said. "Fetch clean water."

She sat on the stable floor amongst the hay and debris from the loft, and laid Kain's head in her lap. She could now see the small cut and swelling behind his right ear. It wasn't deep but concussion could be serious. Some she had treated never awoke.

Her hands shook as she held a handkerchief to Kain's head. She had been trying to save him, knowing a split second before the loft fell that danger was imminent. But now she had caused a possible fatal injury.

Kain groaned and his eyes fluttered, his throat convulsing in a swallow.

"Where is the water?" she asked again

Someone handed her a cup of cool water from the spring and she moistened the handkerchief and laid it against Kain's head.

"Ahh," he said and swallowed again. "What happened?"

"You can't remember, General?" Alique asked. It wouldn't be a bad thing if he didn't recall who had shoved him to the ground. "You fell and hit your head."

There was a quiet laugh from one of the soldiers.

Alique bristled. "This is not a laughing matter," she said. "A blow to the skull can be a serious injury."

"They laugh because they know my skull is the hardest part of me," Kain said weakly. "Lucky it was my head that took the worst of the blow." He attempted to get up.

"Stay where you are." She was able to keep him prone with light force on his shoulders.

"We've lost too much time already," he said.

Alique looked at Sergeant Blas and raised her brows. "Do you think the men could finish the check of the outbuildings, Sergeant? Let me know if you find anything unusual. And check the tracks, I want to know where all the horses are."

"Lady, those are my men you're ordering around," Kain growled, squinting his eyes in pain.

"I can help your headache at least," she said, shifting out from under him and placing a square of hay as a pillow. She stood and fetched her medicine bag from Ebony, along with her water skin.

Alique mixed two powders into a cup of water and added honey, for she knew Kain would complain about the bitter mixture. It was one of her trademarks that she liked to make her medicines palatable, and carrying honey was the easiest way to do so.

Alique gave the cup to Kain. "Drink it all." She looked around the stable as he complied.

"That wasn't as bad as I expected," he said, handing the cup back. "Somehow I thought any medicine you brewed for me would taste so bad it would be impossible to swallow."

"And what good would that be?" she asked. "Men are as finicky as children when it comes to medicine."

Kain grinned, which was the last thing she expected.

"You did this to me, didn't you?" he asked.

Alique stood. "I don't know what you mean. The loft ladder was rigged to collapse." She frowned at him. "See if you can sit up while I pack away these medicines. We should be on our way."

While she fiddled with the ties on her medicine bag and strapped it back onto Ebony's saddle, the men gathered at the front of the stable.

"The place is deserted, Lady Zorba," Sergeant Blas said. "Darin scouted around and found the footprints of horses and men, at least a couple dozen each, heading up the road." He pointed to the road that ran through the estate. "The footprints aren't booted, but nor are they bare. They appear to have been made by a soft-soled shoe."

Alique puzzled over that last remark as Kain walked slowly from the stable. "*Lenweri*," he said. "Dark elves. They clad their feet in soft leather. Dolf suggested it was the elves who were responsible, but I doubted him until now."

"But why?" Alique asked. "Why this estate? What do they hope to gain?"

"As to that," Kain said, "I can't say, but we've had increased activity in recent months." He looked at Alique. "Apart from this stable, which of the other buildings are large enough to accommodate all the people on this estate?"

Alique blinked. Dark elves, her family held hostage, and Kain injured. This day wasn't the best she had seen recently. She knew exactly where the elves would be. "The hay shed."

CHAPTER 4

KAIN'S head throbbed but he'd not allow Alique to know of it or she'd find a way to leave him under a tree somewhere. His vision was no longer double, and the herbs had made the ache ease. All he needed now was a good long sleep. He'd found himself dozing in the saddle on their trek down the farm road. Perhaps Alique would be right to plant him under a tree.

The sun was going down and the breeze had picked up. Kain drew his cloak around him a little tighter and noticed Alique do the same. She didn't complain. He was beginning to respect her toughness; strength she had no doubt picked up living on this land. Perhaps she was different to his sisters after all. He couldn't see them facing this challenge with quite the bravery Alique brought to it. In fact, she might be the one woman he knew who could have done what she did today, except for his mother, of course.

He spied a large shed in the middle of a field to his left and called a halt. "Lady Alique, I assume that building over there is the hay shed?"

She stared at the structure as if it held all the answers to her problems; as if she could see right through the walls. "Yes."

"It'll be dark soon," Kain said. "We'll wait here, and when the sun sets, Darin and Atan can scout around the building and report back." The men nodded and dismounted, pulling their rations from their saddle bags.

The rest alighted and made themselves comfortable as best they could. They tethered the horses to the trees that lined the road. The beasts would be comfortable for the night if need be; they'd been watered an hour ago. Kain gazed at the building in the fading light. There was no movement. What if it was empty and the elves and their hostages had moved on? *Not likely.* They wanted a confrontation; no point them running from it. But what did they hope to gain?

Kain found Alique seated on an old tree trunk and joined her. She nodded at him as he sat down. They ate in silence for a time.

"How is your head?" she asked.

"Not wonderful but I'm dealing with it."

"Is the ache getting worse? Do you have double vision, nausea?"

"I had both immediately after, but they've settled. I'll be fine with some rest."

Alique nodded. "What do you know of the elves, General?"

Kain frowned. "Not enough, I'm afraid. They call themselves the *Lenweri* and come from the rugged mountain forests to the north. Their skin is dark, and they're tall and slim with pointed ears. Their fighting strengths are with the knife and short bow. The elves are stealthy and fight well in the forest. You'll remember Brightcastle lost a group of soldiers to them, month before last."

Alique nodded. "Of course, my brother Ramón and Princess Benae were the only survivors."

Kain frowned. So much had happened in the last two months. With the kingdom in such turmoil, it wasn't difficult to see why the *Lenweri* would choose this time to attack. "Before that ambush, the dark elven activity had been restricted to the areas west and north of Brightcastle."

Alique remained silent for a time. "What's your plan?"

"I'll send the scouts in and confirm who we're dealing with. Then we'll determine the best time to strike."

"Surely the best time is as soon as possible?" She rubbed her arms through her cloak.

"The best time is when I say so," Kain said. "You'll have to trust me on that."

Alique nodded. "Very well."

Kain bit his tongue, tempted to explain her opinion didn't matter; that he was in charge and she would do as she was told. His head throbbed too much to bother arguing with her. He chewed his bread and cheese and contemplated the strange feeling that had come over him in the forest earlier.

As he rode through the trees toward the homestead, whispers and visions had started. At first, he'd tried to ignore them, but they had become more insistent. The voices had been just that at the start, the words unintelligible. As he listened longer and harder, he'd been able to understand some of it. The same word had been repeated over and over. *Lenweri. Lenweri.*

Kain still had no inkling where the whispers had come from. He'd tried closing his eyes but that had led to the visions: dark men with pointed ears creeping through the forest, the very forest they'd been riding through. He didn't know how, but he was certain of this.

"Are you well, General?" Alique's voice intruded and he dragged himself from the memory.

"Just thinking," he said.

"Try to get some rest while you can." She handed him a cup.

"More potions?"

"Only a pain tonic. I want you fit when we rescue my family."

"Lady—"

She held her hand up. "Don't say it. I know what grave danger they're in. Don't ask me to be realistic about their chances."

Kain nodded. There would be time enough for realism later.

* * *

Alique sat in the dark, wrapped in her own thoughts, trying not to imagine what her parents were going through. She hoped her sister and nephews hadn't visited the estate that morning. She might appear to be in control of her fears but Alique held her nerve by a thread. Her mother had always said it helped no one to go all to pieces, so that was what she focused on. Lady Zorba senior would be holding the hostages together, keeping them calm. Alique must do the same.

General Jazara dosed against a nearby tree. She could just make out his dark outline and hear his soft snores. In a way she wished she hadn't spoken to him today. The more she learned, the more difficult she found it to dislike him, and there was no room in her life for *this* man. But her eyes followed him of their own accord, and she tuned into his voice whenever he spoke. He was careful too, not speaking unless it was wise. Alique would swear he had wanted to put her in her place several times today and had held his tongue.

But her embryonic interest in him must stop now. They could never mean anything to each other – she a lady destined for a good marriage or perhaps a life of service, and he a common-born soldier, albeit the top soldier in Wildecoast. No, it could never be, and General Jazara wouldn't consider her for a moment. He barely tolerated her. But he did try to accommodate her, and for that she was grateful.

A branch moved nearby and Alique jumped. Darin and Atan appeared out of the dark.

The general's voice floated out of the darkness. "What do you have to report?"

Darin glanced toward Alique but spoke to his superior. "There are dozens of hostages, mainly farmers, but I think I saw Lady Zorba as well."

Atan carried on. "We got real close. They've moved the hay bales to create cover and have the breeding stallions crammed into a couple of small stalls. Some of the hostages are asleep while others are clearly distressed. Some are wearing bandages."

Alique stood. "Is my sister there? She is heavy with child and has three small boys."

Atan frowned. "I did see a pregnant woman. I think she might be birthing the babe. Lady Zorba was holding her hand."

Alique couldn't suppress the groan that escaped her. Poor Nyon! And what of Mama? She had already lost one daughter in childbirth. What she must be going through! "I must get in there!"

Kain appeared beside her. "Calm yourself, Lady Alique. It will help no one to go on an ill-planned rescue mission."

She knew he was right, but she was on the edge of panic thinking of her family, let alone Nyon and her mama dealing with such an emergency. "We can't afford to wait,!"

"This I know," Kain said. "I don't suppose there's any chance of leaving you here?"

Alique glared at him.

"I didn't think so." He turned to the men. "We'll split again into five groups, that way at least some of us might be successful." He looked at Darin. "How many elves hold the hostages?"

"It's hard to say, General, you can't get a good look at them. I saw about a dozen." Darin looked to Atan and raised his brows.

"I saw five on guard at the back and another five at the side."

"That's half our number," Kain said, frowning. "We should assume they at least match our force. I'd be happier knowing what they want. We might be able to predict how they'll react then."

Alique's hands clenched her skirts. "What can I do?"

Kain turned to her. "You'll come with my group." He included the men in his instructions. "My men will be one of two groups on horseback. Three groups will surround the barn on foot. Jer, your men can come in from the north. Darin, you guide a group in from the east, and Atan, the same from the west. We'll approach from the south overtly and hopefully they'll think that's the sum of our force. Osar, your men will wait in reserve on horseback, so you can get to us quickly if needed. Stay out of sight. I'll sound the horn when we need you." He looked around the group. "Move out."

Alique marched to Ebony and mounted, gazing to where the barn stood in the concealing darkness. "We're coming, Mama."

Alique's nerves stretched taut as their group moved closer to the barn. Dim lights shone through cracks but there were few windows. They looped around so they could approach from the south, not too careful of the noise they made. Their aim was to draw attention. More light was visible from this side, with two windows emitting a feeble glow. Alique shuddered at the thought of Nyon trying to birth her babe in a barn in the dirt and dark, frightened enough of the situation, let alone trying to save her child.

She squinted in the dim light and made out shapes moving. A shout rang out. They had been seen.

"Halt." A voice floated from the night, ahead of a tall dark man whose flashing white teeth were all the detail she could see. "What is your purpose here?" The accent was strange, the tone musical.

"That's rich," Kain said. "You've seized citizens of the kingdom and held them hostage. You've injured a man and sent him as messenger. Surely you expected us sooner or later?"

"Who are you?" another voice asked. A second elf moved to stand with the first.

Kain got down from Snow and stepped forward. Alique stayed in the saddle.

"I desire to know your name first, elf," he said. "You're a trespasser on this land. State your name and your purpose."

"You think you can deal with us like this?" the first elf said. "You think you have more rights to this land than our people?"

Kain remained silent and the second elf spoke up, his hand on the arm of the first.

"Peace, Celri, I will offer this man my name and see what he makes of it."

Alique longed to see the expression in the second elf's eyes, to read his intent. All this was taking too long!

The second elf stepped forward. "I am Niel Gorin, prince among my people and leader of this band of the *Lenweri*. Our purpose should be easily guessed. We are here to claim land that is rightly ours. I have heard of the Thorian King's fearless battle leader. Is that you?"

"I am General Kain Jazara of the King's Army," Kain said, his voice tight.

Alique's teeth pressed into her bottom lip with the effort of not speaking. It would not help.

"Jazara," Gorin said. "Yes, that is the name I was told. I give you notice, General. One wrong move and the captives die. So, if you have any men waiting in the dark, make sure they stay there."

Alique threw herself off Ebony and strode forward. "Touch a hair on their heads and you will have the king to answer to."

Gorin smirked and the other elf, Celri, laughed outright. Gorin addressed Kain. "A fearless she-cat is this one. Is she yours, General?"

Alique snarled, outrage making her careless. There was a knife in her hand before she knew she had reached for it.

"Hold!" Gorin snapped, but seven arrows were still raised against them. "That would not be wise, Lady. We hold your loved ones. This will not persuade us to release them. Drop the knife."

Alique felt the tension in the air as the arrows wavered and Kain's arm rose in front of her. She glared at Gorin, her hand tensing and relaxing on the handle of the knife. She could do this! Kain and his men would back her up. And then she came to her senses. She would never make it. Those arrows were real – Alique could almost feel them pierce her skin. She shuddered and the knife fell from her hand. Kain visibly relaxed beside her.

"This will be on our terms, General. I send this notice to your king and all the rulers in the kingdom of Thorius. This land once belonged to the *Lenweri* and we will be its masters again. We have come down out of the mountains where we were pushed in years past, and we will assert our rightful place."

"I don't understand, Prince Gorin," Kain said. "Why take hostages?"

"We wanted also to meet you and hoped this would lure you from your refuge."

Kain stepped closer to the elven prince and Gorin gasped, waving his archers forward. "It must be him!"

Kain was suddenly surrounded by elves who pushed Alique aside. The soldiers pressed forward on their horses.

"Stop!" Kain shouted. "Stand down, men. I won't have a massacre on my hands." He turned to the elves. "You had better tell me what just happened, because I'm confused."

"We search for you, traitor!" Gorin snapped. "We had heard the leader of the kingdom invaders was a half-breed and now we know the rumors are true."

Kain shook his head. "Have you taken leave of your senses? Why do you call me traitor?"

"Can it be you do not know?" Gorin studied him.

Kain struggled in the grip of his captors and Snow stamped his foot. Another elf emerged from the dark to take the horse's reins and the beast aimed a vicious bite at him. Alique privately applauded the horse's good sense.

"Your elven heritage is clear for all to see, kingdom man," Gorin said, walking closer to Kain. "I would give much to know your story."

Alique's heart beat so loudly she thought all might hear it. Kain a dark elf? Had she heard correctly? She studied him – dark hair and eyes, swarthy skin, lithe, almost graceful body. He could be part elven…

Kain stared at Gorin, appearing shocked beyond speech. The soldiers muttered amongst themselves, perhaps too far away to hear what caused the fuss.

"General?" Alique spoke in a whisper so the soldiers wouldn't hear. "Have you nothing to say to this accusation?"

* * *

Kain's mind had frozen at the accusing words. *Traitor.* He rejected the label absolutely. He was no traitor and he had no elven heritage. He looked at Alique, to find her studying him, eyes narrowed, wondering if it could be true. His men looked confused but not angry. Could it be they hadn't heard? He hoped so.

"It's not true," he said to Alique. He turned to Gorin. "The elven prince speaks a lie."

"We will sort out the matter of your parentage later." Alique turned to Gorin. "What do you intend?"

"Lady, I cannot pass up the opportunity to have this man" – he gestured to Kain – "in the palm of my hand. I do not intend to let him go."

Gorin turned to his elves. "Bring them all inside, brothers."

The soldiers were made to dismount and escorted inside by more elves who appeared from the darkness. There was no sign of any of the other men who surrounded the barn. Kain hoped, with no signal to call them, they would keep their distance. His head buzzed with questions brought on by Gorin's accusation. He couldn't be elven, could he?

They were ushered into the warm and dusty barn, past two stables where the stallions bit and squealed at each other in the close confines. Groups of estate farmers clustered in rooms partitioned by hay bales, each with two elves standing guard. The eyes of the hostages varied from scared in the women and children to resentful in the young men and elders. Some called to Alique as she passed and she murmured words of comfort, though she must have been frantic with worry.

Finally, they came to the last section where more elves and the Zorba family were housed. Alique launched herself toward a woman lying propped up in a corner, obviously in labor. Her sister, with her mother beside her, Kain assumed. Three small boys latched onto Alique's skirt, tears making tracks down their grubby faces. She tried to settle them, but they wouldn't let her go. Kain gently disengaged them and drew them to the side as Alique joined her sister and mother.

"Mama, Nyon," she said, "I'm here now and I won't let them hurt you." She turned to Kain. "This is General Kain Jazara of the Wildecoast army."

"Fear not, Lady Zorba," Kain said. "I'll see you out of this mess."

Gorin laughed, muttered some instructions to Celri and left them.

Alique's mother didn't look reassured by his words so Kain turned his attention back to the boys. The oldest was very blonde, much like Alique, but the other two, twins by the look, were darker. All were scared witless. He introduced himself and set to asking them about their lives in the hope he could distract them. He also watched Alique, whom he found more and more intriguing. She had so many facets. The last thing he had expected was for her to draw that knife. She looked like she knew how to use it too.

"Mama," she said, "where do things stand with Nyon. Is she in labor?"

Lady Zorba closed her eyes and clutched at Alique's hands, nodding. "Nyon's distress is prolonging things. Her waters broke many hours ago and this is her fourth. It should come quickly, but it is not."

"Where is father?" Alique asked.

"I don't know," Lady Zorba said, her voice breaking. "They took him out soon after we were moved here. I haven't seen him since."

"Never mind," Alique said, "we must concentrate on getting Nyon through this. The babe is lying correctly?"

Lady Zorba appeared to pull her thoughts back from her husband to her daughter. "Yes, yes, I cannot understand why the child is not here. Please, Alique, it cannot happen again. You must not let it happen again."

Now Alique was here, Lady Zorba appeared to collapse in upon herself, allowing the grief and worry to overcome her.

Kain got up and went to Celri. "Please go and find two women to help here."

"And why would I do that, traitor?"

Kain felt the label like a physical blow but this couldn't be about him, not now. "Do you wish for this unborn child's death to be on your hands?"

Celri snarled but stalked off down the corridor and was soon back with two women. One moved straight to Alique's side and helped Lady Zorba to her feet, amid objections from the older woman.

"I am fine, Raila," Lady Zorba said. "Nyon needs me."

"You're exhausted, My Lady," Raila said. "Alique will take over and will send for you if she needs help."

Alique looked up and nodded at her mother and Raila. "Go, Mama, all will be well. Jonena will help me."

Lady Zorba slumped in Raila's arms and was led away with her three grandchildren. The other woman, Jonena, knelt beside Alique who murmured soothingly to her sister. Alique looked up and smiled at Kain then went back to work. Kain settled back for a long wait, trying not to dwell on his personal revelations but to make plans for their escape.

From what Gorin had said, they had walked right into a trap. This had been a fishing trip and Kain had landed in the net. But they were wrong about his heritage. He was Thorian, through and through.

As Alique mixed a potion and Jonena massaged Nyon's shoulders, Kain reviewed what he knew. A fifth of his force was here in this barn, along with around thirty elves and the whole population of the Zorba estate. He didn't know where the rest of his men were; hopefully somewhere out in the dark waiting to launch a rescue.

Nyon cried out and Alique moved to examine her.

"I can see the head!" She threw Nyon's skirts back and Kain looked away. "I need you, General!"

"Me? I've never delivered a baby." His heart fluttered with more panic than he'd ever felt in a fight.

But Alique wouldn't be denied. "Wash your hands in that pail and prepare to help me should I need it."

When a woman spoke like that, no man would dare refuse. Kain soon knelt at Nyon's feet, close enough to see the baby's head amongst her womanly flesh. Nyon cried again and Kain nearly followed her. The head bulged out and slipped back again as the contraction passed. Kain's gaze was now riveted to the birth canal and the baby's head. He swallowed emotion and steeled himself to help.

Alique pulled back her overskirt to reveal her petticoats and ripped a large section away, laying it between Nyon's legs. "One more big push and the head will be through," she said. "You've done this before, Nyon, and you can do it one more time. Next contraction must be the most forceful yet. Push until you can't endure anymore." She looked up and nodded at Jonena who levered Nyon into a sitting position.

Kain was amazed by Alique's calm in the face of her sister's pain, not to mention the drama of the surrounding events. With the next contraction, Nyon screamed. Kain wanted to look away but he couldn't, as the baby's head pushed and pushed, then popped into the world. Nyon slumped against Jonena and Alique wiped a shaking hand across her brow.

"Good girl, Nyon, the head is free. Rest now and you'll be ready for the final stage." She looked across at Kain and frowned. "Are you well, General?"

He shook his head. "No, I mean yes. I never saw anything like it."

Alique smiled. "It's new life and precious." She turned back as Nyon groaned. "One more push!"

In a gush of fluids, the babe slid free of the birth canal and into her hands. The little face was pale, the skin all wrinkled, and the child was still.

Alique immediately swung the baby by its feet and slapped it on the bottom, then laid it over her knees, face down, and massaged the back. She rolled the child over and Kain realized it was a girl. Alique bent to breathe life into the tiny nose and mouth – two or three quick breaths, followed by another swing by the feet. Fluid trickled from the tiny blue lips and a loud cry followed. The chest heaved and Alique clutched her niece to her breast, eyes closed, tears leaking from the corners.

She stayed thus for several long breaths as all in the room reveled in the sound of new life. Then Alique opened her eyes and looked at Kain, and he saw the depth of her fear and relief shining in her stunning eyes.

"Good work, My Lady," he said, placing a hand on her shoulder.

She smiled and lay the babe on Jonena's shawl, then wrapped her up and handed her to her mother.

Nyon was crying too. "My dear sweet babe." She looked to Alique. "Did I see a girl, Ali?"

"You did, Sister. Finally, you have a daughter."

"I cannot thank you enough for being here," Nyon said. "I will never be able to repay you."

"That's what families are for." Alique smiled, her hand on Nyon's belly. "Once I deliver the afterbirth, I'll leave you be. Place the babe on the breast. It will help with the next stage."

Nyon did as she was told and Kain watched the rosebud mouth latch onto the nipple.

"How much you have learned, Ali." Nyon's attention was distracted watching her daughter feed.

Kain stood and walked to the corner of the enclosure. Celri had witnessed the whole birth and still gazed at mother and daughter.

The two men locked eyes.

"A touching scene, half-breed. Now the brat is delivered, we can put the rest of our plan into action." He rubbed his hands together. "Our band will be well rewarded for delivering you to the lord and master."

"I'm not going anywhere with you," Kain said.

"You will, or these folk will pay the price. The prince wishes to strike a deal."

"What deal?"

"Your life for your people." Celri's eyes turned cunning. "You have a force of forty men surrounding this barn. We hold the upper hand while inside, but once we leave, we are vulnerable. The prince suggests you negotiate for the release of the hostages. Tell your men to stand down and allow us to leave with you and we will ensure the safety of these people."

"You won't get far."

The elf grinned. "The lady here will accompany us. I'm sure that will guarantee us some breathing space."

Alique's eyes met Kain's. He couldn't risk her life on a mission like this, but did he have a choice?

He began to pace back and forth across the small space. Eventually his men would attack, resulting in casualties on both sides, perhaps even children. The men he had passed looked angry enough to try to force their way out. If Kain could avoid a fight, they had achieved what they came out here for: the release of the hostages.

He tried to puzzle out the elven plan. Was he really so valuable to them? Rather, they *thought* he was valuable, but they were mistaken.

Alique joined him. "We must do it," she whispered. "It's the answer to my prayers. I don't care what they do to me, but I must have my family safe."

"Lady, I don't think you understand what we'll face."

"I don't care. Have you taken a moment to imagine what will happen if your force tries to storm this place with all the children here?"

Kain glared at her. "Of course, I have, but there must be another way other than to go meekly with them."

"Go meekly, and we'll escape later."

He shook his head. "They'll expect that. We'll be guarded closer than the Queen's Jewels."

Alique's eyes hardened. "It's still better than all these hostages. Goddess, Kain, there are only two of us!"

Kain nodded. "You're right, as much as I hate to admit it."

Alique crossed her arms over her breasts. "Does it gall you so much?"

"Hang on! I didn't mean that." He grasped her elbows. "This isn't exactly an ideal outcome. Think what the gossipmongers will say; that the great Kain Jazara allowed himself to be captured along with the queen's lady-in-waiting."

"Your ego will recover." Alique smirked, and despite the dust and dirt, Kain thought she had never looked so beautiful.

He started at the thought. She could not mean more to him than a thorn in his side. They were on different paths, from different worlds. As much as he was coming to respect her, that was where it had to stop.

He cleared his throat and turned from her. "Elf, get your prince!"

CHAPTER 5

ALIQUE wasn't as brave as she tried to appear. The thought of going with her elven captors struck fear into her heart. As she waited for the elven prince, Gorin, to appear, she tried to distract herself with her new niece.

"What will you name her, Nyon?" Alique asked, crouching to run her hand over the drying fuzz on the baby's scalp.

Nyon's tired eyes met hers. "Something that echoes the difficulty we had this night. Or perhaps after you?" Nyon smiled. "You were truly amazing. All those years of your silly games… I never imagined you could perform such an important role as you did this day."

Alique didn't like the backhanded compliment but smiled anyway. "You know I would do anything for you and yours. Rest now. Soon this will all be over, and you can return to your husband with your family. Won't he be astonished to see his daughter?"

"He'll be beside himself with worry is what he'll be," Nyon said. "It's a wonder he's not here already."

Prince Gorin approached, with Celri in tow. Alique joined them.

"Are you ready to negotiate, General?" Gorin asked, folding his arms across his chest.

Kain cleared his throat. "Take myself and the lady here wherever you desire but leave the rest to return to their homes."

Alique held her breath, hoping her family would be spared.

Gorin's eyebrows rose. "That was an easy capitulation. I accept your offer, but be warned, my men will be vigilant. There will be no chance of escape."

Lady Zorba approached from behind. "Please, you cannot take Alique. You must see how we depend on her." She wrung her hands.

Alique's heart broke for her mother. "Mama do not fear. I'll come to no harm."

Prince Gorin laughed. "You should not make promises, My Lady." His gaze was sharp with amusement and something harder. "When we leave here, you will be under our control, subject to our law." He looked at Kain. "Your men had better not follow, General, or I will not be responsible for my actions or those of the brethren."

Lady Zorba slumped at his words and Alique put her arms around the older woman. "Don't worry, Mama. Here, meet your first granddaughter." As Alique had hoped, the sight of her first female grandchild had Lady Zorba riveted. Alique helped her mother down beside Nyon and tucked her shawl around the frail shoulders. She tried not to dwell on the aging that had come upon her mother in the last twenty-four hours.

"You will give instructions to the men who came with you," Gorin was saying to Kain. "Tell them to pass the word that we are leaving with two hostages and are not to be followed. We will take the stallions as well. They will make fine sires for our new breed of mount."

Celri stepped close to Alique and gripped her arm. "Come, Lady."

"Don't I get a moment to say goodbye to my family?" she asked, turning to Nyon and Lady Zorba.

"Do not push your luck," he said. "Come!"

Alique cast her mother a last look and allowed herself to be led away down the aisle behind Kain and the prince. "Papa!" she said, throwing herself into her father's arms when she saw him standing before the outer doors.

Yaral Zorba seemed to have withered too, and the elves holding his arms made it impossible for him to return Alique's hug.

"Here's my little flower," he said. "You are foolish for coming."

Alique released him and brushed the tears from her cheeks. "How could I stay in Wildecoast when I knew you and Mama were in trouble?"

"Look where it has got you!"

"I don't care, Papa." Was he truly angry with her for coming to the rescue? How could she have done otherwise? "I heard what happened to Dolf and I had to come."

"How is Nyon?"

"She has birthed a strong daughter, Papa. So, you see, I was needed." Why was it she always sought approval? Wasn't she old enough to make her own way in the world without concern for the sanctions of others, even her parents?

Lord Zorba nodded. "And your mother?"

"Tired, Papa, but well."

Celri pulled Alique away from her father and ushered her outside to her horse. "Mount."

She did as she was told and sat, drawing deep breaths until her racing heart slowed. Kain spoke quietly to his men before watching them mount and ride away. His eyes sought hers. She couldn't detect an ounce of fear.

"Mount up, General," Prince Gorin said. He sat his horse awkwardly as if unused to riding. Alique filed the small observation away for future use.

The four stallions, two blacks and two bays, were led by elves on horseback. They were fractious in the cool morning air, the dew slippery under their hoofs. The elves leading them soon realized they would have to be kept apart to prevent chaos on the trek. Alique took a last look at her father as he was shoved back inside the barn and the door closed. *Is that the last I will see of him?* She remonstrated with herself for being gloomy. If she and Kain were not resourceful enough to extricate themselves from this mess... well, it wasn't an option to fail. She *would* see her family again.

Kain and Alique rode away from the barn, surrounded by thirty elves, heading north-west toward the forest. When they reached the trees, Alique looked back one last time and spotted a figure on a horse charging after them. At first, she thought it might be one of their soldiers come to rescue them, but then she realized it was an elf. Alique looked beyond him and her heart stopped.

"Smoke!" she said, turning her horse. "The barn is on fire!"

Celri grabbed her reins and she looked frantically for Kain. Elves surrounded him, holding his horse under control.

"My family," Alique screamed. Her horse danced around but more elves helped Celri to restrain her. She strained to see what was happening and could just make out riders around the barn. The soldiers? Would they be able to save her people, put the fire out before they all died of the smoke? The remaining hay was old and dry; the place would go up in seconds.

"Control yourself," Gorin said. "There is nothing you can do for your people now. The kingdom soldiers will rescue those they can, and we can continue on unhindered by any rescue party."

"Bastard," Kain spat. "Those are innocent farmers, women, children. We came willingly. How could you betray them?"

Alique fought elven hands that reached to restrain her as she struggled to get off her horse and break free of the men surrounding her. The sole thought in her mind was to help those she could. *Nyon, Mama, Papa!* She couldn't allow herself to think of her nephews and new niece, exposed and vulnerable.

"Your people are nothing to me," Gorin said, "just as it is obvious the elven people are nothing to you. Those hostages have served their purpose and now I have the prize: you. I will be greatly rewarded, as will my men."

Celri smiled and nodded as he struggled with Alique.

"Move into the forest, brethren," Gorin said, and they passed under the trees, Alique and Kain hustled along in the middle of the group of horses.

Alique kept glancing behind her even though the forest now hid the barn and the smoke. From her knowledge of fire, it seemed the barn must have burned to the ground. The only way she could deal with the turn of events was to believe the soldiers had rescued every one of the farmers and her family.

She looked at Kain, who was weaponless, while all the elves wore large knives and carried horse bows, the type of short bow easily fired from horseback. The two of them were jostled amid the elves, making their passage along the forest track painfully slow.

She burned with hate for the *Lenweri*. Better that than allow herself to succumb to the terror that lurked within. Her family *would* be safe, and what happened to her didn't matter at all.

* * *

Kain pondered a way out of their dilemma. He'd been able to tell his men to send half their force to raise the alarm and help resettle the farmers, and the remainder to follow a half day behind and stay out of sight. That plan would've been thrown out as soon as the barn was torched. He hoped none of the soldiers had left too soon. They'd all be needed to rescue the captives from the fire. Kain kept seeing the newborn girl at her mother's breast. Surely one so young couldn't perish before her first day was over?

He reached across to Alique and grasped her hand that held the reins. It trembled and he squeezed it. He couldn't even imagine his anguish if his parents and siblings had been trapped in that situation. The gesture was never going to be enough, but when he raised his gaze to hers, she smiled tremulously. He nodded his approval and encouragement.

She straightened in the saddle. At their first stop he'd try to reassure her. In the meantime, he had to put aside his fears and guilt and work out a way of leaving a trail. Sooner or later, the elves would start to cover their tracks. He figured the men following would include Darin and Atan. They were the best trackers he had, but still, no point leaving things to chance.

The further they traveled into the forest, the more unsettled Kain became. The voices in his head increased and there was a continuous rustling from the branches overhead. Feelings of excitement coursed through him until his body thrummed with a tension he'd never felt before. *Am I losing my mind?*

"What is it, General?" Alique asked from her position beside him.

"Silence!" Celri snapped.

Kain shook his head, barely able to register her question, so jumbled were his thoughts, images and feelings. As he tried to tune into the voices, he began to make out the words: "Welcome, *Lenweri*, welcome, *Lenweri.*" Was it the elves communicating with each other? But no, he had heard this when the elves were nowhere close, before they arrived at the Zorba estate. It seemed unlikely the dark brethren were the origin of the sounds and images.

The elves were looking around as if they too heard or sensed something. It disturbed Kain to imagine he had that in common with his enemy. *I'm nothing like them.*

Celri seemed particularly unsettled. He cast glances into the canopy of the forest and looked around him as if expecting trouble. The other elves began to do the same.

"Gorin," Celri said, pulling the prince out of the convoy and stopping at the side of the track.

They all halted while the conversation ensued, and Kain took the opportunity to look for a way of leaving a trail. The elves would see anything obvious. Perhaps he could cut a notch on the boles of trees and branches they passed. At the thought, a surge of anger tore through his mind and the branches overhead shook as if a storm wind had seized them. A hail of dead winter leaves and old bark settled upon them.

Alique dusted the vegetation off her shoulders and out of her hair. "Where did that come from? There's no wind."

Kain glanced at her. "Something is occurring in this forest that I don't understand, My Lady. There is anger, amongst the trees." *Anger toward me for thinking of cutting the trees?* No, it was ridiculous.

She looked at him as though he had lost his mind. *Great! What would she say if I told her what I'm experiencing?*

"Surely you can't be saying the forest is angry?"

"I don't know. The elves are spooked, and the rain of leaves wasn't natural. What would you attribute it to?"

Now it was Alique's turn to appear unsettled. "I've traveled these forests all my life and never felt a thing. I still don't feel anything."

"But *something* is happening," he said, darting a glance at Gorin and Celri who were arguing in hushed tones. "If the trees would keep up their hail of leaves and bark, we'd have a trail of sorts that might lead the men to us."

"Now you wish for the impossible," she said. "I'd prefer your men concentrate on the rescue of my people for now. This whole scheme was constructed to spare them, and instead all may have perished. How do you stand knowing this is all because of you?"

Kain stared. Her accusation cut deep. The elves had been searching for him and he had fallen straight into their trap. "You're right. I feel responsible."

She let out a long sigh. "No, I'm sorry. You couldn't have known why the hostages were taken or what would transpire after we left the barn. We dealt with the forest people in good faith and they have betrayed us." She tried to smile.

"Is there anything I can do to make it easier for you?" he asked.

"I'm trying to believe they were all rescued. It's all I can do for now." She fell silent, a frown on her face.

Kain was content for the silence. He needed to sort through the sensation of words, images and feelings bombarding him. They were stronger this time, and if the reaction of the elves was anything to go by, they might be experiencing the same thing. But Alique heard nothing. Kain chose to believe it was the forest and not insanity that caused the phenomenon. He closed his eyes and allowed the sensations to suffuse him.

"*Forest Mage.*"

Kain's eyes flew open as the words echoed through his mind. *Forest mage? What the hell?* He looked around. Celri and Gorin were on their way back to the group and all the others sat at rest in their saddles, except for Alique who stared at him.

"What's wrong? You nearly jumped out of your skin then."

"Must have dozed off and woke with a start. Looks like we're back on the road." Where had the words come from? It appeared he was the only one to hear them.

The party moved off and the sensations in Kain's mind again jumbled. In order to deal with them, he tried to lock them in a compartment in his mind. It was a practice he used to prevent distractions during fighting. The technique worked to a degree and he was able to muffle the disturbing awareness.

* * *

They continued for two hours until Gorin called a halt. Alique dismounted and sat on a log, leaning back against the bole of a tree. The track widened here, and the sun shone on them. It was close to midday by her reckoning. Celri passed a water skin around and she drank. Kain joined her on the log.

"How do you fare, My Lady?" he asked, flexing his shoulders and rolling his neck from one side to the other.

The muscles in Alique's own shoulders and back were on fire. "I'm trying not to think about it. You?"

"I feel a hundred years old."

"Does your head still trouble you?"

Kain frowned, as if considering. "Head is good, mostly."

"You'll tell me if it should trouble you, won't you?"

He smiled. "I surely will."

She doubted he would, but relaxed against the tree and closed her eyes. Instead of rest, she saw her father shoved through the door of the barn, and the smoke as it billowed into the morning sky. She swallowed hard as a wave of emotion swept over her. Tears welled and she gulped to control them. Kain's hand landed on her shoulder, warm and surprisingly comforting. It was almost her undoing.

"We'll find our way out of this somehow," he said. "And your family will be safe. My men were right on hand to help."

"The hay in the barn would have gone up quickly."

"They *will* be well," he insisted.

Alique wondered who Kain was trying to convince, her or himself? *Change of subject required!* "What did they mean when they declared you had elven heritage?"

"I swear I have no idea."

"They seem very sure of their claims," she said, studying him.

"They can say what they wish," he snapped. "I have no knowledge of this so-called elven heritage they speak of."

"I had never thought of it before," Alique said, "but you could have elven blood."

He frowned. "Anyone *could* have elven blood, Lady. That doesn't mean it is so."

"I'm sorry," she said. "You clearly reject this claim being made by the prince and his cronies."

"Of course, I reject it! I can't see how it can be true. I don't care if I look a little like a dark elf! I'm not one and will never believe it." *Then why do I hear the voices as they seem to?* There must be some other explanation.

Alique threw her hands up in surrender. "Forget I said anything. I'm sure you'll get to the bottom of this in due course." She leaned toward him and lowered her voice further. "What plan do you have for our escape?"

"I'm working on leaving a trail for our soldiers to follow."

"Oh? What trail?" She looked back where they had come from but could not see any markings. Of course, Kain wouldn't leave anything too obvious.

He looked sheepish. "I haven't exactly worked out a solution yet."

Now it was Alique's turn to frown. The great General Kain Jazara with no proper plan?

She relaxed against the tree again. Perhaps she'd have to work on a plan of her own. She had weapons, and there were two of them and thirty elves. Not such overwhelming odds. If the soldiers were following, their chances of overpowering the elves, if carried out at the right time, were good. Alique would just make sure the men could find them. Perhaps her calendula potion might be used? In the meantime, she'd gather all the information she could regarding the elves she traveled with.

The leader, so-called Prince Gorin, was the tallest of the group, but all were above average height when compared to human men. Celri was the shortest and appeared the most aggressive. He would have to be watched as he seemed the type to act before he thought.

The prince had a regal bearing, so perhaps he truly did have royal blood – or as royal as dark elven blood could get. The remainder of the elves shared similar features – dark skin, hair and eyes, lithe bodies and ears that were pointed to a greater or lesser degree. Alique tried to catch a glimpse of Kain's ear tips but he caught her at it.

"What?" he asked, his eyes narrowed, suspicious.

"Nothing."

"Tell me."

"No, you'll just be angry. I've been thinking on how to leave a trail. Your earlier idea of a dead leaf trail seems silly to me."

"Well, I wasn't being totally serious," he said, frustration edging his tone.

She looked above her. The oaks and beech in this part of the forest were truly beautiful. If not for their situation, this would be a place of peace.

"What's occurring in the world, General? I don't like this trouble we've had with the dark brethren of late. And then there's the death of the prince, and the problem of an heir for the kingdom, not to mention the assassins at the prince's funeral. Thorius seems to have become a place of danger."

Kain studied her. "Welcome to my world, Lady. I can't think of a worse time to be away from Wildecoast. Perhaps that's the purpose of all this; to get me away and attack the castle. The king is hardly in a good frame of mind, grieving as he is for his brother."

"Even so," Alique said, "the queen will see Wildecoast is defended. As for Brightcastle, Ramón and Benae are both capable of defending their territory."

Kain frowned. "If you don't mind my saying so, the queen, Ramón and Benae are all untried in a time of threat. It isn't easy to formulate battle plans and strategies."

"You must have capable men under you. Won't they keep their wits about them?"

"Many of them will be searching for us." He sighed, resting his head in his hands. "What a mess."

"You carry the weight of the kingdom on your shoulders, Kain."

He looked up; his gaze sharp. "That's the first time you've used my name."

"Social niceties scarcely matter in this situation," she said. "Do you mind?"

"Not at all, but..."

"Don't worry. I won't fall in love with you or any such thing. My future, if I still have one, is with Doctor Mosard and medicine. I've given up on the idea of a family."

Kain smiled. "You're what? Twenty-one years old?"

"In your world that's young, but for a noblewoman, she is usually betrothed by now. She generally has some prospects at least. Mama is beginning to despair I will ever make a suitable match. She has her grandchildren anyway." Her heart ached at the thought that none might still be alive. "At least I hope she does."

Kain reached out again, his hand grasping hers. "Stay strong, My Lady. As to love, I don't think I'm qualified to give advice."

A thrill ran through Alique at the simple gesture and she gazed down at their hands locked together. He began to draw away, but she held on to the comfort. "Don't." It might have been the lack of sleep but when Alique raised her gaze to Kain's she felt as though she was falling into his dark orbs. It didn't unnerve her as it once might have. Of course, she would never admit he had ever made her uncomfortable.

"So touching it is to watch the two of you." Celri had sidled up to them undetected. "It is time to mount up," Celri said. "We have a long ride ahead of us if we are to make the camp by late tomorrow."

The elf turned away but Alique looked at Kain. "So now we know when we'll arrive. It might be valuable information."

He nodded. "Just what I was thinking. Somehow I don't believe the prince would approve of Celri giving that much of their plan away."

"Perhaps it's wrong information to throw us off the track?"

He smiled at her. "You would've made a resourceful soldier, My Lady."

"If I'm to call you Kain, you should call me Alique."

He stood and reached out a hand to help her to her feet. "Perhaps in private."

She nodded. "I think this counts."

He smirked and went to turn away. Alique reached for his arm to stop him.

"Yes?" he asked.

She held a dropper bottle so his body protected it from the elves' view. It contained a dark liquid. "I may have the solution for our trail dilemma. One drop of this onto the path will leave a circle a hand-span wide and the color of copper. It won't appear immediately but over the course of the hour after it is dropped."

Kain's eyebrows rose. "What is it?"

"A plant extract, calendula, plus certain other additives. It's used for providing a healing and protective skin for large wounds and burns. Its effect is almost magical."

Now he frowned. "Are you sure there's no magic involved? I couldn't condone that."

Alique made an unladylike snort. "Don't be such a prude. We'll use whatever we must to escape this situation. But I know no magical link with the potion."

He nodded. "Seems we might have different philosophies when it comes to some things."

Alique smirked. "When shall I start laying the trail?"

"My men will have no trouble following in this country but when it gets stony, you'll need to leave a drop every mile. If we cross a creek, leave a drop on both sides so they know where we left the creek." He concentrated on her. "Are you confident of hiding it from the elves?"

"Supremely confident. Riding side saddle I can drop it straight off the edge and hide the bottle in my skirts. Also, I don't think they'll watch me as closely as they will you."

"After that trick with the knife I'm not so sure."

She grinned and went to find Ebony. Mounting, she secreted the calendula bottle in her skirt pouch until it should be needed. She watched Kain mount his horse with more spring than she'd seen from him since his head injury, admiring the way his breeches molded the muscles of his thighs and backside. He was certainly a fine example of the male form.

She shook her head at where her thoughts had slipped and turned her eyes toward the trail, meeting Celri's suspicious gaze. *Stinking, murdering dark elves!* Alique would see that every one of them was driven from Thorius, never to venture here again.

* * *

Kain battled more of the dark whispers and feelings as he traveled through the afternoon forest and into the early evening. After two hours of trying to keep them away, he had given up in exhaustion. He now allowed them to wash over him, and found them strangely comforting. He had also concluded the feelings, sounds and images came from the trees themselves. Again, he had heard the words, *forest mage*. The words literally meant forest magician or sorcerer.

If the images and words were coming from the forest itself, why? Alique didn't experience anything, but Kain was sure the elves sensed something by the way they behaved. Celri was decidedly jumpy, though the elf was naturally skittish. Prince Gorin was too composed to give much away, but the others appeared distracted, it seemed to Kain. The awareness that he and the elves might have this in common nagged at him. It was simply not possible he was elven. He didn't want it to be true, especially not with this threatened invasion by the brethren.

The shadows under the trees had begun to deepen when Prince Gorin called a halt for the night. They had reached a large clearing on the other side of a creek crossing, surrounded by the biggest trees Kain had yet seen. He vaulted from Snow and hurried to help Alique down.

"Thank you," she said, giving his hand a squeeze before releasing it.

"The trail is being laid as planned?" Kain asked.

She frowned as if he had annoyed her. "I had no trouble following your request," she said, so low he strained to hear and had to bend closer. It brought her uncomfortably near and Alique placed her hand on his chest.

Kain turned away when the prince approached them. "You will make your rest over there," he said, pointing to a patch of moss between two large tree roots. "I want you in the center of the camp so we will be able to ensure your safety. Make haste, food will be ready momentarily and then we will bed down."

As Gorin stalked away, Kain pulled Alique's bag from behind Ebony's saddle and guided her to the appointed area. He retrieved his own roll and spread it on the ground. Alique circled the huge tree they were preparing to lie under. She ran her fingers over the smooth bark and Kain heard a sigh in his mind. He looked up sharply. Surely the tree couldn't respond to Alique's touch? Once he wouldn't have had the thought, but lately? No more sighs followed, even though Alique now had both hands on the tree trunk and stared up at its canopy.

"It's so beautiful," she said, laying her forehead on the trunk, eyes closed. "I've always loved the forest. I keep thinking, were it not for the circumstances, this trip would give me real pleasure." A tear squeezed out from amongst her thick honey lashes and glimmered in the torchlight.

Kain stepped closer so he could place his hand on her shoulder. "They'll be safe, Alique. The elves didn't truly want to hurt them. It was a delaying tactic."

Her eyes flashed open. "I hate them! Even with so many rescuers, we could be dealing with a catastrophe when we return." She swallowed hard and looked up at him. "I don't think I could cope with it, especially if the children are hurt."

He pulled her close, her head under his chin, and after a moment's resistance, she softened against him. "We'll deal with whatever we must," he said. "Please just concentrate on getting through this. It won't help to imagine the worst."

"I know," she said. "It's just so easy to believe everything will go wrong."

Kain smiled and felt her hair snag in his whiskers. "I've been in many a hopeless situation and fought my way clear. Nothing is ever as bad as it appears at first glance, and sometimes what seems terrible becomes something to be grateful for."

She looked up at him and Kain thought her even more beautiful with tears in her eyes. Somehow it made her eyes more startling.

"You're trying to tell me we might look back upon this and be glad we were taken hostage?" she said. "Somehow I doubt it."

"Nothing is ever as it appears, and yes, we might be glad of this one day."

"I shall only be glad when these people are driven from the kingdom, for good."

There was a noise beside him and Kain turned to see Celri with a plate of food.

"I told the prince we should starve the prisoners," he said, sneering. "This is too good for you." He shoved the plate at Kain and stared at Alique. "You, Lady, I will particularly enjoy *your* death. You could never live peacefully in the kingdom with my people. There is only hate in your heart."

Alique pushed away from Kain, toward Celri. "Hate! You should know, elf. You've taken hostages, beat an innocent man so he might never recover, and then set a barn full of women and children on fire. Where is the hater here? I'll personally see your people driven from Thorius and up into the farthest reaches of the mountains."

Celri sneered. "Do not make promises you are unable to keep." He held up a hand and flexed his fingers into a claw. "One touch around your pretty white neck and we shall see who will triumph over whom. You are not in your palace now, queen's servant."

Alique tried to launch herself at Celri but Kain threw an arm around her waist and held her back. Celri laughed at having exacted such a response from his captive, which only served to enrage her further. Kain pushed her away from Celri and toward their resting place, one hand still gripping the plate of dinner.

The elf walked away, still laughing, while Kain waited for Alique to cease struggling.

"Stop it, Alique. He wants to make you mad, make you crazy so you'll do something stupid and he can be justified in killing you."

She tried to shake Kain off. "Leave me be."

"Not until you calm down. Celri would poke a knife in you in a moment. Then what would I tell the queen? How would I tell your parents that a dark elf killed their daughter?"

Too late, he realized it was a bad example, as Alique flared up at the mention of her mother and father.

"There might be no parents to mourn me. That's the whole point. I want revenge and I'll get it one way or another. They've made this personal."

Her eyes flashed blue fire and her body strained against his hand. Kain put the plate on the ground and gripped both of Alique's elbows. He gave her a little shake and she glared at him. At least he had her attention.

"Take it from someone who knows, Alique. Your revenge needs to be cold. Keep a cool head and you won't make the mistakes you're likely to make if you charge at your enemy in a rage, especially now when we're in such a precarious position. We'll get through this and we *will* triumph over them. It may take a little time and planning."

Alique relaxed under his hands and Kain heaved a deep sigh of relief.

"You're right," she said. "It's just when I think of what they've done…"

He wrapped his arms around her, trying not to focus on the places their bodies touched. She was so soft, yet firm in the right places, and…

"Do you have a knife in your cleavage, My Lady?"

She smirked up at him. "Guilty as charged. I didn't think they'd search there."

Kain frowned. Alique was turning out to be a most surprising woman. He'd never expected her to possess this depth of character. Her beauty had caused him to underestimate her and he almost felt he should apologize. But that would be giving too much away.

He stepped back and gestured her toward the bedding he'd laid down. "I'm starving. Let's sit and have something to eat."

She followed his lead, sitting on Kain's bed roll and leaning back against the trunk of the tree she had earlier admired. "What have they prepared for us?"

Kain sifted around in the food on the plate, trying to identify the contents of the dinner. "Looks like nuts. That's a cloud berry, and these are –"

"Crowberries," Alique said, picking up a deep purple fruit with the appearance of a blueberry. She popped it in her mouth. "Mm, that's quite delicious."

"How do you know that's not a blueberry?"

"They're sweeter than blueberries," she said, selecting another.

"How do you know it isn't a sweet blueberry?" He enjoyed talking about something other than the situation they'd found themselves in.

"I just know, Kain. If I had one of each here, I could demonstrate for you. What I don't understand is where these came from. We haven't had crowberries here for months, except in jars. They produce in autumn, and we're fast heading into spring."

"The elves come from the mountains far to the north. They must have carried them along in their sacks. Personally, I'd kill for a tasty roast rabbit, or some crusty bread and cheese. This fare is for forest creatures, specifically birds." He picked up a handful of berries and nuts and chewed them without enthusiasm.

Alique smiled. "This food is good for you. There are excellent properties in berries and nuts that will keep you healthy. That's why we principally use this type of plant material for our medicines, along with herbs, of course. You wouldn't believe the myriad of different fruits, and not just in the forest. I fossick along the beach and in the open plains, and Doctor Mosard travels north on occasion to collect plants and fruits from the high-altitude forests and tundras. He has promised to take me with him next time." Her eagerness dimmed. "Now his trip will be postponed, and all due to the mischief of these damned dark elves."

"Let's not start into that again," Kain said, sensing another outburst building.

She scowled, but even then, looked charming. "As long as you promise we will have our revenge for all the trouble they've caused."

He shook his head. "I can't guarantee that, but I'll be trying my damnedest to see they're sent running back to their forests."

Alique's frown didn't ease.

"What now?" he asked.

"What if it's true that you have elven blood?" She leaned forward. "How can you act against your own people?"

"They aren't my people!" he said. "No matter what I look like, I'm not elven."

"But what if you are? They seem very certain."

Kain's jaw clenched with the effort of not snapping her head off. "I'll never accept that. Never." His gaze bored into Alique, letting her know the subject was closed. It was the look he used on recalcitrant soldiers and never failed to intimidate. Until now.

She met him glare for glare, the food forgotten. Damn but she was fine. There wasn't a soldier in Wildecoast who could have stood up to him, and yet she did it without raising a sweat.

"Let's agree to disagree for now," she said. "I am merely saying I foresee troubles ahead for the kingdom if what the elves say is true."

Kain kept his mouth shut and went back to nibbling on the less than satisfactory fare. Then he remembered something. He reached for his saddlebags, opened a flap and pulled out a small wrapped package. "Cheese!"

"A masterful change of subject, General." She took the offered slab of cheese. "This will stick to our stomachs much better than the elven meal. Make sure you save some for the morrow."

"Saving some for later," he said, allowing a little sarcasm to show through. Honestly, how did Alique think he managed his soldiers while on a mission if he couldn't think ahead to save a prized addition to road fare?

Celri swaggered up. "The picnic is over. It is time to bed down for the night. There will be sentries on patrol so be warned."

Kain's hand grasped Alique's. She remained silent but he felt the tension in her body.

The elf turned away and she relaxed somewhat. Sagged was what she really did.

"He infuriates me," she said, "but you're right. He'd take any opportunity to harm either of us and I nearly walked right into his trap."

"He thinks he has something to prove." Kain still held her hand. It was a good feeling. The skin of her fingers was a little rough, unlike most ladies. He supposed it was due to the work she did, grinding herbs and bandaging wounds. Alique wasn't soft as he had thought, nor was she spoiled.

She was a woman to be admired and one who clearly wanted to make her mark on the kingdom, if her threats to the elves were serious. And she carried knives. That had him wondering if she hid other weapons amongst her clothes, besides the one nestling in her bosom. Just the thought of it had his manhood stirring. And now he must sleep next to her.

He released Alique's hand and cleared his throat. "Finish your meal and then we must settle. If you like, I'll sleep on the other side of this tree."

She snorted, albeit in a ladylike fashion. "We were told to stay together. Besides, it will be cold tonight. We need to conserve body heat, or at least I would appreciate yours – in a purely medicinal way, of course."

Kain stared. *Medicinal?* The mere thought of bedding down with Alique was… distracting, enticing… "I'll offer my body heat, My Lady. Back to back?"

Alique finished the last fruit on the plate. "That will do."

* * *

Alique longed for a bath, or even a wash, but apart from splashing some of her drinking water on her face and hands, she had to go without. She thought longingly of the steaming baths below the castle at Wildecoast and vowed to spend a morning there as soon as she was freed. She immediately felt guilty. How could she be thinking of bathing when her family could be dead? But Kain was right. She had to anticipate the best outcome, and perhaps dreaming of a hot bath was merely a diversion during a difficult time. Kain knew about distractions and survival. She would take her cues from him.

She lay down with her back to him and pulled her cloak over them both. At first it was cool, even cold, but his body heat began to permeate her gown. His hard buttocks kept hers company and her face grew warm imagining how it would feel if there were no clothes between them.

He shuffled a little. "Are your feet cold?" he asked, his voice deep and resonant beside her.

"They are," she said.

"Take off your boots and stockings and press them against me."

She stilled, shocked at his suggestion, even though she had just been imagining their skin together in a much less innocent way.

"Go ahead, I won't bite," he said.

She did as she was told and smiled at his gasp when her icy feet pressed against his legs.

"I can feel them even through my breeches," he said. "How have you endured this?"

"I have always had cold feet, so I'm used to it. It's only when I go to bed that I really notice it." She heard him move. It was her turn to gasp as his rough hands chafed her feet. Warmth surged through them.

"Oh," she said, "that's so good." She allowed her head to loll back as circulation and warmth returned to her feet. He even replaced her stockings afterwards and then lay down again beside her, pulling the cloak over them.

"Thank you," she said. "That's one of the nicest things anyone has ever done for me."

He grunted in response and she closed her eyes, no longer disturbed by cold feet or the dark and dangerous man beside her.

CHAPTER 6

KAIN woke at first light, warmer than he had ever been when camped out overnight. He soon discovered why. His body was curled around Alique's, his front to her back, and his chin nestled in her golden curls, his arm looped over her waist. As he breathed in her heady scent, a tight hand of need clenched his gut. He hadn't even known it was there until he had his arms around this woman; this beautiful, complex, infuriating woman.

When he thought about moving, he discovered he didn't want to let her go. What he did want was to lie here with her and forget their predicament. And by *lie* here, he meant something a lot more intimate than just having his arms around her, nice as that was.

He resolved to remove his arm and his body from her person, but instead, his arm tightened around her waist. Alique squirmed and nestled back into him, murmuring something unintelligible. He froze, not wanting to wake her any earlier than he had to, and not wishing to be caught with his arm about her. What would she think if she knew he snuggled so close? Hell, she could probably feel the hard length of him pressed up against her backside; if she was awake.

Alique wasn't awake, he knew full well, for she wouldn't accept this closeness if she were. All she would accept was functional warmth from him, not this intimate nestling that was so much more than practical. *Goddess, I'm falling under her spell!* She wouldn't want him developing an attachment for her. He was army and she was nobility. More than that, she had her sights set on a career as a healer. He could see her now, running her own hospital, and leaving no stone unturned in the search for ways to cure people of their ills.

Something squirmed in his gut at the thought of Alique moving on, perhaps loving a man who wasn't good enough for her. She was brave and intelligent, but beneath that he sensed a need for love. She wouldn't long be able to deny her desire for someone to share her life. His friend Niko wasn't available to her. In trying to ensnare him, she had exposed a foolhardiness which reared its head again when she goaded Celri. She might be a lady but Alique had passion and anger to burn.

As he lay there, pictures of Alique in the moments he had known her flashed through his head: galloping her horse side-saddle across the cliffs of Wildecoast, sending him spare with fear that she'd plunge over its edge; gently tending Niko's wounds in his rooms at the castle; cavorting in the ballroom, every male eye riveted to her; brandishing a knife at the dark brethren; delivering Nyon's baby. Kain hadn't realized he'd stored such a wealth of memories of her. When his imagination kicked in to create daydreams of a future which included the woman resting in his arms, he bit back a groan.

He wouldn't torture himself! He liked to think he had a well-developed sense of self-preservation and it didn't allow him to expose himself unnecessarily. Not to mention the fact that daydreaming of a future with Alique was plain stupid. She might allow a flirtation, perhaps even take him to her bed, but she would *never* see him as a permanent part of her world.

He sighed, disgusted at his pathetic thoughts. He knew the cause. He hadn't bedded a woman in weeks and being so close to Alique triggered unused libido. That was all. He resolved to remedy the situation when he broke free of these damned elves.

* * *

Alique lay as still as she could, feigning sleep, keeping her breathing slow and even as she enjoyed the feel of Kain's arm around her more than she should. He was awake. She could almost hear his thoughts.

She liked to think he enjoyed the feel of her body too – he must, if the hint of hard manhood at her backside was anything to go by. She smiled when she thought how mortified he'd be if he knew what she could feel. Her imagination naturally wanted to go to the next step!

I could roll over and face him and this moment would be over. At least she thought that would end it. But what if he leaned in for a kiss? What if she allowed him to get his hooks into her heart? She already felt more for him than she should. He used to annoy her. She used to puzzle out the best way of getting under his skin just to punish him for the grief he gave her. But on this trip, she had seen another side to Kain. He was a leader of men – she had already known that. He was sensitive to the suffering of others – she hadn't suspected that. He was a man under a mountain of responsibility. It weighed on him, and Alique sensed a future crisis if he didn't look after himself. For some reason she wanted to be around to look after him. To remind him to be kind to himself.

His barbs had already wormed their way under her skin, and they were fast moving toward her heart. Where would they be once they extricated themselves from this mess? And what if Kain did indeed turn out to be a dark elf? What would that do to his world? What would it do to her feelings for him? She had to distance herself before she got in too deep.

Reluctantly, Alique stretched as if waking from sleep and gave him a few minutes to pull away. Then she rolled over and propped herself on her elbow, looking down at him. He was a vague outline in the dawn gloom.

"Morning," he said. "How did you sleep?"

"Like a baby, thanks to you."

He grunted. "I did nothing but give you some body warmth."

She smirked, knowing how much more he had done. "Still, I was toasty warm and that helped. How about you?"

"I must admit it was one of the best sleeps I've had out of doors."

One of the best! Huh! "I assume I can take some credit?"

He sighed. "Perhaps."

Oh, so frosty this morning. She still loved getting those digs in and keeping him on the edge. It was one thing that wouldn't change between them. It was too much fun scoring points against him. She knew he was at a disadvantage, her being a lady and all, but it was still fun to infuriate and surprise him.

"What do you think today will bring?" she asked.

"Today we meet the orchestrator of all this," Kain said. "I for one can't wait to confront him."

"Or her," Alique said.

"Perhaps, but I doubt it."

It was becoming lighter and she could just make out the burning light in his eyes. Kain needed to draw the elves out on his supposed heritage, and Alique doubted he was ready to have his dark elven roots confirmed.

"Females are as capable as men, you know."

His brows rose. "I didn't mention capability. I get the feeling elves don't bow down before females."

"You could be right."

"I know it."

"What if we are rescued before we get to the stronghold of this elven leader?"

"Then our confrontation will be at a later date," Kain said. "Don't fear, Alique. I don't intend to let these dark brethren get away with what they did on your estate. One way or another, they *will* pay."

Alique's heart surged with pride at his words. "Together we'll defeat them."

He frowned. "I didn't say anything about together."

She clutched his shoulder. "You must allow me to be a part of this. I will have my revenge."

He tensed under her hand. "I see there are 'discussions' ahead on that topic."

"I don't care what I have to do, I *am* going to be a part of this."

"I don't think the kingdom will accept a lady on the battlefield, let alone your brother and family."

"Why bring Ramón into this?"

"As caretaker of Brightcastle the king will value his opinion, especially relating to the role of his sister in any war."

"You think it will come to that? War?"

"And that proves my point," he said, sitting up to face her.

Alique's hand dropped away from his shoulder as his muscles flexed beneath her fingers. It really was a very fine shoulder.

"You make statements about revenge without comprehending what it means," he said. "Leave the fighting to the experts."

"I'm ready for war," Alique said, feeling his scorn deeply. "I'm trained to defend myself, and I can train more."

"Your role will be as healer. The kingdom doesn't need you to fight." As her head dropped, his fingers gently raised her chin, so her gaze met his. "I don't mean to be harsh, Alique, but you must use your skills where they'll be most needed. What would you say if I suggested I was going to offer my services to Doctor Mosard?"

He was right, but she didn't have to like it. "I'd tell you that your talents were best used fighting and organizing men."

"Exactly!"

"I need to *do* something, Kain."

"And you will. Just be patient."

Without warning, Celri's voice sounded from behind them. "You are required to be up and break your fast. We are on the road in ten minutes." Celri shoved two wooden bowls of oatmeal at them and walked away.

* * *

They were on the road inside the ten minutes Celri had stated. By then it was fully light, though the trees blocked all but the brightest rays. Kain was more optimistic than he had a right to feel in such circumstances. Part might be the restful night but another very large part was Alique's presence. That was unexpected! She was no longer a thorn in his side, and the somewhat fragile friendship they shared was becoming important. Was he growing dependent on her? Had she brought some balance back into a life that was all about conflict, strife and court intrigue?

It was too early to tell. And while there were positives in their association, there was risk as well. This crisis provided a good opportunity to investigate whether she was someone he wanted in his life. The question remained; what place could she legitimately have in the life of a soldier?

Today Alique rode ahead of him and he watched as she left her drops of calendula formula which would lead the rescue team to them. By his reckoning, she marked almost exactly each mile. He couldn't have done better himself. It was as if she was trying to prove her worth, but he realized she'd have no thought for him in this. She was a perfectionist who did all tasks well when she put a mind to it. She'd be an asset anywhere.

Except in my army. Women didn't belong in the fighting ranks. Kain had come across the occasional woman in battle and he hated it. He'd been raised to respect and protect females. Fighting them only distracted him from the process of engagement. In his two fights against women, he'd been the victor and both times had been haunted by their deaths. Their reach was smaller, as was their strength, and it was too much of a disadvantage. Considering that, along with their natural role as nurturers, it was wrong to use them as soldiers.

He imagined Alique in soldier's breeches and tunic and his groin tightened. Damn but she would look good. This wasn't working for him. Perhaps sensing his eyes upon her, she flicked him a look and raised one brow. The sooner he got back to Wildecoast and his normal routine the better.

This time when the forest began to talk to him, he welcomed the distraction from his thoughts of Alique. He tried to tune into the voices and feelings as they presented and rode in a trance most of the morning. By lunch he felt in tune with the trees. They were excited to have elves amongst them again. *Again!* Some of the younger trees didn't remember the dark brethren, but the ancient trees remembered many centuries ago when this land had been only forest and the elven people had roamed its entirety. *What?*

Kain tried to digest this recollection. He wasn't willing to call it fact yet. As he had this thought, the branches overhead shook, raining down small twigs and leaves. It seemed the forest might not appreciate his skepticism.

So, what of the words "forest mage"? What did the continuous repetition of the phrase mean? Was there a magician amongst these elves that the trees paid homage to as he passed? Kain would give anything to ask these questions and many more of the elves, but he'd have to reveal his encounters in the forest and he wasn't willing to open himself up to that kind of derision. Best to be guarded with his enemies. Besides, he didn't want Alique getting wind of his strange experiences amongst the trees. He could just see her face if he told her the trees were talking to him.

They lunched beside the trail and were back in the saddle and moving before Kain had a chance to allow his muscles to stretch and loosen. He wasn't getting any younger. Prince Gorin rode up beside him after they hit the trail.

"You have been model prisoners, General," he said. "I am sure that will bode well when they decide the manner of your death."

Kain glanced sideways at him but the elf seemed serious. *We'll see whose death comes first!* Kain held his tongue rather than give Gorin the satisfaction of responding.

"I expect to arrive at our camp before sunset and then we shall see what our leader makes of you. Prepare yourself."

"What do you mean 'prepare yourself'?" Kain asked.

"You are right, General," Gorin said. "How can you prepare for interrogation and accusation? My leader could bring any number of charges against you, could ask you any question about the kingdom and its strategies for our people. How could you prepare?"

"You're mad," Kain snapped.

"No General Jazara, I think it is you who is mad. I have watched you on this trip. You do not act like a sane man; muttering to yourself and casting glances around, as if hearing things that others of us cannot hear. Yes, I have watched you. It will be like killing a mad dog when you die."

Gorin's words brought a ripple of dread down Kain's spine. He prided himself on keeping his feelings within, and yet this stranger had read him like a book. He had to be more watchful. "You're mistaken, Prince Gorin. There's no need for you to fear me. I'm as sane as the next man."

Gorin's brow arched. "Oh, believe me, I do not fear you. And I am not mistaken."

He trotted forward leaving Kain deep in contemplation, worried he had underestimated the elven leader.

Gorin stayed away for the remainder of the ride and it was nearing dark when Kain began to hear the sounds of a camp ahead. They soon found themselves in a large clearing, picketed horses and tents on all sides. Cooking fires burned through the middle of the clearing and they pulled to a halt at the nearest of them.

Celri sidled up to Kain. "You and the woman get down and keep your eyes lowered," he said. "You are in the presence of royalty."

Alique made a low snort and Kain frowned across at her. He knew she had no respect for her captors but surely she could show some restraint? She opened her eyes wide at him as if she didn't know what she had done to upset him. He glared at her and dismounted. If he could keep his eyes lowered, so could she.

They stood side by side. Alique's hand brushed his and for a moment he thought she would slip it inside his. It didn't eventuate and he convinced himself he imagined it. There was no further time to contemplate as they were ushered away from their horses and toward a smaller clearing nearby.

This space was dark and menacing, with a fire to one side, before which sat a large *Lenweri* male of middle years, tended by a beautiful elven woman.

Kain had forgotten to keep his eyes down as he approached the elven leader and Celri elbowed him in the back. He made a show of ducking his head but still peered at the leader through his lashes. Alique, of course, wasn't cowed by Celri's demands and stared at the elves.

Celri bowed low. "Mighty Prince, I bring you the kingdom army general, Jazara, and his woman."

Alique spluttered in protest. "I am not his woman," she said, glaring at Celri. She turned back to the elven prince and offered a small curtsy. "I am Lady Alique Zorba, handmaiden to the queen herself."

Kain stared. After the anger Alique had displayed toward the elves, the last thing he expected was any show of respect.

The *Lenweri* prince nodded. "It is refreshing to meet someone of the kingdom willing to show deference to our race."

Kain tensed, expecting a denial from Alique but she remained silent. *Thank the Goddess!*

The prince continued. "I welcome you to my humble camp. Failora, fetch a cushion for the lady to recline on." The elven woman hurried off and returned with a large purple and red cushion which she placed next to the prince. Alique settled herself upon it as if she were visiting a local royal.

"Thank you, Prince…?" she said.

The elven leader smiled a self-satisfied smile.

I'm going to have fun pulling you down from your roost! Kain could already taste the satisfaction.

"I am High Prince Elvor Faenwelar," he said, "the closest thing our people have to a king. Gorin is my son."

"I would say I'm pleased to meet you, Your Highness, but clearly I am not," Alique said, her voice as cold as a winter stream.

Kain flinched. Now this was what he'd expected.

Prince Faenwelar didn't seem to take offense. "Of course, Lady, I must apologize for the circumstances. These are difficult times, calling for measures I would not normally condone."

Alique's chin rose and she looked down her nose at the elven leader. "We both know that isn't true, Your Highness. You'll do whatever it takes to secure your goals."

"I am not at liberty to discuss that with you."

"Even if your men killed my family?" Alique's voice had taken on an edge of hysteria.

"I will make no comment on that at this time, Lady. For now, the general and I have business to discuss. I have long waited to meet with him."

Kain found himself the subject of the golden gaze of the elven prince. It was quite a stare, considering most of the elven people had the dark eyes of Gorin and Failora. There had to be a story behind that.

Kain determined to wait until the elf spoke again.

"I see this will be a rocky association, General," Faenwelar said.

"If it's rocky, *you* have created it," he said. "It's you who've captured us, not the other way. What do you want?" Kain had run out of patience.

"I want many things from you, and you are lucky that one thing I do not need is respect," Faenwelar said. "You are so far below me it is of no moment if you defer to me or not. I will use you for our cause, then discard you and never think of you again."

"I will decide when and how I'm to be used," Kain said.

"You seem to think you are in control here, General."

Kain folded his arms across his chest, determined not to be led by his captor.

"You will tell me about the movement of kingdom forces," Faenwelar said, "of your defense plans, and anything else I need to know. If you do not, there will be consequences."

Kain quirked one eyebrow. He was on solid ground here. He knew full well there was no torture that would make him divulge secrets about the kingdom. All his soldiers were trained in managing torture techniques and Kain was better than almost anyone at enduring pain. "Do your worst, Prince."

Faenwelar flicked a glance at Alique. "I don't think the lady will be quite so encouraging, General, since it is she who will be providing the incentive for you to speak your secrets."

Kain's heart almost stopped. "You can't mean to torture *her*?"

"I can and I do. As I said, 'hard times'. I hope neither you nor she will condemn me. I am doing what must be done."

Alique had gone very still and Kain was surprised he couldn't hear her heart from where he stood across the fire. Her pupils dilated in fear, but she lifted her chin again.

"I would never allow the general to betray the kingdom," she said. "It simply cannot happen."

Faenwelar didn't stand or raise his voice but menace rang through the clearing. "You are both at my mercy and will do as I say. Neither of you have any choice in the matter."

"There is always a choice, Faenwelar," Kain said, though he felt far less confident than he portrayed to the prince. He should have realized why Alique was taken with him. They would threaten to hurt her in order to force him to betray his people.

The elven prince narrowed his eyes as if trying to assess whether Kain was bluffing. Then he shrugged. "I will not argue with you tonight, Jazara. We will begin the interrogation tomorrow."

Kain let out a quiet sigh of relief. That gave them more time to escape or be rescued.

"However, I do have another matter which needs clarification," Faenwelar said.

"Oh?"

"Your reputation precedes you, General."

"What do you mean?" Kain asked, thinking he spoke of his army career but not certain.

"The *Sis Lenweri* have heard of a part elven, part human who may be in this region. I think that man is you."

Kain grunted even as Alique's ears seemed to prick. "I've never heard of anything so insane. My parents are Thorian through and through. I have a brother and two sisters. I'd know if I had elven blood."

Faenwelar stood and walked around the fire to confront Kain. The elf was taller than him and several pounds heavier. In fact, this being was the largest elf Kain had ever seen. He wore the customary tight-fitting browns and greens and moved with awesome grace. The dark hair at his temples carried a dusting of grey.

Kain bore Faenwelar's scrutiny. The *Lenweri* were like a dog with a bone. What else had he called them? *Sis Lenweri*? What did it mean? A different tribe?

Perhaps if he allowed the prince's close inspection, this would pass, and he could look back upon it and laugh at the absurd accusations. He glanced at Alique who studied him almost as closely as Faenwelar.

Scrutiny was something Kain wasn't accustomed to. As the leader of the army he was much more used to dishing out this type of treatment than running the gauntlet of it. He steeled himself to the probing gaze of the elven prince and didn't flinch when the ruler brushed the hair from the top of his ears.

Kain heaved a long sigh when the inspection was completed. "Well?" *Damn, that sounded like I care what Faenwelar has decided.*

"I think there is no question our information is correct, General. You are at least half elf. Your lithe frame, dark skin and dark eyes confirm it. I know the look of the half human and half elf. I do not know how it came to pass. You must take that up with your family."

Kain hadn't been prepared for the words. He'd convinced himself the prince would laugh at the accusation when he'd had a chance to study Kain. How could he accept this when he had no idea how it might even be true? He'd had a normal upbringing. His father had taught him to fashion furniture and run the family business. His mother had raised him with good manners, his siblings had teased him ceaselessly. True, none of them had the olive complexion he had, and their hair wasn't as dark, but that could be explained in other ways. Couldn't it?

"It's not true." Kain's voice no longer held the ring of conviction it once had and Alique noticed. Her eyes widened as she took it all in.

Kain couldn't worry about that now. "What does it all mean? Surely a half-breed elf is nothing unusual?"

Triumph lit the prince's eyes. "Hah, so you might be prepared to admit I am right?"

"No," Kain said, "I wish to know what it means for me here and now."

"We need all our people in this troubled time," Faenwelar said. "My mission is to unite the *Lenweri* so we can conquer the kingdom. I do not think there is any harm in telling you that, as you will never be allowed to leave us."

Alique gasped and tried to stand but Failora held her down.

"This is ridiculous," Kain said. "You won't succeed. The king will never stand for it."

"I care nothing for your king, General," Faenwelar said. "I care only that one day soon I will be ruler of all the elven people, and we will drive the race of men from this land. We will take back what is rightfully ours."

Kain stared in horror. This was much worse than he'd imagined. These elves were united, or soon would be, under one leader. They weren't just isolated pockets of trouble. He had played right into their hands by going to the rescue and worse, had exposed Alique. But they still had a choice; they could and would refuse to give in to *Lenweri* demands.

"I tire, General," Faenwelar said, "and so I will send you and the lady to your beds. We will begin again tomorrow." He nodded to Failora and walked into the forest.

"I will show you to your tent, General, Lady," Failora said in her exotic elven accent. "You will need your rest. Tomorrow is to be a long day."

* * *

Alique stared at the ceiling of the tent. She had long given up on the idea of sleep. Her eyes were gritty with fatigue and she was ashamed to admit, even to herself, that she had cried during the endless night.

It was not like her to weep, but she'd never been in such a dire situation.

It appeared Kain had slept. At least she had heard gentle snores issue from her companion. She was glad. He'd need all his wits about him if he was to stay a step ahead of the elves. Ha! What was she thinking? They hadn't been a step ahead of these people for many months, if not longer.

The tent lightened and she heard the camp stirring to life. Her heart quickened its pace, dreading the moment when she'd have to face the *Lenweri* again. For all her bravado, declaring she would get her revenge, Alique had to be realistic. She could cast her anger at the dark brethren but how was she to succeed in her plan to thwart them? Kain would certainly help, or more to the point, *he* would see the race of forest people driven from the kingdom. Her heart quailed; already she doubted they'd ever be free of the elves.

Kain stirred and opened his eyes. "Morning." He sat up and rubbed at his face. The bristles made a pleasing sound against his skin.

"Did you sleep at all?" he asked, studying her.

"Perhaps a little," she said. "I did hear snoring from your side of the tent."

"Sorry," he said, pulling on his shirt.

Alique sighed as his ridged abdomen disappeared. It was such a shame to cover a body like Kain's.

"We had better be up and ready to deal with the prince," he said.

"What do you think will happen?" Alique's stomach churned so badly she felt sick. "You can't divulge sensitive details to the elves. I'll stand torture before I see that happen."

"No, Alique," he said, reaching for her hands. "You won't withstand torture. I'll tell them what they wish to know."

"Kain –"

"You have no say in this," he said. "I'm a creature of conflict and I know how this works. Please tell me you'll let me handle this. It's the only way I can protect you and the kingdom."

Alique swallowed the bile that rose in her throat. She was willing to be tortured but he was right. She would not last long when the hot knives came against her. But what did he plan to tell them?

* * *

Kain sat outside their tent under a tree and watched as Alique picked at her breakfast. First, she had barely slept and now she wouldn't eat. He needed to know she'd be safe. That wouldn't be the case if she didn't look after herself. He wolfed down his meal as if it were his last. After years on the road, eating battle rations in all kinds of conditions, he'd learned to take his food and rest where he could. It was the only way to survive, and Alique's response to their situation was a stark reminder of how far apart their worlds lay.

"Eat," he said, "you need a full belly to face this day."

She grimaced. "My stomach is in knots. I don't know how you can eat with such relish."

"Necessity." Kain popped the last nut into his mouth and rinsed it down with a mouthful of water. "You never know when the next opportunity to eat will present itself. Also, it helps you think if you've fueled your body. You have a lot to learn."

She glared at him. "Well excuse me for failing to meet your exacting standards. I'll try to do better in future."

He knew he was being hard on her, but better that than for her to fall into a hole of her own making. "I'm trying to teach you some survival skills. You say you wish for revenge. So far all I see is empty talk."

"You really know how to kick a person when they're down."

Are those tears in her eyes? Goddess, things are worse than I thought. "Believe me, Alique, I don't wish to hurt you, quite the opposite. But you have a lot to learn about survival and toughness."

"Of course I do," she snapped. "I'm unused to being on the road and in situations that risk my life, not to mention fearing the loss of my family." She seemed to pull her composure together before going on.

"But I can learn, and if I need to stuff myself, no matter how unsettled my stomach feels, then I'll do so."

She began to push fruit and nuts into her mouth, chewing furiously, and Kain had to suppress a smile. She wouldn't appreciate him laughing.

"Perhaps I can teach you techniques to help you manage your fear and enable you to settle your nervous stomach." He leaned against a tree trunk. "Finish that mouthful and make yourself comfortable."

Surprisingly, she complied.

"Close your eyes," he said, doing the same. "Concentrate on your breathing – slow in, hold, and then slow out. Think about how it feels when the breath fills your chest and the movement of air in your body. Do this until you feel calm." He continued to breathe as he had instructed Alique, and within a few more breaths he had dropped into the trance that helped him relax and rest when on the move.

In moments, Kain was as relaxed as he ever was, aside from when sleeping. He waited a few more breaths, until he thought Alique might have calmed down, and opened his eyes. She had her eyes closed and her breathing was slow and full.

"Does your belly feel better now?" he asked.

She didn't open her eyes but replied, "The churning has settled."

"Good," he said. "Now imagine the muscles of your body relaxing one by one, the bones settling into the ground. In your mind tell yourself 'relax' or something similar."

She didn't reply but one eyebrow tweaked as if she was skeptical the technique would help.

Kain followed suit, relaxing all his muscles, and felt himself floating away like a leaf on a stream. He kept the image in his head until he had achieved the calm he sought, then replaced it with a flame. Into the flame, he fed all the anger, frustration and fear of the last two days. When the process had finished, he had achieved that perfect place where nothing could disturb him.

"What now?" Alique's voice crashed through, shattering his calm. *How the hell does she do that? She shouldn't be able to smash my composure so easily.* He swallowed down a moment of dread. He would *not* allow her to alter his world like this. He *would* be immune to her.

He drew a deep breath and opened his eyes. What he saw soothed his unease. The frown had disappeared from her forehead, her shoulders had relaxed away from her long, slender neck, and she wore a smile on her luscious mouth.

"It worked," Kain said, smiling back at her. "How's your stomach?"

"I think I can finish my meal now without vomiting. Thank you." She returned to her plate and it was soon empty.

"Such a technique will need to be used several times a day. The more you practice the better and quicker you'll be able to relax. In turn, you'll sleep soundly, make better use of your food, and think through problems with greater efficiency."

"It all sounds too good to be true," she said, her familiar mocking tone present in spades.

"You've seen the results for yourself. Imagine how effective the technique will be when you're adept at it."

Prince Gorin approached. "I love to watch a teacher at work, but we have some answers to gain today."

Kain stood slowly, stretching out the kinks from a night sleeping on the ground. He helped Alique rise and watched her straighten her skirts. He winced at the dirt on the once fine gown. After two nights sleeping rough, not to mention the birth of her niece, he thought the only fit ending for the dress would be the bonfire. But somehow Alique managed to look elegant despite the dirt and muck and wrinkles.

Although he wanted to ask what the prince intended for them, Kain remained silent. All would be revealed soon enough. Prince Gorin, Celri, and two other elves surrounded him and Alique as they walked to the center of the larger encampment.

A wooden pole had been erected and the two elven soldiers grasped Alique, one on either arm, and led her toward the pole.

"What are you doing?" Kain asked, striding after her. He was blocked by Gorin and Celri who roughly held him back. Alique sent a fearful glance his way as she was hustled up to the pole. Her hands were tied in front of her then pulled high over her head and secured to a large nail hammered into the wood.

"There's no need for this, Gorin," Kain said.

Alique's earlier calm had been shattered. Her eyes were wide, and her chest rose and fell in rapid gasps. The elves bound her waist to the pole with thick rope which they wound around her several times, as if she were a giant who could snap her bindings with a flex of her muscles.

But Gorin merely ignored Kain and turned to Faenwelar, who had seated himself on the stump of a huge oak. Failora arrived at his side and stood behind his left shoulder. Fury swelled in Kain. He was sick of wondering what these people had in store for him, and what they had to do with his past.

"Faenwelar!" Kain's voice echoed through the clearing and all turned to look.

The elven leader's eyes narrowed. "So, the general is capable of anger?"

"You've pushed too far this time, High Prince." He breathed deeply, trying to bring his rage into line. When he looked at Alique, tied to the tree and with fear in her eyes, he wanted to tear these elves limb from limb. It wasn't like him to feel battle rage. He released a ragged breath. Much about this *adventure* was strange. "I'll answer your questions without the need to torture the lady. Let her go." He wouldn't say "please" to these invaders.

Faenwelar snorted. "You men have not changed; still trying to lord it over our people." He stood and threw his hands out. "This is our land and our words hold sway here. If I say the lady is to be bound, then she is bound. If you do not answer to my satisfaction, she will pay. Perhaps that will keep you honest. You see, General, I know torturing you would prove futile. This woman, on the other hand, will not hold out very long and I do not think you could bear to see her hurt."

Kain's gut tightened. He'd have to be careful how he answered these questions or Alique would pay. "Ask your questions," he snapped.

Failora handed Faenwelar a steaming cup of tea, and he sipped, releasing a long sigh of contentment. Kain's patience stretched thin, and he fed the frustration into the flame as the moments ticked by in silence. By the time Gorin spoke, Kain had achieved some measure of control.

"What is your understanding of the *Lenweri* presence in the kingdom?" Gorin asked.

At least Kain could be truthful on this one. "Up until you held the lady's estate hostage, I had no real idea of the extent of the *Lenweri* incursions. Now, of course, it's a different matter."

Faenwelar stared at Kain. "And that is why you can never return to your former position, kingdom man. You, or the lady here."

Kain had suspected as much. "My options are limited then."

"You might say so. Your place would be assured amongst my people if you were to help us."

"And if I will not?"

"Then it will be a quick end for you after we have gained what we can." Faenwelar frowned. "Or perhaps we might keep you around to milk more information from you. I cannot, however, allow you your freedom."

"What of me?" Alique called. "You seem to be lumping me in with General Jazara as if I don't have a mind of my own. I could also be of help, skilled in healing as I am."

"You must think me stupid, Lady," Faenwelar said. "The only reason for you to stay alive is to ensure the general cooperates. If he dies, you do too. You would not betray your people, whereas Jazara has elven heritage."

"I dispute that," Kain snapped.

"It is fact. You bear an uncanny resemblance to a certain elven king. I hear he has recently departed to the halls of the dead. Please accept my condolences. He was your father."

Kain's stomach took a dive. He shook his head and staggered back until Celri stopped him. The elven high prince sounded so certain that he, Kain, looked like a past elven king.

"Resemblances are often in the eye of the beholder," Kain said, hardly aware of what he said at all.

Faenwelar shot to his feet and strode around the stump, seeming at the end of his tether. "You are stubborn enough to be the old king's son, that is sure."

"You're not making sense," Kain said. "If I'm an elven king's son, why has no one ever claimed me? Why is this the first I'm hearing of it, after being kidnapped by you?"

Faenwelar sighed. "I cannot answer those questions." He sat and turned to Gorin. "Proceed with your interrogation."

"What are the kingdom's strategies relating to the elven invasion thus far?" Gorin asked.

"We were still in the process of gathering intelligence," Kain said. "There has been trouble in the north with raids on our farmers. Recently one of our convoys, traveling between Brightcastle and Wildecoast, was attacked. Since then we've stepped up our patrols, particularly of the forests west of the capital."

"The news is that the king has lost his brother," Gorin said. "Brightcastle is vulnerable and the inheritance of the throne is under threat."

Kain shrugged. "Prince Zialni is dead but there is a steward in Brightcastle until the heir is born and comes of age."

"And what of Princess Alecia?" Gorin asked, his eyes narrowed. "We hear she is still at large, as is the army captain Anton."

"That is my information," Kain said, wondering where this line of questioning was going. So far, they had asked nothing that couldn't have been known by routine intelligence gathering. But he wasn't volunteering anything more than he had to.

"So, if the princess were to be located, would she be declared heir to the throne, as the prince's only child?" Faenwelar asked.

"Only kings have ruled here for at least two hundred years," Kain said. "Princess Alecia wouldn't be eligible to take the throne."

"And her offspring? Would her son not be an heir?" Gorin asked.

"Prince Zialni's widow is with child," Kain said. "If she produces a son, he will be heir before any child of Alecia's." He could see where they were going with this. If the elven nation could destabilize kingdom rule or corrupt its natural ruler, their invasion would be easier, or perhaps even unnecessary, if they could install a puppet king.

"Ah, Jazara," Faenwelar said, "but what if the child is a girl, or if something should happen to it? Then the line of succession is cut short. I believe there is a nephew of the king, Piotr, lurking somewhere. It seems more and more likely that, should something happen to the current king, this nephew might step into the breach."

"You won't succeed in sneaking in the back door, Faenwelar," Kain said. "Brightcastle is well defended, as is Wildecoast." At least he hoped Brightcastle was safe.

Faenwelar stood again and approached. Kain felt the high prince's breath on his cheek. "The kingdom is ripe for the picking, Jazara. Your people have fallen asleep on the job. Your king has failed to produce an heir, in fact, he has only lost them over the last year. He is soft as are you – soft and lazy. My people will walk into your cities and towns and burn them to the ground. We will obliterate the race of man from the kingdom. And you, my dear general, will help us."

CHAPTER 7

ALIQUE felt as though she was still tethered to the pole. Her wrists smarted and she was sure the rope had left bruising on her lower torso. The hour of interrogation had seemed like a day and she feared there was worse to come.

Kain sat in the opposite corner of the tent, lost in his own thoughts. He had been morose since being escorted back to the tent, and she didn't blame him. The elven prince's summary of the situation in the kingdom was sobering.

"We've been too complacent," he said. "*I've* been too complacent. How could I have let the kingdom come to this?"

"It's not your fault," she said. "You merely follow orders."

"It's my duty to analyze the kingdom's threats and defenses." He rubbed his restless fingers through his spiky dark hair. "I should've seen this coming."

"The king has other advisors. It's not only you who's to blame."

He shook his head. "What a mess! And now I'm not even able to help us dig our way out of it."

Alique crawled over and knelt before him. "Somehow we'll extricate ourselves and the kingdom."

"That's ridiculously optimistic."

"Perhaps," she said, "but what's the alternative? We can choose to believe there's a way out or we can give up now. I don't think you'll give up."

His dark eyes found hers. How had she ever thought them cold or remote? They were many things but never that. Currently they held a heat she hadn't seen before. He swept his hand down her cheek, the knuckles brushing her skin. She shivered. His gaze dropped to her mouth and her heart leapt into a gallop. She sucked in a sharp breath. "What are you doing?"

His hand dropped and he let out a long sigh… "I'm sorry. This is driving me crazy. I don't know what I'm doing." He covered his face with his hands.

Alique took a deep breath to quiet the tumult within. "It has been a difficult few days, but things will get better." She got no response from him, so she leaned forward, pulling his hands away from his head. "They will."

His dark gaze raked her face. "Has anyone ever told you you're magnificent?"

She gave her head a small shake and her heart lightened a little. "No, never."

"Well, let me be the first." He placed his hands on her shoulders and gave them a gentle squeeze. "Lady Alique Zorba, you're magnificent, and don't let anyone ever tell you otherwise."

Alique's heart swelled. This hard-bitten leader of men thought her worthy of praise. How little of that she had experienced in the past. As far back as she could remember, no one had paid her such a compliment. She swallowed the lump lodged in her throat.

"You can't imagine how much that means to me." She leaned forward and captured his lips before he could react, her hands sliding up along his jaw, her fingers entangled in his hair.

He gasped and froze for long seconds during which Alique wondered if she'd been too impulsive this time. *Will he reject me?*

And then both of his hands looped around the back of her neck as his lips found hers. Alique had expected mastery and passion but not this sweet, tentative exploration. His mouth was soft and succulent, and she sank into it, giving herself to the moment. She sighed, relaxing against him, her hands on his shoulders; shoulders broad enough to shelter her from a myriad of dangers if she required it. He deepened the kiss, his tongue thrusting past her lips, urgency mounting. The hands that cradled her head moved to her back, and he pulled her against his chest and rolled over, so Alique was on the ground under him.

She undid the ties of his shirt and slipped her hands inside to caress his chest, then pulled the shirt up to explore the muscles of his back. He moaned and his hand cupped her buttock. His fingers strayed breathtakingly close to her sex and Alique stilled, aching for the moment when he'd touch her there. He pulled her tighter against him, the bulge of his manhood nudging her thigh. Her body arched against it.

Kain gasped and drew back. "What am I doing?" His pupils were huge with arousal and he swallowed. "I'm sorry, Alique. That was inexcusable."

She froze at the apology. "I was enjoying myself." She reached for his hand and placed it back on her bottom.

"We can't do this," he said. "You and I are from different worlds; we need to keep perspective."

"This?" she said. "It's a kiss between two people in a dire situation who are attracted to each other. For once on this mission I wasn't fearful. What's wrong with that?"

"Don't you see how dangerous this is?"

"No," she said. "I only see a man I desire, a distraction. We could be dead tomorrow."

"Let's hope it doesn't come to that." He placed more distance between them, and she reluctantly let him go.

"But you see what I mean. There's no one to stop us from acting on our desires. I know you want me." She rolled onto her knees and seized his face in both hands before he could stop her, planting a kiss on his startled lips. Immediately she invaded his mouth, sliding her tongue over his and then along his teeth.

Kain sucked in a breath, as though being strangled, and broke contact with her. He looked startled beyond belief. "You have a reputation to maintain. I'll keep it for you even if you won't."

"I'm my own woman, and if I wish to tumble the general of the King's Army, then I shall."

She reached for him again but Kain held her off, his hands on her forearms. He gave her a little shake.

"If we act on our desires, you'll come to rue the decision."

"Ha," she said. He gave away so much with his words. "You never said *you* would regret it. Is it only me you're concerned for?"

He sighed. "You're a beautiful woman and I'd welcome you in my bed in other circumstances."

"The circumstances are perfect. No one need know. We can both walk away at the end of this and have no regrets."

He frowned. "Are you certain?"

Alique stared, thrown off kilter by his question. Could she walk away unaffected after a romantic tryst with Kain Jazara? "I know the difference between real feelings and what exists between us, Kain: the attraction between a man and woman."

"Are you a virgin, Alique?" he asked. "I wish to know where I stand."

"So, you *are* considering a fling with me?"

His eyes narrowed. "Perhaps, in the right circumstances."

"Then I'll answer your extremely rude question," she said. "No, I'm not a virgin. My first sexual encounter was with one of the farm hands when I was fifteen, and I saw no reason to stop there."

"You've been lucky to avoid a child," he said.

She tried to shake off his hands. "Enough of this idle chat. We're wasting time on words when we could be giving each other pleasure. Pucker up, General."

Kain's eyes widened as if he had difficulty believing his ears. "I will *not* make love to you, or tumble you, or even kiss you when you're in this mood. We'll be on the road in a few minutes."

He looked so annoyed she almost laughed. Something about this situation they found themselves in made her reckless; urged her to take a risk with the dark and dangerous General Jazara. Who knew when the next opportunity would present itself?

"Just kiss me, Kain."

His hands tightened on her arms and he drew her against his chest, his lips claiming hers with a mastery she hadn't felt before. Something within her answered his urgency. She wrapped her arms around his neck and pressed her womanly curves against his hard lines. The frantic beat of his heart told her Kain was very much affected by her body. He pushed her over until she again lay below him, and when his hand reached under her skirts, her hips bucked against his.

Kain groaned. "You'll be the death of me," he said, but his fingers continued their slide, first up the outside of her leg, then sweeping across to her inner thigh. Alique held her breath as his hand meandered closer to her core. She was wet with need, ready to accept his manhood, eager for the release the act would bring.

"Yes, Kain," she moaned. Let him not be in any doubt that she wanted this. She thrust her hips against him and the movement, as her pleasure spot encountered his taut manhood, nearly made her come. She had it bad for this man. His fingers stopped their wandering.

"Don't stop," she said, pulling his lips against hers and wrenching his shirt open to play with his nipples.

He was hot and hard and Alique was more than ready for him. His fingers crept closer to her moist folds and she moaned as his roughened fingertips slid over her engorged center.

"Oh, yes." She pushed against him. He continued, gliding his thumb over her core as Alique mounted higher and higher, until she hovered on the edge of a precipice, but Kain took her higher still. Just when she thought she could take no more, he slid two fingers into her, thrusting until she shuddered into oblivion.

She came back to reality, Kain's fingers inside her, her core trembling with the aftershocks of her completion. She gazed up at him, lost for words. His dark eyes seemed troubled.

"What's wrong?" she asked

"Nothing, except I'm not sure that was wise."

"Oh, it was wise, Kain, it certainly was. It was also amazing."

"Glad I could be of service," he said, a mocking tone to his words.

He pulled his fingers from her and Alique felt bereft. She wanted to give him as much pleasure as he had given her. "I'd be happy to return the favor."

He shook his head. "Get yourself tidied up. We'll be leaving soon. I wouldn't want anyone walking in on us."

Alique pulled her skirts down and straightened her bodice. "They know what we've been up to, unless they're deaf."

He shrugged and she realized he regretted his moment's weakness. Perhaps he'd never allow her to love him as he had just loved her. She was sad at the thought.

* * *

Ten minutes later they were on the road once again, Kain acutely aware he had stepped over the line with Alique. He couldn't erase the feel of her body against his hands, the scent of her arousal, the urge he had to make her his own. For a man who guarded his heart so closely, this was new. No one had forced their way past his defenses as Alique threatened to. She had wriggled through the barriers he had tried to erect. Perhaps it was the situation they found themselves in; emotions were running high and confidences were natural. Confidences led to closeness, and to caring. He must put a halt to this before one or both got hurt.

Content with his decision, Kain turned his attention to the trail, wondering why a rescue hadn't yet been mounted, and then berating himself for needing one. He doubted he had ever felt so vulnerable or so useless. His hands curled in the reins and Snow threw his head up. That earned him a sharp look from Celri. Kain shot him a hard look back.

He'd been told they were moving to the stronghold the elves held to the northwest. It was a journey of around ten days. Surely along the way they could disentangle themselves from the brethren. The elves called the city *Elvandang* but to Kain it sounded like the abandoned city of Amitania.

Alique rode ahead of him, her body slumped in the saddle. It had to be difficult to ride for long hours side saddle. Perhaps some trousers could be found so she could ride astride. He would give up his saddle for her and ride bareback as many of the elves did. His groin tightened as he imagined hours on the bony back of a horse, but chivalry demanded it.

* * *

Two days later, Alique rode with Kain and her elven captors deep in the forest to the northwest of Wildecoast. Brightcastle lay to the southwest, and they would soon head due north to Amitania. She had heard of the fabled city, doomed to destruction and moldering away in the forested mountains north of Brightcastle. There were conflicting stories regarding what had led to its downfall but the most popular was an uprising by the people against a tyrannical ruler. Not much had survived the civil war that rocked the city. It seemed the elves had chosen it as their stronghold.

Kain had organized elven leggings and a tunic for her so she could ride astride. He had given up his saddle as well. He now rode on a horsehair pad that couldn't be comfortable. So, even if he was withdrawn, she knew he thought of her, if only to regret his decision to offer up his seat. It irked to be attired in the clothing of the forest people, but Alique had to concede that side saddle was not for long trips. Her endurance had improved considerably, and since they tied her up each day and interrogated Kain, she had enough aches and pains to worry about without adding a stiff back to her woes.

The elves grew more frustrated with each inquisition. Kain had been masterful in sparing her. Each time she feared torture was imminent, he would offer up a tidbit of information which appeared to satisfy them. Alique wondered if they were capable of hurting her, but when she looked into Failora's eyes, she didn't doubt the elven woman could and would do her harm. Failora was a constant at the interrogations and often whispered into the ear of the high prince.

The nerves of all the party were stretched taut. Not knowing the fate of her family was slowly killing Alique. Since their intimate moment in the tent two days ago, Kain had been distant. She knew he was concerned no rescue had been forthcoming but also that he schemed their escape. If he would tell her what he planned, she might rest easier. She still left the markers, but her supply of calendula would soon run out.

Midmorning, they rode through a dense patch of forest where the trees blocked most of the light. Burning brands were lit to disperse the dark but despite this, Alique began to feel a prickle at the base of her skull, as though she was being watched. She glanced behind to Kain and caught him peering into the shadows beneath the trees with fixed concentration. Their captors appeared similarly alert.

The forest around them was quiet, even though at this time of the day the feathered inhabitants should be most active. Alique slowed her horse and fell back beside Kain without anyone noticing – another strange occurrence.

"Something is afoot," she said.

Kain nodded. "Perhaps our help is finally here."

"It must be so!" Her heart leapt with hope. She might see her family sooner than she thought.

"Stay close to me," he said. "Whatever it is, the situation will be dangerous."

Alique struggled to rein in her excitement, taking deep breaths until her thundering heart slowed to a more respectable pace.

They traveled further into the forest, alert for any sign of what might come next, as the light grew dimmer. Hardly anyone spoke but no one noticed Alique's position beside Kain. She battled harder than she ever had to keep her uneasiness in check, using Kain's relaxation exercises to good effect. She had to be ready for anything.

A blood-curdling scream echoed through the woods and the two elves who rode in front of her tumbled from their horses, arrows protruding from their backs. The horses reared and charged, causing chaos in the forward ranks. Alique gathered her reins even as she avoided the bodies of the fallen. Her mind swirled with the images before her. Horses panicked and bolted, and elves sawed at reins trying to control their mounts, as arrows sliced through the air to rip the hearts out of their captors. It had to be their rescue party.

An arm slid around her waist and she screamed before she realized it was Kain.

"Stay down." His arm slipped away. "Follow me."

He hustled Snow past Ebony and down a narrow path to the right of the track. Alique followed close behind, keeping her head low over Ebony's withers to avoid arrows and branches. Sticks grabbed at her cloak and legs, but the sound of the battle faded quickly as they moved into the dense trees, following the track.

"We've done it," she said. "We've eluded them!"

"Halt." The order came from an elven woman who appeared on the path twenty paces in front of them, an arrow aimed directly at Kain's heart. Two other elves, a woman with silver hair and a man, stood behind the first, also with arrows at the ready.

"You had to say it," Kain muttered. "You had to tempt fate by saying we had eluded them."

Alique frowned. "You're not that superstitious, are you?"

"All soldiers are."

"Cease the talk and dismount before I place this arrow between your eyes, kingdom man," the first woman said. She was tall and lithe with shoulder-length, dark hair and dark eyes. The customary elven breeches and tunic fit her like a glove, displaying her long-muscled legs and tiny waist to great advantage. Alique suppressed a stab of envy. If only she could carry off the costume with such aplomb. If only she had such thighs!

The elven woman studied them as they dismounted. "Step forward so I can see you." Her voice held all the authority of a queen.

Alique and Kain dismounted and made their way forward, as sounds of the fight carried through the trees. The elven woman didn't look familiar. Had she been with the party who had taken them hostage?

"You are a long way from home," she said, lowering her arrow a fraction. The others didn't follow suit.

"Not so far," Kain said, standing with his hands on hips, feet apart. Alique glanced at him, so calm and cool beside her, while she trembled. Who were these elves?

"And this woman with you?" the elven woman said. "Who is she?"

Kain frowned. "Who the hell are you first?"

Alique was confused. The woman's words seemed to imply she hadn't been with the elven group who had held them captive, and yet…

"I am Gwaethe Arenil, kingdom man, and you still have not answered my question."

"My name is Kain Jazara, and the lady with me is Alique Zorba, but you should know that."

"Why would I, when we have just met?" She nodded at Alique, her eyes running over her elven clothing. "The costume suits you well, My Lady."

Alique's breath caught. "Thank you," she said, feeling silly that she could not think of any compliment in return.

"I have looked long and hard for you, General Jazara," Gwaethe said, her dark gaze shifting back to Kain. "You will please come with me and know I mean you no harm."

Gwaethe turned and strode up the path. The other two elves stepped back, arrows still trained, allowing Kain and Alique to lead their horses past. Whatever Gwaethe said, they were still prisoners.

CHAPTER 8

KAIN followed the elven woman, Gwaethe, as she negotiated the narrow trail, his mind mulling over reasons for her intervention. He was almost positive she hadn't been in the original group. Was it her people who had attacked Faenwelar's party or was Gwaethe simply taking advantage of the confusion? If so, why? There was a teasing familiarity about her which he couldn't place. She had volunteered she meant them no harm, and had been polite to Alique. But no matter how she appeared, he couldn't afford to relax his guard.

Gwaethe veered off the narrow track and onto an equally narrow path which began to wend its way to the southeast. Before he could ask any questions, the track opened out into a small clearing beside a brook. Several other elves were waiting there with horses, including three without riders. Gwaethe marched straight up to a golden stallion with silver mane and tail and ran her fingers through his blond forelock.

The elves on foot behind them moved to the right and left of him and Alique, arrows still nocked and trained. The elven woman with the short silver hair wore tight black leather leggings and tunic. Her eyes were a brilliant pale blue, like the sky, but they were cold as a winter's night. The man was unremarkable, typical dark skin, short black hair and dark eyes.

Kain waited with impatience while Gwaethe greeted her horse. Finally, she sighed and turned to face him, folding her arms across her chest, accentuating generous breasts; very generous for an elven woman.

"As I said, I have searched long and hard for you over many months and now I have you before me, I do not know how to begin." Her face looked troubled which made her appear young.

"At the beginning is usually a good place," Kain said, his frustration growing. *This elven race could try the patience of a holy man.*

"Not here," Gwaethe said, turning to vault onto her horse. "Mount up, we ride for our camp." So saying, she spun her horse and left the clearing via another narrow trail on the north-eastern side.

They galloped through the dense forest, angling to the east. Kain estimated they were now moving to a position due north of Wildecoast. His gut was in turmoil. These elves were like the other *Lenweri* who had taken them hostage, and yet subtly different. For one thing, there were female elves who were apparently warriors. Gwaethe seemed to be in command of the group, which grew with the addition of another dozen riders about an hour after the ambush. Some carried wounds. They gave a hushed report to Gwaethe and then took up position in the band.

Apart from a short break for a meal, they rode non-stop until it was near dark, alternating between walk, trot and canter to save the horses. Alique looked ready to drop from the saddle by the time they rode into a large clearing surrounded by burning brands on poles. Several tents had been erected, and there was a picket line where a handful of horses were already tied.

"See to the horses," the silver-haired elven woman said as she slipped to the ground and came to stand beside Gwaethe. Six elves scrambled to do her bidding.

Kain dismounted and helped Alique down from Ebony. Gwaethe joined Kain, patting Snow on his velvet nose.

"He is a beauty," she said.

Kain frowned at her. "I assume you didn't bring us here to admire our horses, Lady Gwaethe."

She looked sharply at him. "You use sarcasm to your advantage, General. I like that."

"I don't care what you like, I need an explanation."

Gwaethe shook her head. "In case you had not noticed, you are our *guest*. You will not be making demands."

"What am I," Kain asked, "guest or hostage? Have I left the frying pan to jump into the fire?"

"That is for you to decide."

"Cease the cryptic comments and tell me who you are and what you want," Kain snapped. Alique put her hand on his arm as if to calm him. He flashed her a look and her hand dropped away.

"What do you know?" Gwaethe asked. "Why were you taken by the other *Lenweri*?"

"They also said they searched for me. They wanted information about the kingdom's defenses, some rubbish about taking their rightful lands back."

"Did they tell you anything else?" Gwaethe asked, seeming a little desperate.

"A story about me having elven blood," he snapped. The idea still made his gut churn and his hands shake.

Gwaethe took a deep breath. "It is true," she whispered.

"It *can't* be true!" He stalked back and forth across the small space, needing to find an outlet for the frustration and fear inside. His life had been certain before this and that was the way he liked it. He arranged his life to suit himself and ordered others to do the same. Now he felt as if he were suspended over a chasm and all that held him was a thread of cotton.

"You look so much like him," Gwaethe said, her voice low as if talking to herself.

"They said that too," Kain said, "that I looked like some elven king."

"Orionkael," Gwaethe said, "that is his name. He was my father."

She walked over to a nearby fire and sat gazing into the flames, her arms wrapped around her body. She looked young and vulnerable, too much so to be leading a raiding party through enemy territory. Despite his reluctance to deal with these people, Kain joined her.

"I look like your father," he said. "And are you saying this Orionkael is related to me?"

Gwaethe nodded. "We share a father. It is why I have sought you. Orionkael is dead, and our people need a leader – someone who can guide us through our troubles and help us find a place in this world."

"You think that person is me?" Kain's mind refused to accept that here was his half-sister. He looked across at Alique who studied them, her eyes narrowed. She raised her brows and shrugged.

"All I know is that it cannot be me," Gwaethe said. "Females are not given positions of leadership amongst our people, at least not the role of supreme leader." She looked at Kain searchingly. "But I should explain myself."

"Please do," Kain said, making no effort to water down the sarcasm. The last few days had been the craziest he had ever endured, and it seemed his world was about to be further turned upside down. What would all this mean for his life, his family, if it were true?

"You have met Faenwelar," Gwaethe said. "He leads the *Sis Lenweri*. *Sis* means 'chosen' and they are dedicated to regaining the lands of our people lost to the kingdom. If the truth be known, he intends his reign to extend further, but that is his starting goal. Bitterness drives him, and now he has passed his bitterness on to me, for he killed my father."

"I'm sorry," Kain said.

"Faenwelar and Orionkael never saw eye to eye. Faenwelar was influenced by a powerful wizard who drove him to conquer the lands of men. With increasing raids by *Sis Lenweri* forces, my father traveled from deep in the mountain forests to the north to meet with Faenwelar in *Elvandang*, the city you call Amitania."

"I know it," Kain said. "It was where we were headed when you raided the party."

"Correct," she said. "The two leaders fought, and my father was wounded." She swallowed hard several times before she could go on. "When he made it back to his mountain home, he was near death from blood loss. I did what I could for him, but after lingering for a week he finally traveled to the halls of the dead."

Kain reached out to grasp Gwaethe's shoulder which vibrated with a fine tension. "It must have been hard losing him." The words felt inadequate.

"The only thing that kept him going until he reached home was the message he carried to me. He had one last request to make on his death bed. One last troubling announcement."

"Which was?" Kain asked, the hairs on the back of his neck standing up.

"That he had a son somewhere in the kingdom, born of a woman he loved decades ago, when he was a young man. My half-brother. You." Gwaethe stared at Kain. His heart pounded what sounded like a death knell; a death knell for his world as he knew it. If this was true...

"I assume you can prove this," he said.

"No, I cannot, not yet," Gwaethe said. "I only hope your mother is still alive to confirm she had a son by Orionkael. She might not even have known he was an elven prince then."

"My mother lives."

"Thank the gods," Gwaethe breathed. "When can I speak to her?"

Kain shook his head. "You won't speak to her. I'll do it."

"But there is much I would ask, not just about you, but about my father."

"A lot of water has gone under the bridge since then, if this is true. My mother might not wish for her mistakes to be dredged up."

Gwaethe stared. "You think your birth was a mistake?"

"What else could it be? My mother couldn't have wanted a half-breed child to tarnish her life." Disgust and anger threatened to rob Kain of his breath.

Alique spoke. "Kain, you don't know the circumstances. Can't you reserve judgment until you speak to your mother?"

She could be soft at times, gentler than he had ever anticipated.

"How could she do this?" Kain snapped. "My whole life she has lied to me."

"Kain!" Alique said, gripping his forearms.

He shook her off. "You don't know how it feels to find out your life has been a lie."

"This might be a lie too," Alique said, glaring at Gwaethe. "We only have *her* word for it."

"She seems sincere."

"So, you would take the word of a strange elven woman over that of your mother, your family?"

"You all keep saying how elven I look." Kain pointed at Gwaethe. "*She* says I look like her father. Faenwelar says I look like the elven king. All my life people have remarked on how I look nothing like my father and not much like my siblings. I didn't think anything of it, laughed it off. Now I begin to understand why I might seem the odd one out. But it's not only that."

Kain thought of the trees and their murmurings. His abductors *had* heard that. It was another reason to believe he had elven ties. He turned to Gwaethe. "You hear the trees, don't you?"

He felt Alique stiffen beside him.

Gwaethe inhaled sharply. "All elves hear the forest whispering. They listen to the trees from childhood. It is integral to our being."

Kain closed his eyes, trying to take in this latest confirmation of his heritage, the strongest evidence yet that his father was elven.

"Why didn't you tell me what you were experiencing?" Alique said. "All this time when you were acting strangely you were listening to the trees?"

Kain looked at her to find her eyes narrowed.

"You didn't trust me!" she said. "You thought I'd judge you! I deserved to know what was happening."

"This isn't about you, Alique!" Kain snapped. "I was hearing voices, being accused of elven heritage and of being a traitor, dealing with being taken hostage, and trying to keep us alive. I had to hold something close to my chest, to allow myself time to process it. I'm sorry if that upsets you."

Alique stared at him, hurt blazing from her eyes. "Just don't make a judgment until you've spoken to the woman who gave you birth."

"I'll think on what you've said." It was a hard possibility to swallow, that the most important woman in his life had kept such a significant secret. *Lies!*

He looked from Alique to Gwaethe, who stood with arms crossed, watching his reaction. "What now?" he asked.

Gwaethe let out a long breath and dropped her arms. "We escort you back to your home in Wildecoast. Perhaps you can find me somewhere to stay while you talk with your mother. I would like to know the outcome."

Kain swallowed hard. This was getting more complicated by the second. His half-sister wanted to hang around to find the truth. He'd give anything for this not to be fact, but something deep in his gut told him Gwaethe's declaration was true.

"So, we're still prisoners?"

Gwaethe shook her head. "Of course not. I would never hold my own brother hostage. However, you are still not safe, and I must insist on this escort. There were some survivors of our raid on Faenwelar's party, including the high prince and his son. They will not give you up easily."

Kain considered. He didn't have much choice in the matter and Gwaethe was correct in saying that the other elven faction was still a threat.

"Lady Alique and I would be grateful for your help in getting us back to Wildecoast. As to your accommodation, it must be only you and perhaps one other. I can't have Wildecoast swarming with dark elves. The king wouldn't appreciate it."

Gwaethe grinned at Kain's words but there was no answering mirth in his heart. The need to escape and mull the revelations over in his head rose to engulf him.

CHAPTER 9

ALIQUE was filthy and exhausted, but uppermost was fear as she rode with Kain toward the gates of Wildecoast. They had traveled for almost three days south with Gwaethe's party, leaving the elves in camp in the forests to the north. They wouldn't be safe there for long. Kain was to deliver gowns and bonnets for Gwaethe and her diminutive silver-haired companion, who turned out to be her cousin, Isiloe. They would enter the city and stay in one of the inns in the northern quarter. The remainder of the party of elves would retreat further north to await Gwaethe and Isiloe's return.

Alique thought it a plan fraught with flaws. At any time, the king's patrols could discover the larger party of elves as they waited in the forests, and the elven women would hardly be inconspicuous on the streets of Wildecoast. Their skin was too dark for one thing, and Isiloe's hair shone like a beacon, guaranteeing her plenty of attention. Alique had tried to say as much to Kain, but he had been almost completely silent since the conference in the forest after their rescue. She supposed he had much to think about, but it upset her after the closeness they had shared.

She tried to focus instead on *her* family. After days of being on the road and not knowing, now she would discover their fate. They had to be well, they just had to be.

The city gates loomed above them and a rotund sergeant held up his hand.

Kain emerged from his silence. "Ho Grif!

"General Jazara!" Grif saluted, a broad smile creasing his face. "The king has half his army out looking for you and here you turn up at the gates unannounced. Glad I am that you and the lady are safe." His gaze found Alique, but he didn't quite meet her eyes. "My Lady, you will be anxious to know of your kin. They are well, although some received burns. Your father was a hero, ensuring all escaped the barn."

Alique let out a sigh and looked to the heavens. "Thank the Goddess, Sergeant, and thank you for relaying the news so quickly. I've been sick with worry."

Grif still looked uncomfortable. There was something he wasn't revealing.

"What haven't you told me?" she asked.

Grif avoided her gaze and instead looked to Kain. "General, I think you and the lady should speak with the queen."

"Just spit it out, Grif," Kain snapped. "We don't have time or patience for your games."

Grif muttered under his breath and then squared his shoulders and looked at Alique for the first time. "Your father is missing, My Lady. No one knows where he is."

Alique's heart thumped, bringing an ache in her sternum. "Missing? What do you mean missing?"

"The morning after the rescue, he wasn't found anywhere on his estate, and no one had seen or spoken to him."

Alique stared, unable to take in the news. "How could he just vanish?" She turned to Kain. "General?"

Kain grasped her above the elbow. "Don't think the worst, My Lady. I'll get to the bottom of this." He looked at Grif. "Are the search parties also looking for Lord Zorba?"

Grif nodded. "They are. I'm sorry, My Lady."

Alique barely heard him. Her father was gone, and nobody knew where. His last deed had been to rescue his people. *I must find him!* The first place to start was her estate. She turned Ebony about, ready to gallop to the south.

Kain grasped her reins. "You can't do anything to find him at the moment."

"I have to know!" Alique had never felt so reckless, so overcome with the need to act.

Kain pulled her mount away from Grif and lowered his voice. "I'll find him, Alique, just don't do anything rash."

"You can't be sure you'll find him alive," she snapped. "I've worried about him all this time and just when I think he is well, he is not."

"There are any number of reasons for his absence. He could be looking for you!"

"The woods north of here are crawling with dark elves. It's too dangerous. And what if he *has* been taken by them?"

"Stop it!" Kain snapped. "Stop imagining the worst. The bulk of your family is safe. Focus on that and on being strong for them."

She took a deep breath and tried to slow her racing heart. It was good advice, but… her father! She couldn't lose him! "I'll try."

"Come with me." Kain walked his horse back to Grif. "Can you get us an escort so that we may be conveyed to the castle in haste?"

"Already done, General," Grif said, "they should be here shortly."

Kain turned to Alique. "I'll go to my rooms and change. Organize the clothes for Gwaethe and Isiloe as soon as you can and send word to me. I must have time to think on what I can tell His Majesty. In the meantime, find out what you can about your father. Say nothing of your ordeal."

"I do know how to hold my tongue," she said, and then her heart softened at the look of desolation on his face. His world might be crumbling. "When will you speak with your mother?"

"Tonight."

"I could be with you when you speak to her, if you like?"

He seemed surprised at her offer. "No, this is something I must do alone."

"Again, I beseech you," she said, "don't judge her too harshly. She was a young girl then. Let her explain… and try to understand."

"I can't promise you that."

"Please try. She deserves your respect."

His face hardened but then he nodded. It was all Alique would get from him, she suspected, but it was something.

The escort arrived in the form of Alique's cousin, Lieutenant Josef Formosa, and his men. She almost groaned with frustration. *Of all the rotten luck!* Josef was a pompous ass of a man whom she had never warmed to. He was Ramón's age, but annoyingly full of his own importance.

The lieutenant saluted Kain and they formed up around the two wanderers. Josef fell in beside Alique, which was natural enough she supposed, considering they were related.

"I'm sorry to hear of your family trials and your father's disappearance," he said. "It's good to see you returned in safety though."

"Thank you, Josef. It's good to be back. Can you tell me anything of father?"

He nodded. "I'm privy to certain details and have led several search parties. It appears your father took one of his brood mares and left his estate the morning after he was released from the barn. None of your family or estate workers spoke to him before he left."

"Then he hasn't been taken by the elves?" Alique asked.

"It's unlikely, unless he came across them in his travels."

Kain called back to them. "What did he take with him?"

"As far as we can tell, enough provisions for two weeks, and his long bow and arrows."

"He *is* searching for me," she said, dismay making it difficult to breathe. "Why didn't he stay put?"

"He loves you," Kain said. "How could he just sit when his daughter was in danger?"

"He could have trusted me *and* you," she said. "He has responsibilities. I hate to think what will happen if he dies."

"He's only thinking of you, My Lady," Kain said.

She turned to Josef. "Have you found any trace of Papa?"

"He appears to have headed north into the forest," Josef said. "We have our best trackers on his trail but no news from them yet."

Alique mulled over her options. Kain would want her to sit quietly waiting for others to search, and even he had personal matters to sort through before he went looking for her father. She couldn't sit by and wait while every hour carried her papa into elven hands.

"I'll join the very next search party that leaves Wildecoast," she said.

Kain and Josef cast each other worried looks.

Kain cleared his throat. "You won't be joining any search party, My Lady. We have matters to resolve first."

Josef looked at them with interest. "You'll need to speak with the king and queen, on the subject of what passed during your captivity." He peered at Alique. "Your return alone with the general will be a source of speculation. It seems your side of the family are quite adept at causing a scandal."

"I hope you'll quash any malicious rumors." Alique could well remember when her brother Ramón and the Lady Benae Branasar had ridden into Wildecoast after being attacked by dark elves on their way from Brightcastle. It was a bare three months ago and even she had teased her brother about his relationship with the beautiful Benae.

But this situation was different. Alique was a free woman and the troubles with the dark elves were now well-documented. Benae had been betrothed at the time to Prince Zialni. Of course, now, with the prince dead and Benae pregnant and sharing stewardship of Brightcastle with Ramón, Alique had to wonder what the truth of their relationship had been when they were in Wildecoast.

Her face burned as she imagined the rumors that might be circulating already regarding herself and Kain. All she could do was crush anything that started and hope the damage was not too great.

Josef raised his brows. "I would never allow wicked gossip about you, Cousin. You have been through a great ordeal, as have your family. As part of the Zorba clan, I have no wish for the name to be tarnished."

"I assure you nothing improper happened between myself and the general." Damn that heat she felt in her cheeks. It would reveal her for the lying woman she was. And damn Josef and all his type, for it was none of their business. The trouble was, it did matter what people thought of her. It could affect her prospects and her life in all sorts of ways.

News spread quickly in the city and crowds already lined the streets to watch the arrival of the freed hostages. Kain looked composed but his shoulders were tense. He wouldn't relish this attention when he had so much on his mind. His withdrawal from her hurt, but it was clear to her that he needed space to think and work through the revelations of the last days. Also, there was the looming meeting with his mother. She wished he didn't have to go through it alone.

They made it past the inner gates to the castle and Alique noted a visible relaxing of Kain's shoulders. He dropped back beside her.

"Send a maid with the money and clothes, well wrapped, to the barracks," he said, for her ears alone. "This must be done with the utmost secrecy and as soon as possible."

"I realize the urgency and discretion required." She couldn't help her annoyance. After what they'd been through, didn't he know she understood what was at stake? "You can trust me."

Josef looked on with interest and so she added, louder. "I'll never be able to thank you enough for extracting me from that predicament, General. You have my deep thanks."

"I was only doing my job, protecting the citizens of Wildecoast. I'll also do my best to see that your father is returned." He bowed from the saddle and cantered back through the gates, heading for the barracks.

"An interesting man, the general," Josef said, looking after Kain's retreating form. "Not many know him well. Yes, a man of mystery indeed." Josef sounded as though he would like to uncover every one of Kain's secrets. Alique prayed he wouldn't. She couldn't bear it if her family caused Kain a moment of regret.

"If you'll excuse me, Josef," Alique said, dismounting unassisted, "I'm anxious to speak to the queen. Thank you for your escort. Please give my regards to your parents when next you see them."

Josef hurriedly dismounted and bowed before her, deeper than she deserved. "You're welcome, Alique. Tell my aunt I'll do all I can to help find Uncle Yaral."

Alique nodded and turned away. The sooner she got those clothes to Kain, the sooner she could be on the path to finding her father.

* * *

Kain stomped into his quarters in the barracks, having first seen to Snow. The horse appeared to have suffered no ill effects from trekking through the forest for days. Kain wished he could say the same for himself. He was bone weary and his nether regions ached like the devil. Riding with no proper saddle was for the elven bastards who had taken him hostage. He'd be sore for days and hoped the bruising ride had done no lasting damage.

A pang of regret struck when he thought of his family life as a child. Were his happy memories about to explode into a million fragments? He crossed to the small mirror on his wall. Finally, he could examine the face that had looked back at him for thirty-odd years. His skin was dark, but he had always thought it tanned. His face was lean as was his body. He swept the hair back from his ears to reveal blessedly rounded tips. In that regard he was fully human.

Listen to me! I'm taking them at their word when I have no good reason. No good reason except it made sense in a weird way. He didn't look like his siblings. His father had always said he took after his mother's side of the family. If this was true, did his father know?

A shiver ran through him. He couldn't wait any longer to ask the questions that had been building for days. The king had asked him to present himself at the earliest opportunity, but he could wait. Kain stripped off his clothes and gave himself a quick wash and a shave, then dressed in civilian attire. He threw on his hat and a cloak and left the barracks, trying to attract as little attention as possible.

Once out of the castle gate, he took the central avenue and entered the city. His muscles ached at the punishment, but it would do them good. He turned left off the avenue about halfway along, into a wide street full of craftsmen. His family's shop was only a short distance on the right. There was a large workshop at the front and a comfortable residence above.

The bell rang as Kain stepped through the door. "Father?"

Lamps lit the interior of the shop, revealing the glowing timbers of various items of furniture. His father stuck his head around a large cabinet with ornate carving, another of his specialties.

"Kain! Thank the Goddess!" He hurried forward and enveloped Kain in a hug. Kain stiffened but then relaxed into his father's arms. It was good to be home. "Your mother has been beside herself with worry."

"You should both know by now that I can take care of myself."

"Doesn't stop us from worrying, Son. Let me look at you." He stood back and examined Kain from top to bottom. "You've lost weight. Only to be expected with what you've been through."

"Father, I need to talk with Mother," Kain said. If he didn't get to this now, he'd snap from the tension.

"Of course you do. Go up and I'll be there soon. Have dinner with us. Your brother is out, bringing in a load of timber."

Kain climbed the stairs and found Astelle Jazara getting dinner ready.

"Hello, Mother," he said.

"Kain!" She threw herself at him, wrapping her arms around his waist. "I was so worried. I've hardly slept since I heard you were missing."

She did look tired and thin. In fact, his mother looked her age.

"Well, I'm all right now, but I need to ask you something."

She stepped back from him, a wary look on her face. "That sounds serious."

Kain swallowed hard, begging for the rumors not to be true. "I was taken by dark elves, Mother." He watched for any sign that the news might make her nervous and was devastated to see her gaze drop for a second. His stomach tightened.

There was nothing else but to come right out and ask. "Was my father elven?"

Astelle turned her back on him and walked into the kitchen. "I feared it would come out one day," she said, kneading the bread as though she wanted to strangle it. "I worried about that too when I heard who had you."

"So, it's true?"

She nodded. "Your father was a dark elf. His name was Orionkael Arenil."

Kain imagined he had prepared himself, but her words turned his blood to ice. Suddenly he felt the need of a good thick coat. He crossed to the fire, rubbing his hands before it as he struggled to bring his panic under control.

"I'm half elven," he said, thinking if he spoke the words it might become more real. *No.* "Were you ever going to tell me?" He couldn't look at his mother; had to keep his feelings tight inside so he could bear this.

He heard her approach. "No, I wasn't. What was the point? I see now what the knowledge is doing to you and I was right to withhold it." Kain heard her shuffle closer. Perhaps reach out for him.

He straightened his shoulders. "You should have told me." His voice belonged to another man – an angry, frightened, cold man. "You had no right."

She came to his side, but he wouldn't look at her. "It doesn't make any difference to who you are as a man, Kain. You're still my son and your father still loves you."

"He's not my father," Kain snapped. "My father lies in a grave in the mountains and I never knew him." He snapped his mouth shut before he said words that would crush her.

His mother gasped and now he looked at her; saw the grief etched on her face.

"Orionkael is dead? You're sure?"

Kain nodded. "His daughter told me... my half-sister, Mother. You thought I didn't need to know my family? That my heritage wouldn't come back to haunt me?"

His mother had her hands over her face and when she dropped those hands, tears filled her eyes.

Had he ever really known her? "You clearly had feelings for Orionkael."

Astelle sat in a chair by the fire and Kain took the other.

"Yes, I had feelings," she said. "I was in love with him." She glanced at the doorway as if fearing to be overheard. "I was very young, only seventeen, when I met him. I lived with my parents in a town far to the north-west. Sometimes we traded with the elven people. They were gentle, musical. I used to travel out with my father to help him harvest the wood from which we made our living. One day I was washing at the stream and felt eyes upon me. When I looked up, there was Orionkael."

She looked again toward the door and then, arms wrapped around herself, she went on. "I loved him on sight, and I think the same could be said for him." She blushed. "He wooed me for the time my father and I camped in the forest. Those days were magical." The years fell from her face and Kain was easily able to imagine the young, vulnerable girl his mother had been.

"But inevitably the time came for my father and I to return to town, and Orionkael and I shared one last night. He promised we would be together one day and it's why I never worried about a child. We were in love and it didn't matter."

"You never saw him again?"

She nodded. "Oh yes, I did. Several months later, I returned to the forest with father and during that time, Orionkael and I found each other again. I don't know how but he seemed to know I was there. Perhaps he kept watch for me. I liked to think so." She rubbed her abdomen as if reliving that time.

"I told him I was with child and he was overjoyed. He said he couldn't wait to watch me grow large with his babe. He promised to present me to his father and mother the very next day, and we would live with his people. I was frightened at the thought of all that strangeness, but he seemed so excited I couldn't disappoint him."

"What happened?" Kain asked, his hands clasped tight between his knees.

Astelle drew a deep breath. "He didn't return the next day, but I kept watch for him for two weeks, despair lacing my heart. I loved him and I was carrying his child – you."

"Gwaethe said Orionkael knew he had a son," Kain said, his voice cold even to his own ears. "Gwaethe is my half-sister."

Astelle frowned. "Gwaethe," she said. "A pretty name."

Kain snapped. "How did Orionkael know he had a *son?*"

"The story didn't finish there," Astelle said, her eyes sadder than he had ever seen them. "Soon after Father and I returned home, I could no longer hide that I carried child and told my parents the whole story. They were horrified and angry. They forbade me to speak of it, and Father said he would handle everything. I was ashamed and hid myself away from the eyes of my community."

"Father went on a trip into the mountains and returned with a sack full of gold. He told me that Orionkael's father – an elven king, no less – had given it to him in reparation for his sins. Father said Orionkael wanted nothing to do with me or my child." She placed her fist to her mouth to stifle a sob. "My heart broke that day. I felt so alone."

A small crack of pity opened in Kain's heart. His mother had been young and vulnerable, and her love had been true. It was Orionkael who let her down.

"But how did Orionkael know he had a son?" Kain asked.

"When you were born, Father again ventured into the mountains and returned with another sack of gold. He said it was the final payment for Orionkael's indiscretion, and that the elves never wanted to see or hear from any of us again. If you had been born dead or lost during the pregnancy, there would have been no more gold."

Kain's gut shriveled with shame. "Where did Father come in?"

Again, Astelle took a deep breath. "You must not blame him, Kain. He has been a good man to me and to you. He did not have to rescue my honor."

"What happened, Mother?"

She pursed her lips. "Soon after my pregnancy became obvious, Guile and I were betrothed. My father arranged it. Guile was an apprentice to my father, almost finished his study."

The voice of Guile Jazara floated from the doorway. "I had long admired your mother," he said. "I couldn't believe it when Master Ambon came to me and offered her hand in marriage. He promised a large dowry and all I had to do was accept another man's child."

Guile looked at Astelle, love shining in his eyes. "I didn't need the gold. I was already in love with this wonderful girl and didn't care if she was with child. We all make mistakes, you see."

"Right," Kain said. "That would be me, the mistake."

Guile shook his head. "I've never once regretted the day I married your mother, and I've never regretted calling you son. Any man would be proud to have you."

"But not Orionkael," Kain said.

"There is no need for shame," Guile said, stepping further into the room and coming to stand beside Astelle's chair. He placed his hand on her shoulder. "You are as much mine as any of the others."

Kain surged to his feet. "That's hardly the point, Father!" He stumbled over the last word. What if he could never be comfortable saying it again? "I'm half elven. I have no place in this society. I have no place in any society. When the king finds out –"

"There is no reason for him to know," Guile said.

"I can't hide this," Kain snapped. "I was targeted because of who I am. The elves were looking for me, hoping to draw me out. They succeeded. The only reason I'm free now is because of Gwaethe."

Astelle stood. "I must meet her."

"No!" Guile faced his wife, and Kain saw fear in his eyes. "I forbid it."

Astelle gripped his elbows. "What harm can it do, Guile? Orionkael is dead. All these years I wondered how he could cast me aside. Perhaps now I can understand."

"Does my love mean nothing?" Guile asked.

"You know what?" Kain asked. "I'm going to leave you to this discussion, because I need to be alone."

He had their attention now. "Don't go, Kain," Guile said. "Let us explain."

Kain shook his head. "Perhaps later."

"At least tell us more of your ordeal," Astelle said.

"Mother, you've kept this secret from me for decades. I can't stay in this room with the two of you any longer. I'm sorry." He turned and bolted for the stairs, taking them two at a time. He was through the shop and out the door in seconds, heading for the nearest tavern.

CHAPTER 10

"I DIDN'T know who else to tell, My Lady," Sergeant Grif Tyne said as he led Alique up to the barracks, a sprawling building that lay outside the palace walls. "He's had a skin full of ale, wouldn't let me call his folks. I brought him here and then fetched you."

"You did the right thing, Sergeant," Alique said. "Show me his room, and then you must wait outside."

"He isn't expecting you," Grif said.

Alique drew in a sharp breath. So, he hadn't called upon her for help. For some reason it deflated her. She had sent a maid earlier with the package for Kain, and the girl had returned with her parcel, saying she couldn't locate the general. Now Alique knew why. His urgency to speak to his parents had been so great, he had gone straight there and must have forgotten the clothing for the elven women. Alique had the parcel with her. Perhaps something might be salvaged from this debacle.

Grif led her through a warren of passages to a door at the end of a corridor. He knocked. "General, it's Grif." He cracked the door and looked in. Alique heard snoring.

She entered the room behind the sergeant. Kain's quarters were large with a fireplace at either end. A bed stood near one fire while a desk and chairs were arranged before the other. Kain lay on the bed, fully clothed, though he appeared to have changed from the filthy clothing he had worn during their ordeal.

Alique walked across the room and poured a tankard of water for Kain.

"General," she said, shaking his shoulder, "Sergeant Tyne has brought me to tend to you."

"Go away," he said, without opening his eyes. "Did we not see enough of each other to last you a lifetime?"

Alique's stomach clenched at the alcohol on his breath. "Oh, so you remember our adventure?"

"I'm not in the mood for talking."

"I'm not going anywhere," she said, pulling a chair to the edge of the bed and taking a seat. She turned to find Grif looking at them with a frown. "You may wait outside, Sergeant. I'll be quite safe here."

He nodded and left.

A wave of exhaustion swept over her. No wonder Kain was in this state if he felt anything like she did.

"I assume this means you've spoken to your mother and confirmed your elven heritage?" she asked.

"It would seem so," he mumbled, rolling over so he faced away from her.

"And now you're feeling sorry for yourself?"

Kain spun back and groaned, seizing his head. "Can this wait?"

"No," she said. "You were supposed to deliver these clothes." Alique held up the bundle. "What will your sister think when you don't arrive? What if she comes looking for you and falls foul of the guard, or worse?"

"I'm doing the best I can."

"It's not good enough!"

"I'll get the clothes to Gwaethe tomorrow. She'll understand."

Alique sighed. "What happened?"

He took a deep breath and slowly released it. "Everything up to now is a lie," he said. "My mother was in love with Orionkael, when she was seventeen, and became pregnant. Seems he didn't want to know about the child and paid my mother and her family to make the problem go away. My father – my stepfather I mean – agreed to marry my mother and raise me. Guile Jazara settled for someone else's woman. He was bought and I was sold, like a piece of property."

Alique reached for his shoulder and found it rock hard with tension. "Nothing I can say will make this better for you."

"Then say nothing. I'm not your concern."

"I thought perhaps we might have meant more to each other, after what we endured." Alique knew she shouldn't have been hurt by his words, but it cut her that he was shutting her out.

"Didn't you hear what I said, Alique? I'm half elf, and not only that, my father was an elven king. I don't know what ramifications it will have, but I'm sure you should stay well away."

She swallowed hard. "As your friend, I can't just walk away. You need help. You at least need someone to talk to about this."

"It's fine. I got drunk. I'll sleep it off and then I'll get up in the morning, dust myself off and get back to work; that includes finding your father. You don't have to concern yourself with me."

Alique stood. "If that's how you feel… I can see you're dealing with your news the best way you can. Let me know if you need anything else for Gwaethe. I wish you well, Kain."

She turned and walked toward the door. Perhaps she could escape before the facade of composure she had wrapped around her shattered. She reached for the handle of the door, but he was there before her.

"Alique, wait."

She looked up into his eyes, the pain she saw there enough to break her heart. "I shouldn't have come." She stared at his chest, fighting tears. Why couldn't he just have allowed her to leave?

Kain was silent and she eventually looked back up at his face. He warred with some emotion. Fear, or uncertainty?

"What is it?" she asked.

"The truth is," he said, cupping her cheek with his palm, "I would love to talk this over with you, but I don't wish to hurt you. The past days have shown me the extraordinary woman you are, and I don't want to pull you down."

She swallowed the lump in her throat. "Can't I be the judge of what will hurt me if I'm so extraordinary?" She pressed herself to his body, her hands sliding up his chest and around his neck. "I want to be here to support you, even to take your mind from your troubles." She wove her fingers through the longer hair at the base of his skull and stared up into his eyes.

Patience, that was what was required here. He needed time to work through his troubles but Alique instinctively knew Kain's cautious nature would hold him back from her. She waited, hardly daring to breathe, and witnessed his struggle. His body drove him toward her, but his honor and independence held him rigid. Perhaps the drink in his body was enough to tip the balance, for finally his lips descended upon hers. There was nothing gentle in his caress this time. As Alique sighed into his mouth, Kain pushed his tongue past her lips, molding her tight to his body.

A fever seemed to have overcome him. He said nothing but swept her into his arms and strode across the room, laying her on the rug in front of the fireplace. He stood over her, his breathing ragged and pupils dilated, his hands bunched into fists.

"Is this truly what you want?" he asked, his voice harsh to her ears.

Alique didn't have to think twice. She nodded.

He fell to his knees and kissed her with an abandon he had not shown before. He showered kisses on her face then moved on to her neck, nibbling the delicate skin below her ears. She shivered and arched her hips to meet him. He undid the fastening of her cloak and growled as her nightgown was revealed. His hands wandered over her breasts, tracing their outline, and Alique was glad she hadn't dressed for her trip to the barracks.

She undid the buttons of her bodice one by one, Kain's eyes riveted to her fingers. When she had finished, he slipped his hand inside, finding her breast, while his other hand slid up her leg, bringing the skirt of her nightgown with it.

"You're beautiful," he breathed against her throat. Alique's stomach clenched with desire. He kissed her, savoring her lips, then slid his mouth down her throat to her chest and across to one breast, then the other, sucking and tonguing her nipples. Meanwhile his other hand reached the apex of her thighs and his fingers explored folds slick with desire.

"Please, Kain," she said. He flicked his tongue against her nipple and plunged two fingers inside her. She was gone in moments, her body racked with a pleasure so intense that she forgot herself and cried out. "Yes, oh yes!"

Kain chuckled, smothering her cries with his mouth, her body shuddering under his ministrations until she lay limp beneath him. He gave her one last lingering kiss then rose to undress, discarding his garments one by one, until he stood naked before her. "It's not too late to say no, My Lady."

Alique raised her knees and pulled her skirts to her waist, allowing him a clear view of her gleaming flesh. "Is that answer enough for you, General?"

He fell to his knees and plunged himself into her, his eyes growing wide as her tightness engulfed him. Alique thrust up to meet him, feeling another climax mounting as he drove into her. She gripped his thighs and locked her legs around him, achieving a closeness she had never dreamed of. As their bodies rocked together and Kain plunged deeper, Alique's body tightened and she went soaring to another peak, this one so intense she lost all sense of where she was. Kain followed soon after, but she was vaguely aware of him pulling out from her body at the very end.

As she regained her senses, he rolled away and cleaned himself up with his discarded shirt. He hadn't looked in her direction.

"That was earth-shattering," she said, gazing up at him.

He flicked a glance at her, his jaw clenched. "Cover yourself," he said before looking away.

"Why?" she asked, "I know you like what you see. Come back and we shall see what else we can get up to."

He turned to her. "You told me you had lain with a man! Now I find you lied!"

"You wouldn't have touched me if you knew I was a virgin," Alique said. "Now I'm no longer one, we can do as we like."

He shook his head. "You should've told me."

"I chose to give myself to you, Kain. I don't regret it."

"Well, I do," he said, pulling on his breeches. "I think you should leave now."

Alique stared. Slowly she lowered her skirts and did up her buttons. She stood, still unable to believe his reaction. "Didn't you enjoy yourself?"

He gripped her forearms and pulled her against him. "Lady, I enjoyed bedding you very much indeed, but can't you see how wrong it was? I could have left you with child."

"You pulled out. Besides, I have a tea I can take to ensure no pregnancy." Alique's dream of lying with Kain was fast turning into nightmare. "You don't have to fear I'll be a stone around your neck."

He closed his eyes. "I fear only for you. We were unwise, and you a virgin to boot." He looked sadder than ever. "You should go."

"I was trying to leave when this happened," she said, marching to the mirror and attempting to tidy her hair and clothes. She turned to him. "I don't regret any of this, Kain, and if you do, you're a fool." For the second time that evening, Alique walked to the door, fighting back tears. This time, he didn't try to stop her.

CHAPTER 11

K AIN faced his opponent, one of his sergeants, with the practice sword. The sun crept over the horizon, making vision difficult. It was how he liked to train, with the conditions as challenging as possible. His men hated him for it, but it kept them alive. As he swung the sword against his weaker opponent, he struggled to focus on the task at hand.

Gwaethe and Isiloe were in residence at an inn near his parents' home. He had organized that much, but since then, had stayed far away from the elven women and his family. Some force prevented him from taking the step that would bring them all together.

The meeting with the king had gone better than expected. King Beniel had seemed content with the vague answers Kain had been able to supply regarding his kidnapping. The monarch was distracted by the news that previous elven skirmishes signified a much larger threat to Thorius than previously thought. However, Kain suspected he hadn't heard the last from Beniel and if the queen became involved, he doubted she would be content with the answers he had supplied thus far. At least his position was safe for the moment.

He hadn't seen Alique. He lamented the weakness that had led to their encounter and even more that she had given him her most precious gift. He knew his reaction in the aftermath of their lovemaking had hurt her, and guilt simmered in his gut. Alique would be a willing and exciting partner in the bedroom and in life. But she was too young and too noble. The union would never work, and besides, she didn't want him as a permanent fixture in her life. Kain shook his head before the thought could take hold. There could be no thoughts of permanency.

This wasn't like him! He did *not* moon over women. He didn't allow them to get under his skin, creating unwelcome distractions that could endanger him and his men. *You're getting soft, man!* Surely it was the recent experience and revelations that had brought this on? Anyone would be shaken to find that all they believed was a lie. Once he sorted through his feelings and settled into his new reality, life would return to normal.

His opponent's practice sword scraped Kain's shoulder and he rallied to bring the fight back under his control. In real battle, that could have been a killing stroke. He brought all his concentration to bear and launched a blistering attack that had the sergeant on his back, Kain's sword against his throat, in seconds.

He took a deep breath and stepped back to allow his subordinate up. He couldn't continue to do this. Becoming distracted at the wrong moment could kill him, or someone else. He placed the practice sword in the rack and stalked out of the yard to find Nikolas Cosara leaning against a rain barrel.

"Niko." He grabbed his friend in a bear hug. "You've returned sooner than I expected!"

Nikolas pushed back from him. "Not a moment too soon, if my eyes and ears don't deceive me." The huge blond man studied his friend. "I'd like to hear the story."

A cloud descended on Kain. "Bad business."

"Is Alique unharmed?" Nikolas asked. "I heard she was taken too. What did they want?"

"Lady Alique is well," Kain said. "The plan was to lure me out into the country."

"They wanted inside information?"

"Seems so." Kain didn't like keeping anything from Nik, but better that than saying the wrong thing. "I couldn't tell them anything they didn't know already, and eventually we were able to escape."

"Walk with me, Kain."

The two men fell into step and headed out of the army compound and into the city. It was only a short distance to an inn which was a favorite haunt of the army and naval officers. Several men saluted as Nikolas and Kain entered and took a seat in the corner.

They ordered breakfast and Nikolas leaned back against the wall, again studying Kain.

"There's something you're keeping from me, isn't there?" Nikolas said.

Kain should have known his friend would notice. "There is," he said finally.

"Talk to me."

"Last time I talked to you I didn't get a good reception," Kain said.

"You came to warn me off Merielle. It was none of your business."

"Perhaps this is none of *your* business?" Kain said.

Nikolas shook his head. "I have a feeling it's not just personal. You were distracted back there, and I've never seen you like that. He could've seriously hurt you, even with a practice sword."

"You're not telling me anything."

"So, I'm wondering what it takes to distract Kain Jazara to the extent he nearly gets his head taken off by an opponent?"

"Just got a lot on my mind."

"Ah," Nikolas said, "it wouldn't be a certain young noblewoman, would it?"

Kain frowned. He didn't want to get into this, but he could sure use a sounding board. Niko had been through a lot lately – he'd been the pariah of Wildecoast for losing a whole ship full of men. Perhaps he'd have a useful perspective.

"I found out something I'm having a hard time coming to terms with," Kain said after a long silence. He looked Nik in the eye. "My father was an elven king."

Nikolas laughed long and hard after the initial surprise wore off. By the time the laughter died, Kain was good and angry.

Nikolas's expression sobered. "You're serious."

"Yes," Kain said, "dead serious."

"Hell, man, that sets the cat amongst the pigeons," Nikolas said. "What are you going to do?"

Kain rested his head in his hands. *Talk about burning questions!* "I don't know."

"When this gets out there'll be hell to pay," Nikolas said. "Dark elves massing on our borders, and the army general finds out he's a half-breed elf."

"Keep your voice down," Kain hissed. "It'd be nice if I could choose the timing of that revelation hitting the public."

"Man, you've got to do some damage control. Who knows about this?"

Kain sighed. "Apart from my family and you, Alique and a bunch of elves."

Nikolas groaned. "Alique! Will she keep her mouth closed?"

"She will."

"You sound very sure," Nikolas said, his eyes narrowing.

Kain faced his friend. "We have an understanding now, since the hostage thing."

"And that is?"

"What we went through bonded us. She was there when I discovered my heritage. She understands what it means to me and the kingdom. She won't do anything to threaten her home. Believe me, she wouldn't help the elven cause by destabilizing the kingdom."

Nikolas frowned. "Seems I must have missed an important piece of information. You say the elves know your identity. How?"

"I'm not sure, but they didn't just lure me out for information. They wanted me, as the son of a past elven king. I seem to be a pawn in their power game, in some kind of civil war."

"That implies at least two elven factions," Nikolas said.

Kain nodded. "My half-sister leads the other faction. It was she who rescued us from those who took us hostage. Both groups were looking for me. Gwaethe is here in the city."

"Your elven sister is holed up here?"

Kain nodded. "I know it wasn't wise, but she wanted to meet Mother. Trouble is, it hasn't happened yet."

"We have to get that sorted before someone realizes we have an elven princess in our midst," Nikolas said. "I can help you."

"No," Kain snapped.

"Look man, you're not dealing with this and I should know. I was in the same position not so long ago. Luckily someone pulled me out of my crisis and that's what I'm trying to do for you now."

Kain stared at his friend as the words sank in. Niko was right. He couldn't allow the situation to slide any longer. "All right. We'll go to the inn, where the elven women are, and take them to see my parents."

Kain was tight as a coiled spring as he ushered Gwaethe, Isiloe and Nikolas into his father's shop. Guile Jazara looked up from his workbench and his face creased in a smile.

"Kain! I am so glad you have returned. There is much to discuss." He looked around at the others. "And Admiral Cosara. Congratulations! It is long since we have had you under our roof."

"You're too kind, Master Jazara," Nikolas said, shaking Guile's hand. "It's good to see you looking so well.

Kain made the introductions. "These ladies are Gwaethe, my half-sister, and her cousin, Isiloe," he said stiffly. "I've brought them to see Mother."

Guile bowed. "I am Kain's father, Guile Jazara, ladies. You are welcome under my roof."

The elven women bowed.

Kain ground his teeth at the pleasantries. The last thing he felt right now was pleasant. Uncomfortable, perhaps; frustrated, definitely.

"Father," he said, "I'll take the ladies upstairs." He ushered the women through the shop.

"I'll stay down here, Kain," Nikolas called.

Kain didn't argue. Niko was already more involved than he was comfortable with. At the top of the stairs, he left Gwaethe and Isiloe and went to find his mother in the kitchen. His younger brother Jans sat at the kitchen table carving an intricate design in a piece of golden-brown walnut. It was no doubt destined for a special order. Jans jumped up and enveloped Kain in a bear hug.

"It's good to see you," Jans said. "We were so worried during the kidnapping."

Kain disentangled himself from his younger brother who was taller and stockier, with light brown hair and gray blue eyes. "You should know by now I can take care of myself, little brother."

"I tried to see you yesterday but was headed off at the pass by one of your underlings." Jans stood with his arms crossed. "You've been avoiding me."

"There's been a lot to deal with since I returned," Kain said. "Speaking of which, these ladies need to talk to Mother. I wonder if you would be so kind as to join Father and Niko downstairs?"

As Kain knew he would, Jans leapt at the chance to see his hero, the admiral. Even when Niko was the pariah of the city after the loss of his crew, Jans had refused to countenance any criticism of his idol. He bowed to the ladies and hurried from the room.

Kain turned to Astelle, who hadn't said a word. She gazed with wide eyes at Gwaethe and Isiloe. "Who have you brought to see me, Kain?"

He drew Gwaethe forward. "These ladies are Gwaethe, and her cousin, Isiloe. Gwaethe is Orionkael's daughter."

Astelle's hands flew to her mouth and her eyes were wide as she took in the daughter of her lost lover. "You look like him," she sighed, stepping forward. She reached for Gwaethe's hand and Kain tensed, not knowing what reaction his mother would get.

But Gwaethe's fingers found Astelle's and in seconds their hands were entwined.

"You were his first love, Astelle," Gwaethe said. "Father told me about you before he died. He wanted me to find his lost son, and I hoped I would meet the woman who had stolen his heart."

Astelle fixed Gwaethe with a challenging look. "Your father abandoned me when he discovered I was with child. He paid my parents off with gold."

"He regretted it, more than you can know." Gwaethe released Astelle's hands. "I often looked at Father and wondered what made him so sad. It seemed he had everything in life – a people who loved him, a good wife, and an adoring daughter. But time and again I found him gazing off to the south as if part of him was there. Now I know where his thoughts dwelt. With you and with his son."

Kain grunted. "He broke my mother's heart. She never got over him."

Gwaethe's eyes softened as she looked at Astelle. "He loved you and he never got over you either, Astelle. I truly believe that."

"Is your mother still alive?" Astelle asked.

"She is. She loved my father very much but theirs was an arranged marriage. My mother would not speak of it when Father was alive, but after his death, I asked her about the time of her union with Orionkael. The old king had come to my grandfather and the two planned for their children to wed. Mother had no choice, and I don't believe Father did either. It all happened in a matter of weeks."

Astelle gasped, her hands over her mouth and more tears brimming in her eyes. "Then he did love me. Father told me Orionkael wanted nothing to do with me or the child."

"He wanted nothing to do with me until I could be useful to his cause," Kain said, bitterness making his gut burn.

Astelle cast astonished eyes at her son. "What do you mean?"

"Orionkael sent Gwaethe in search of me from his death bed. You see, Mother, Gwaethe can't lead the elven people. She needs a male figurehead to lead her elven faction against the *Sis Lenweri* – they who thought to either use me or kill me, or at least stop me from falling into Gwaethe's hands."

Astelle stared at Gwaethe. "Is this true? You would use my son in your civil war?"

Anger flared in Gwaethe's eyes and Isiloe appeared even more furious.

"Do you not think I would do this myself if I could?" Gwaethe asked. "I am a warrior. I am as good as any son but by elven law, I cannot rule, and I cannot become queen, just as my mother cannot bring our people together."

Isiloe stepped forward, her hands clutching her skirts. "You people know nothing of us. You insult my cousin with your words, and she does not deserve it."

Kain reached for his mother and drew her to a chair by the fire. She was pale and her hands shook. He turned back to the elven women. "I think this meeting is over now. We have a lot to think about."

Gwaethe twisted a curious silver ring that encased her right middle finger. "There is more," she said.

Isiloe hissed. "Let us leave, Cousin. I told you the humans could not be relied upon."

Gwaethe lifted her chin and the bearing of the elven princess returned to her. "Silence, Isiloe!" She turned to Kain and his mother. "I have another reason for wanting to see Astelle." She frowned, seeming torn as to whether to proceed, then squared her shoulders and spoke. "My father gave you a gift when you were last together. Do you still have it?"

Astelle frowned. "Do you speak of the wristband?"

Hope flared in Gwaethe's eyes. "You still have it!"

"So many times, in the early days, I nearly threw it into a river or off a cliff. When Orionkael first gave it to me I wore it around my upper arm. It made me feel connected to him. But when he deserted me, I removed it. I let it sit on my windowsill where I could see it each day, reminding me of how stupid it was to love. But then Guile and I wed, and it seemed time to cast it from my life."

Gwaethe wrenched at her ring, her eyes tormented with an unnatural fever. "But you did not, Astelle? Please, I must know."

Astelle didn't seem to hear. "Several times I left the house with the armband, intent on destroying it, but I never could cast off the gift of my lover, even if he no longer cared for me. I packed it away in a small wooden box that Guile had given me for my jewelry. Today is the first time I have thought of it since."

Gwaethe let out a huge sigh. "That is good, Astelle. You did well to keep it."

Kain was at the end of his patience. "Right, so why are you intent on knowing if my mother has this armband?"

Gwaethe turned her sober gaze upon him. "The amulet is yours, Kain. You are the rightful owner. Astelle must pass the band to you."

Kain sat opposite his mother. The elven women were gone, escorted back to their inn by Nikolas. The band Gwaethe had been so determined to find sat on his left wrist. It was an exquisite piece, four fingers wide and composed of intricate metal scrolls encrusted with emeralds. But there was too much else going on to worry about a piece of jewelry.

"I'm sorry, Kain," Astelle said. "I started all this."

"How, by falling in love?"

"I should have told you sooner, and then you'd have been prepared. Perhaps you would have chosen to return to your father's people instead of leading the army. You might have made different choices."

Kain allowed his mother's words to sink in. She had deprived him of many opportunities, including getting to know his father, his real father. But could he allow her to accept all the blame for the trouble he now found himself in?

He drew a deep breath. "You're right, Mother. So many things might have been different if you had told me of my heritage." The anger welled within, making speech difficult. "But I can't let you shoulder all the responsibility. This is something your father orchestrated, and the elves were involved as well, not to mention my… stepfather. You weren't to know where it would lead." He stopped, his voice failing. "I do regret not meeting Orionkael, though."

Kain knew the words would hurt but he couldn't deny them. The reality that he would never know his birth father sliced at his heart, causing a physical ache. He could never satisfy the yearning no matter how long he lived, no matter how close he and Gwaethe grew. In a way, that would add to the pain, for she had intimate knowledge of a man who could only ever be a shadow to Kain.

"I'll deal with this," he said, drawing Astelle to her feet. "I know you'll worry for me but somehow it will all be well in the end." He pulled her into his arms and hugged her. Astelle's body trembled and a sob escaped her lips. Kain had never seen her cry.

"I will forever be sorry for keeping this from you. I pray one day you can truly forgive me."

Guile was at work when Kain made it back down to the shop below.

"I must talk with you," he said, putting his tools down.

Kain swore under his breath. "Where is Jans?"

"He went with the admiral," Guile said.

"Nik wouldn't appreciate you calling him that, Guile."

"And I don't appreciate you calling me that!" Guile said. "I'm the only father you have."

"Yes, thanks to you and Mother I'll never meet my real father," Kain snapped.

Guile looked stricken. "I'm sorry, Son, I didn't think."

Kain paced across the workroom and back. "I know you were only doing what you thought best, but I don't know how to react to any of this." He slapped his hand down onto the work bench and Guile jumped.

"You must know I'd never do anything to hurt you," Guile said, his voice wavering with emotion. "I loved your mother from afar for so long that when her father came to me and offered me her hand, I didn't care that she came with another man's child. I didn't care about the money either. What I did mind was the condition that we move out of the town where we had both lived our whole lives."

Guile pulled a handkerchief from his pocket and mopped at a tear. "There was so much secrecy. We married quickly but Astelle was over three months along. It was decided she would birth the babe under her parents' roof and then we would travel to our new home in the city of Wildecoast. By that time, I would be a qualified carpenter. Part of the deal with the elves was they be told when the infant was born and what the sex was. At that stage, another and final payment in gold would be made."

Kain couldn't believe what he was hearing; his birth had been such a cause for shame that it had taken place in secrecy.

"As soon as you and Astelle were fit to travel, we left on the three-week trip to Wildecoast. We've never seen our families again. We kept half the gold, enough to buy this place and some tools, and the rest remained with your grandparents. It was hard at first. Customers didn't come. I had no references having so recently completed my apprenticeship. And then soon another child was on the way. I wish I had fought for a greater share of the elven gold, but that is another mistake I made."

"Father," Kain said, "you did what you thought was best."

Guile held up his hand. "Hear me out. I never regretted for one second marrying Astelle and accepting you as my son. You couldn't be any closer if you were my blood kin. I thought it would be best that you never knew. I thought it would help you make your way in the world, for I knew, as a half-breed, you would have many doors closed. I never realized the reason the elves insisted on being notified of your birth and sex. They must have always thought they might use you one day, especially if you were male."

Kain nodded. This day may have been thirty years in the making. It took his breath away that his father and grandfather had planted a half-breed pawn in the kingdom, ripe for the using should it ever be required. He shook his head, anger building again, but this time it was not against his parents, but the faceless elves who had set his feet upon this path.

"Don't fear, Father," Kain said. "I will triumph over this, and I'll work to forgive you and Mother. Please support her as you always have. I think she'll need all of you."

Guile nodded and Kain enveloped him in a hug. "I love you."

Kain left Guile mopping more tears, hopeful that somehow, they would find a way forward together.

CHAPTER 12

ALIQUE fumed. There was still no word on the whereabouts of her father and now she was wasting time preparing for a royal reception. She had spent the last day and a half on her family estate, consoling her mother and sister, who had convinced themselves of the worst. It had been hard for her not to set off on her own search, but she was sensible enough to realize it would be foolhardy.

Josef had given her updates on each incursion of his soldiers into the northern reaches of the kingdom, but still nothing had been discovered. He didn't say it openly, but Alique believed her cousin suspected Lord Zorba had been taken by *Sis Lenweri*, sometime after he left his estate. Her chest tightened when she imagined the torture he might be experiencing. How glad the elves would be to snatch another noble hostage.

Tonight's reception was being held in honor of herself and General Jazara. It seemed the king and queen needed to make some gesture of welcome. Alique wondered how hospitable they would be if they knew of Kain's dark elven heritage.

She put the finishing touches to her eyes and took up the brush to paint her lips. She wore crimson tonight in honor of the house of Zialni. It wasn't her favorite color, but the gold lace would highlight her brilliant blonde locks. Her hair had been restored to its former glory, thanks to the queen's hair attendant.

She looped a strand of rubies around her throat and stood back to admire the effect. Not bad. Kain wouldn't be able to ignore her this night.

Alique had brooded over her interlude with Kain for two days. It had changed her, bonded her tighter to him than she had ever imagined. But no matter her feelings, the fates were stacked against them, including Kain's own reaction to his parentage. He had locked her out of his life as surely as if a door had slammed in her face. Stubborn man!

She checked one last time to make sure no stray hairs had slipped from her chignon, collected her small purse, and stepped into the hallway. One of the young squires waited to escort her to the banquet hall. He bowed deeply to Alique, his eyes wide.

"Squire Damon is it not?" she asked.

Her escort nodded and made a grab for her arm as if he feared she would escape. Alique suppressed a giggle. This boy had much to learn.

"Calm yourself, Squire," she said. "Take two very deep breaths… Good, now we shall walk with dignity to the banquet hall and you shall tell me about your family on the way."

* * *

Kain waited outside the hall, steeling himself to set foot inside. He knew once he did there'd be no going back, with at least five hours of festivities and formalities ahead. It was the last thing he needed after dealing with his sister and mother this morning.

He stood near a marble column. Blessedly no one had yet seen him. Somehow, he had to slip inside without allowing the master of ceremonies to announce him. It would be easier that way. They were calling him a hero. Kain winced at the thought. He'd done nothing. Alique was more a hero than he.

At the thought of Alique she appeared at the top of the stairs, a young squire on her arm. She paused, surveying the crowd below, and Kain slipped back out of sight. He felt stupid hiding from her but couldn't help it. As usual she looked magnificent. For a few seconds he drank in the sight like a thirsty horse after a long gallop. She appeared to have bounced back from her ordeal very well if her appearance was anything to go by.

He couldn't help staring as she started down the stairs, the squire a step behind. He felt a sharp stab of jealousy for the young man, little more than a boy, who escorted her. Surely Alique deserved a better escort than a teenage boy after what she'd been through? She deserved at least a lieutenant to escort her. Or him.

As Alique neared the foot of the stairs, she was announced to the crowd. Applause broke out all around as lords and ladies milling around the doorway turned to catch a glimpse of her. She seemed to sway and then started to fall, the boy at her side hopelessly inadequate in preventing it.

Kain didn't think, he just dived forward and somehow caught her before she crashed to the marble floor. He glared at the squire. "I'll take it from here, boy," he said, supporting Alique until she could stand on her own.

"Yes, General." The squire slipped away in the blink of an eye.

Kain kept a hand on Alique's arm. "Are you recovered, My Lady?"

She looked up at him. "I don't know what happened, General. One moment I was listening to my name being announced, and the next I fell."

"Can I escort you back to your room?" Kain asked.

She appeared puzzled. "Why? It was just a dizzy spell. I've been looking forward to seeing… everyone."

"Come inside then," Kain said, ignoring the master of ceremonies as he tried to announce the couple. "I'll get you some food and a drink."

Kain led Alique to the banquet table set along the side of the hall. She trembled and he tried not to imagine it was anything to do with him. Damn stupid to have a reception so soon after such an ordeal. The king and queen had stuffing for brains. He spied Nikolas and Merielle with some other lords and ladies. The crimson-haired lady wore a pale lilac gown that sheathed her body like a second skin. Nik's eyes, as usual, were glued to her.

Kain poured Alique a goblet of mulled wine and handed it to her. She sipped and his eyes were drawn to the delicate movement of her throat muscles. Shaking himself out of his fascination, he piled a plate with meats and savory pastries and led Alique to a seat in the corner. He sat beside her.

"Are you sure you're quite well, Lady?"

Alique's eyes flashed at him. "Yes, *General*," she said, placing a derisive emphasis on the word. "It was merely a dizzy spell. No need for you to belabor the matter."

He frowned. "A dizzy spell that could've had you flat on your face, Alique!"

She smiled. "That's better. I thought we had moved beyond 'General' and 'Lady' as terms of address?"

He dropped his voice further. "We're in public. No point in risking wagging tongues. Haven't you heard the rumors?"

"What rumors?" she asked.

"That you and I had a romantic interlude while we were away. As if we had the time or the inclination."

Alique's eyes grew wide. "But we did, Kain, and it was very nice, as was our meeting in your rooms. More than nice." She ran her eyes over him. "It's good to see you."

Kain swallowed a rising tide of desire. That merely a look from Alique could do this to him was warning that he did indeed need to keep a distance. "I would've said you were looking well until you fell into my arms a moment ago. What's wrong?" He wouldn't lead her on by allowing her to think he'd missed her company.

"It was a momentary weakness. More importantly, I'm desperate to know what has become of my father. I've been to visit my mother and she isn't coping. When will we be on the road to finding him?"

Kain stared at her. "You're staying here. Allow me to retrieve your father."

"You have other things on your mind," she said. "I feel as though Papa is slipping through our fingers."

"It has only been two days, and it hasn't been only me with other things on my mind. The king wanted to see me and then insisted on this reception as you well know."

"It just chafes." She paused to allow another inspection of him. "How have you been?"

Kain grimaced. "I can't get into that here."

"We could dance," she said. "Then you can talk to me without suspicions being raised."

"Damned stupid reception!" he snapped. "What were they thinking?"

"If not for this function, how long would it have been before you made contact with me?"

Kain drew Alique to her feet and led her toward the dance floor. He pulled her into his arms, marveling at the way they fit together. He tried to concentrate on guiding her around the floor but his body, his mind, had other ideas. Pretty soon his imagination sent him back in time to the night in his room, when his hands had wandered over her, his lips savoring her sweet skin. Kain could never have guessed that Alique hid this delicious softness. She was a complete delight. He had to stop it, had to find some way to put her out of reach, for his feelings were inappropriate and dangerous.

"Kain?" she asked. "Josef has achieved nothing much that I can see. I need you to find my father."

He pulled his thoughts away from her tempting body. "Yes, I know. I have approval to mount a force to travel north and sweep the dark elves from the forests. At the same time, we'll search for your father."

"When do we depart?" Alique asked.

"Leave this to me," he said.

"It's not possible for me to sit and wait," she said. "Besides, you'll need someone to care for injured soldiers. Surely the queen won't refuse me if I ask to go along."

"The queen may not refuse you but I will. I'm still the head of this force." He frowned. "At least I think I am."

"What's the matter?" Alique asked.

Kain shook his head. "It begins already. There's talk of sending Lieutenant Formosa, or perhaps Captain Vorasava from Brightcastle along to 'help' me. I suspect it's merely someone to watch over me, make sure I do my job properly."

"You've done nothing wrong besides keeping your heritage a secret, and that's your business."

He huffed. "Not when it might affect the security of the kingdom."

"You'd never do anything to jeopardize Thorius," Alique said.

"I'm glad you have such faith in me," he said, "but it's early days yet."

"What's that supposed to mean? You can't be considering siding with Gwaethe!"

"It's none of your concern."

"Then who will you talk to?" she threw back at him. "I'm the only one who knows."

Kain flinched as she said the words. *Now I've done it!*

Her eyes widened. "You've told Nikolas!"

"Hush," Kain said, catching several curious looks. "Yes, I told Niko. I didn't intend to, but it all came out. I needed advice."

He tried not to notice the hurt look in Alique's eyes. She had to understand that involving her now he had confirmed his heritage would be wrong. Didn't she?

"Listen, Alique," he said, "I'm trying to protect you. It'll do you no good to be associated with me, in any way. Already our names are being linked far too often."

"I *am* listening to you, Kain, and I can't believe what I'm hearing. I thought we had a bond." The last came out as an angry hiss and she pulled away from him as the music died. To anyone watching it would have just seemed the dance ended, but Kain knew better. He'd hurt her. Again. He watched Alique push her way through the crowd, and he turned in the opposite direction.

Nikolas barred his way. "I see you and Alique are still getting on famously."

Kain let out a snort. "Honestly, who can keep a woman happy? I'm trying to protect her and yet she takes it as an insult."

"You've been through a lot together. It's bound to make life difficult for a while," Nikolas said.

Kain examined his friend. "Well, listen to you. Niko, the voice of wisdom. Things have certainly changed for you."

"I was like you, shutting myself away, intent on fending for myself. It was only when I let someone close that I was able to heal. Perhaps Alique is what you need."

"Can you hear yourself?" Kain said, incredulous. "I'm not you. And I'm not shutting myself away. I just don't see the point in dragging Alique down with me. That's where I'm headed."

"How can you be so sure?"

"When the king and the court finds out about my heritage, they won't be able to disown me fast enough. I don't want Alique associated with that."

Nikolas chewed his lip. "I'm not so sure they'll disown you. This isn't your fault."

Kain grasped the shoulders of his best friend. "Think, Niko," he muttered. "I'm the son of a past elven king. My people aren't going to leave me alone. One way or another, I'll be sucked into this conflict. There's going to be collateral damage."

"Boys, boys," Queen Adriana said, sweeping up to them.

She looked ravishing in a midnight-blue velvet ball gown that scooped low over her bosom and hugged her figure to the hips. She wore her favored silver mail necklace and fingered it as she spoke. Kain often wondered if the necklace indicated that the queen had hankerings for the life of a soldier.

"What has you so fired up, General Jazara?" she said, her green eyes admiring Kain's face and shoulders.

Kain bowed deeply before Adriana. "Your Majesty, it's good to see you. I'm honored that you organized this gathering on behalf of myself and Lady Zorba."

"Anything for a party, General," she said, "but you have not answered my question."

Kain suppressed his dismay. This was just what he had hoped to avoid. "Just glad to see my old friend looking so well, Your Majesty," he said. "Niko seems truly happy, and no one deserves it more." There! That should deflect attention from himself to Nikolas, where it belonged. Besides, what he said was true.

Adriana smiled. "You will not get any disagreements from this quarter, General. The love of a good woman has redeemed my cousin, and not a moment too soon."

Nikolas held up his hand. "I'm standing right here. Don't talk as though I don't exist." Merielle wandered up and Nikolas put his arm around her waist. The look he cast his lady raised Kain's hackles. He just couldn't shake the suspicions he had concerning this woman.

"If you'll excuse me, Your Majesty, Kain," Nikolas said, "I promised Merielle this dance." The couple swept away leaving Kain alone with Adriana.

The queen turned assessing eyes upon him. "You do not look rested, General," she said. "Is there anything I can do to help?"

He took a deep breath. "It was an ordeal, Your Majesty, but I'm a soldier used to danger. In time, all will be well."

"My husband admits he does not know what these elves hoped to gain by kidnapping you and the lady. They seemed not to gain much. How did you escape again?"

Kain swallowed. This woman was no slouch when it came to ferreting out information. She might have made a better leader than her husband. "They dropped their guard after some days on the road. The lady and I were able to escape under cover of darkness with our horses."

"It appears you were very fortunate, or the elves inept," she said.

"Perhaps a little of both," Kain said, wondering how he was to escape this scrutiny.

Adriana tapped her finger on her lips, her eyes narrowing. "The dark elves lured you out of Wildecoast to the Zorba estate, where they advised you they sought information, and then you suggested they take you and let the others go?"

"I thought they would spare the estate people. I didn't know they would insist on taking Lady Zorba as well."

Adriana's brows rose. "Yes, Alique – she does not wish to speak much of it."

"The elves threatened to torture her if I didn't cooperate," Kain said. "She was there to keep me honest."

"And yet it appears they did not hurt her," the queen said, "which leads me to believe you told them more than you are letting on."

Kain shook his head. "Truly, Your Majesty," he said, "there was little they didn't already know. I did confirm for them some of the details, but the elves brought them to me: the death of the prince, the questions over Piotr and his intentions, the unborn heir to the throne, our knowledge of elven plans and movements. It was very strange."

"And you can tell me nothing else?"

Kain considered. "I think they would have kept us and used us in some other way. I could have trained their soldiers in sword play."

Adriana straightened and looked down her nose at him. "You would have cooperated?"

"Either that, or watch the lady suffer," Kain said.

Adriana folded her arms under her bosom. "Sometimes we must make sacrifices for the kingdom. Alique would understand."

Kain stayed silent, not knowing how to respond. He could not have carried out her suggestion if it came to that. What did it say about his commitment to the kingdom? Was he already betraying his homeland for the elves?

"Perhaps she would, Your Majesty, but I would have still tried to spare her pain while giving as little as I could. If that doesn't meet with your approval, I'm sorry."

The queen gave him a hard look. This woman would be no pushover at the negotiation table. "The king has signed the papers for your mission to clear the northern forests of elves. You will also find Lord Zorba. Captain Vorasava of Brightcastle will meet you when he can."

She turned away and Kain blew out a long, relieved breath. It would be good to leave this den of suspicion.

He made his way through the crowd, stopped by lords and ladies eager to catch a word about his recent exploits. More than one nudged him and asked about Lady Alique so, by the time Kain slipped past the banquet table and out onto the terrace, he was sweating.

He leaned on the stone balustrade and gazed up at the stars, wishing he could fly off into the night and away from his earthly troubles.

"If we were owls, we could take flight and not have to deal with all of this fuss," Alique said, at his shoulder.

So much for the peace of the balcony. "Just what I was thinking," he said, not looking around. "I thought you were angry with me."

"I am angry, but I saw you speaking with the queen and then you came out here. You looked upset."

Kain breathed deeply and closed his eyes. He had to stop displaying his feelings for all to see. But this was Alique, perhaps she saw more than others. He hoped that was the case. "It's nothing."

"Don't reject me again, Kain. I need you."

Now he turned to her. "One or two kisses and a roll in the hay don't make a relationship. You don't need me, especially not when my whole future is at stake. What do you want? For me to drag you and your family down with me?"

"I see through this, Kain Jazara," Alique said. "It wasn't just a casual encounter between us. I chose you for my first!"

"You tricked me."

"I wanted you," Alique said, her hands gripping her skirts.

"You and I can never be," he said. "The queen has just interrogated me about our experiences and what the elves wanted from us. She wasn't satisfied with my answers. Imagine what the reaction will be when they discover my heritage?"

"Your heritage is this kingdom," Alique snapped. "Why would you betray us?"

"Why indeed? Perhaps it doesn't matter what I'd do. Who wants a half-breed elf in charge of the King's Army? I should resign my post and save them the trouble."

"Will you?" Alique asked.

"Forget me, Alique," Kain said, grasping her upper arms. "I can't be your friend, your confidante. I certainly can't be your lover."

She stared at him, her lips slightly parted, and suddenly all Kain could think of was planting a kiss there. He resisted, instead pulling her body against his so her tempting lips and pleading eyes were hidden. Her arms folded around his waist then dropped to his backside. He felt himself swell, and Alique must have too, for she gasped.

She drew back from him. "You want me, Kain," she said. "Don't deny it."

He groaned. "I won't destroy you, by giving in to this. And I won't allow you to give in either."

"You can't dictate how I will feel. I care about you."

Suspicious moisture lingered at the corners of her eyes. He always forgot how young she was; almost ten years younger than he. "You have your whole life ahead of you – a promising career in medicine, a prosperous family estate, and hopefully a husband and children. If your name is associated with mine when my birthright is discovered, you stand a good chance of ruin. No one will wish to know you."

"So, keep it under cover!" She grasped his face and pulled him down for a kiss and, fool that he was, he allowed it. *You're going soft, Jazara!* How delicious it would be to have Alique love him and care for him, to have his children and know his future was assured. He could retire to the country and raise horses; do the things he had always dreamed of doing. Alique could provide that and more. But she'd never love him like that. Not with the chasm that separated them socially, and now racially.

"I don't know that I can," he said, drawing away from her and looking back out into the night. "I have a sister who needs me now. She's waiting for me to talk to her about the future."

Alique turned him round to face her. "Gwaethe said that?"

"Not in as many words, but the fact that the kingdom is having elven trouble is testament to the likelihood that I will be drawn into it somewhere. She was looking for me. I can't let Faenwelar's *Sis Lenweri* take over the dark brethren when I can do something about it."

"So, you would turn your back on your mother's people? On Thorius?"

"I wouldn't be doing that," Kain said. "I'd be saving the kingdom. I can influence the elves. It's why Gwaethe sought me out. She can't do it on her own. And Faenwelar killed my father. I wouldn't be much of a son if I didn't avenge him."

"Your loyalty should be to the kingdom," she snapped, her voice rising.

"I don't expect you to understand," Kain said. "*You* don't have a leg on either side of a chasm, not knowing which way to step."

"I *am* trying to understand," Alique said, "but how can you even think of supporting those elves? They hurt my family!"

"My kin didn't hurt your family. They rescued us."

Nikolas stepped out onto the balcony. "If you don't wish to be the talk of the city, you'd better keep it down."

Kain turned to his friend, coming back to the present. Goddess, what was he thinking discussing this with Alique out here? "You're right, Niko, I should go."

"You can't go," Alique said. "The queen has a presentation for us. I won't stand up there on my own."

Kain frowned. He wanted out of this and now.

"She's right," Nikolas said. "You can't leave the lady to face them alone."

Kain ground his teeth. Damn it! They were both right! "Fine! I'll stay for the formalities, but then I have business to take care of." He stalked back inside, eager to get the night over with so he could see Gwaethe.

* * *

Alique watched Kain storm from the banquet hall after the formal part of the evening was over. The man was a seething mass of nerves tonight. It wasn't like him at all, and indicative of his inner turmoil. She wished she could help and burned to know what course of action Kain would take now he knew his father was elven royalty.

Alique tried to imagine what she would do in his position, but she couldn't help her emotions taking over. Elves had been cruel to her family and to think of unleashing them on the kingdom was fodder for nightmares. Over her dead body would Kain take their side. She simply wouldn't allow it. But what could she do to stop him?

Should she tell the king and queen all his secrets? It would stop his plans before they even started. She'd like to see him talk his way out of that. He might though. More likely they would throw him in prison while they decided what to do with him. Just the fact that he hid elves in the city and consorted with them was enough to get him hanged. Alique swallowed a hard knot of fear. She couldn't do that to Kain. But did she feel enough for him to keep his secrets? He had shut her out as though she meant nothing to him. Yet they had connected in a deep and meaningful way. She had to make him see sense.

Lady Diseta joined her and Alique cursed inwardly. "Good evening, My Lady," she said. "It's a lovely evening, is it not?"

"I've been observing you this night, Alique, and I'm worried."

"Oh," Alique said, trying to feign innocence, "what has you concerned?"

"You've been through a terrible ordeal, my dear, and one couldn't blame you for acting out of character. I would counsel caution."

Anger flared but Alique beat it down. "I don't know what you mean."

"I see I'll have to spell it out," she said. "General Jazara. Forget him."

"You're mistaken if you think I spare him more than a passing thought."

"I know what I see, girl," the older woman said. "You've let him get under your skin, but he is beneath you. Don't convince yourself a liaison is possible. I'd hate to see you hurt."

Alique frowned. If Diseta saw her preoccupation with Kain then others might as well. "I assure you, I have admiration for the general and nothing else. If you see anything in me, it's fear for my father whose whereabouts are still a mystery. I'm desperate to find him."

Diseta nodded. "I'm sorry for your loss."

"He will be found safe and returned," Alique said. "Now, if you'll excuse me?" She turned away and swept toward the doors and escape, but Merielle stopped her.

"I wanted to ensure you were well after your adventure," she said, studying Alique closely.

She tensed, wondering what this was leading to. "I'm recovered, Merielle, though I'd feel much better if my father was safe and sound."

Merielle nodded, and Alique thought again how beautiful she was, with her exotic red hair and fiery emerald eyes.

"I know we have not always been friends, but I would like to put it behind us. If there is anything Nikolas or I can do to help, please ask."

That was the last thing Alique had expected Merielle to say. For a moment, she was lost for words. "Thank you, Merielle, you're most kind."

Merielle sailed away in a cloud of crimson hair and lavender silk, leaving Alique wondering if the offer had been genuine. Until recently, Alique had her eye on Nikolas for a husband. Surely Merielle had to know? She had expected animosity from the admiral's wife, not an offer of friendship. Was it possible there was some other motive behind Merielle's words or did the lady truly wish for peace between them? Perhaps Kain was wrong to mistrust her?

Alique took a deep breath. Those were questions for another day. For now, she had to find Kain.

Once back in her rooms, Alique entered her bedroom, flinging open her large oak wardrobe and casting her eye over the contents. A riding gown would do – perhaps the russet, which would merge into the night. But who could she turn to for help? She wasn't stupid enough to imagine she could walk the town at night alone, and she didn't know where Gwaethe was housed.

Think, Ali, think! As she dressed, she mused on who would know where Kain had gone. Would Nikolas? Perhaps. She tugged on the bell rope and waited, smoothing her hair and pulling on a pair of riding boots.

When the maid came, she asked for Lord Nikolas Cosara to attend her. "Don't let anyone know what I have asked. And I mean anyone." Alique cast the girl her most intimidating glare and the maid scuttled out the door.

Within minutes, a loud knock sounded at her outer door. Alique hurried to answer it and drew Nikolas into the room.

"What the devil, Lady?" he said. "I got a message that you needed to see me on a matter of urgency." His wary gaze raked over her clothes and he frowned. "What do you want?"

"I'm worried about General Jazara."

He shook his head. "Kain? What about him?"

"I think he is meeting with Gwaethe this night and he shouldn't be alone."

Nikolas went still. "Oh?"

"He is torn between his old world and this new one. It pains me to think what commitments he might make to his sister. I want to be there. I just don't know if he would accept it."

Nikolas started to pace back and forth across the parlor. "He's a man of his own mind. You shouldn't interfere."

"I don't care what you think, Admiral. I can't sit here and allow Gwaethe to push Kain over the edge."

Nikolas stayed silent.

"What do you know?" she asked

"Nothing about Kain and Gwaethe," he snapped.

"But you do have news," Alique said. "What is it?"

"I'm not at liberty to discuss the matter."

Frustration built up in Alique and she took a deep breath to calm her anger. "You can tell me, Nikolas."

"No, I can't. If you wish to know you must ask Kain."

Alique fell silent. She had a feeling this was important and if Nikolas wouldn't tell her, then she must find out by another means.

"You know where Gwaethe is housed, don't you?"

He nodded warily. "Yes, I escorted her back after she met with Kain's mother. You want me to take you there?"

She decided on her approach. "Yes, thank you, Nikolas, that's most generous of you."

"I didn't say I would," he said, rubbing his hand over his whiskers. "Why do you wish to interfere?"

Alique had no clear answer. Why did she need to be there? Why couldn't she trust Kain to solve his own crisis? Was it because she wanted him to tow the kingdom line? Was it because she didn't trust Gwaethe, an elven princess bent on solving her own civil war at the expense of the kingdom's military leader? If Gwaethe had her way, Kain would throw his lot in with the elven woman and he would be lost to his people and his family. *And to me.*

The thought of never seeing him again caused a pain in her chest she had never experienced before. She shook it away and focused on the task at hand.

"I don't understand it myself," she said. "I just have the very certain feeling that if I'm not present, Kain will do something he'll regret."

"He'll do that no matter where you are," Nikolas said. "More likely if you're there, if you ask me."

"Surely he can't be that stubborn?"

"He's the most obstinate man I've ever known." Nikolas looked at her slyly. "Of course, he can't hold a candle to you in that area."

She raised her chin, but then realized it was a compliment of sorts. "So?"

"So, I'll take you, My Lady, if only to stop you from getting yourself into more trouble than you can handle."

"You underestimate me. I *can* look after myself."

Nikolas crossed his arms and raised his brows. "Yes, I'm sure. If you're ready, we should leave now. We'll use the servant's exit. Meet me in the alley outside. I'll go first."

"Wait, I must see someone before I go."

He rolled his eyes. "Fine, I'll wait for you. Don't be long." With that, he left the room, closing the door quietly behind him.

Alique left soon after, her midnight-blue cloak wrapped tightly around her. Perhaps the queen could tell her what Nikolas would not? It was worth a try.

CHAPTER 13

KAIN entered the common room of The King's Rest and approached the bar. The innkeeper shoved a beer at a burley soldier and sidled down the counter to Kain.

"What can I do for you, General?"

Great! The man knew who he was and that meant every man in this common room would know he had visited. Perhaps he could use that to his advantage, make them think he was here for some skirt. It might take the heat out of rumors of him and Alique.

"I want two women, private dining room, ten minutes." Kain slid a piece of paper with Gwaethe's room number, across the bar. He prayed the man didn't suspect the women were elves.

The innkeeper's eyes brightened, and his lips curved in a grin. "Certainly, General. I'll let them know. Come this way."

The man ushered Kain into a private room where a fire burned in a small hearth. The furniture was plush for a place of this caliber. He paced the area behind the chairs that sat before the fire, his mind a churning mess. He didn't have long to wait.

Isiloe preceded Gwaethe into the room. "What is it you want, kingdom man?" Isiloe asked, whipping a silver shawl from her head.

Gwaethe reached for her cousin's hand and shook her head. "Silence, Isiloe."

Kain indicated for Gwaethe to sit and waited as she took a seat before the fire, adjusting the folds of her gray gown. Isiloe stood behind her.

"That's what I wish to know, Sister," he said. "What exactly is it you want of me?"

Gwaethe's dark eyes met his but the muscles of her neck gave away her nerves. "My first objective was to stop you falling into Faenwelar's clutches," she said, shifting her gaze to her hands which lay clasped in her lap. "But it is not enough to save my people from destruction. For that I need you, as leader."

Kain's gaze flashed to hers. "That would mean forsaking all I've held dear for thirty years." His stomach clenched at the mere thought of leaping into that chasm. "I don't know if I can do as you ask."

"What alternative do you have?" Gwaethe asked. "Faenwelar will not stop until he has you in his clutches. Much better you leave now and join the fight against him."

Isiloe sneered. "I did not think you were the type of man to sit and wait for death."

Kain shrugged off her words. He had not achieved leadership of the king's forces by rising to every bait cast his way. "You're right, Isiloe," he said, "I won't be a sitting duck."

Gwaethe's cousin frowned. "Then what will you do?" she asked.

"I leave tomorrow at dawn with a force of three hundred soldiers." Shame flooded Kain at the announcement, remembering his audience with the king and queen. That they should think it necessary to send Josef Formosa to watch over him! A man so inferior to him it took his breath away.

"I told you he would forsake us," Isiloe snapped at Gwaethe. She spun back to Kain. "You will reap what you sow, kingdom man!"

Kain held up his hands. "The force will have two purposes. One to find a local lord who I fear has been taken hostage, and the other to drive Faenwelar from his hideout in the northern forests." He would show the monarchs he could be trusted.

Isiloe frowned. "It is a trick."

Kain shook his head. "It is no trick unless it's the king who plays it. I believe I can achieve both these objectives, that the hostage might well be with Faenwelar. I can't allow your rival to get a foothold in those forests, nor allow him to kidnap nobles."

Gwaethe nodded. "This might fit with our goals as well. But I need you to make a choice, Brother. You cannot sit on the fence."

Kain frowned. "This is the best I can do for now. I ask for your forbearance." He didn't know where all this would end. The revelation of having a sister, of being an elven prince, of being forced to turn his back on everything he had held dear for a lifetime – he pushed it all from his mind for the hundredth time that day.

Isiloe snarled again. "You ask too much!"

"No, woman," Kain said, "*you* ask too much. Place yourself in my shoes. Imagine discovering you were a human princess and being asked to defend Thorius. Somehow I don't think you'd accept it well at all."

Gwaethe seemed to be smothering a smile. Kain thanked the Goddess that Gwaethe was his half-sister and not Isiloe. *That* he could not have borne.

His words were enough to drive Isiloe into silence, which was an achievement. Kain turned to Gwaethe. "Will you come with us? You'd have to stay well away, for fear my soldiers may mistake you for the enemy."

The door crashed open and Alique and Nikolas stood on the threshold.

"What the devil are you doing here?" Kain snapped.

Alique marched right up to him until she stood under his nose. "All elves are the enemy, General. Don't allow these women to deceive you."

Isiloe growled and started toward Alique, her hands bunched into fists at her side. Gwaethe grabbed her cousin above the elbow, restraining her, whispering low words into her ear.

"You shouldn't be here, Lady," Kain said. "And Niko, you should know better than to escort her to this place." He gave his friend a hard look.

"I don't intend to stand here and argue with you," Alique said. "I have every right to go where I want and do as I please. I've heard that you leave tomorrow at dawn with a large force and I'm coming with you."

"Over my dead body," Kain said. No way would he have Alique along on such a dangerous mission.

"I've just come from the king and queen," she said. "Their Majesties have approved it, so it's not up to you, my dear General." Alique crossed her arms over her chest, a smug look on her face.

Kain's stomach clenched. She wouldn't lie about this, would she? "It's too much of a risk. I can't allow you to come."

"My father is out there, perhaps hurt. There will be injured soldiers if you're to achieve your other objective. I can help."

Kain let out a long breath. He turned to Gwaethe. "Do you agree to remain a hidden force?"

Gwaethe studied him through narrowed eyes. The seconds were marked by a grandfather clock in the corner of the room. For once Isiloe and Alique remained silent. "I shall marshal my forces to the east and keep a close watch on matters. It is risky though, Brother. If we are found, we will have no choice but to fight – unless you have already told your king about our people and your link to them."

"Of course he has not!" Isiloe snapped. "He will not burn his bridges. He seeks to come out of this in the best state possible."

"You go too far!" Kain said.

"It is true, kingdom man," Isiloe said. "If not, announce your heritage and work with us for a better future."

"That's enough, Isiloe," Gwaethe said. "You have over-stepped, again."

Isiloe opened her mouth to reply but shut it at the look Gwaethe sent her way.

Gwaethe turned to Kain. "*Have* you informed the king of your heritage?"

Kain again pushed shame aside. He couldn't be expected to embrace this wholeheartedly in a few short days. "No, I haven't. I'm unsure of their reaction. If there were not skirmishes occurring between our people, then perhaps…"

Gwaethe's eyes held disappointment. "We need you now, not in some indeterminate time in the future."

Alique hissed at Gwaethe. "You're not being fair!"

The elven woman turned on Alique. "I do not have time for fair. We go to battle tomorrow, and I do not think either Faenwelar or your king will be fair in war." She turned back to Kain. "I would prefer if all your men knew of our factions. There is no point in them fighting *my* people."

"I'm not going to change things now," he said. "I have faith you'll remain unseen and if things need to change in the heat of battle, I'll find a way to make it right. You'll have to trust me."

Gwaethe considered long and hard. Their relationship was still so new. Instinctively, Kain felt he could trust her, but did she feel the same?

"We will do it your way, Kain," Gwaethe said, "but I am uneasy."

He nodded. "Thank you. You should pack and leave the city, rejoin your people to the north. Nikolas will see you safely on your way." His friend nodded. "I need to speak with the lady."

"Until we meet again, Brother." Gwaethe left the room with her cousin hissing in her ear.

"I'll wait outside," Nikolas said, closing the door quietly behind him.

Kain met Alique's steady gaze. "Go on, tell me why this is all a mistake," he said.

"I don't even know where to start." She marched across to the fireplace. "Were you going to tell me? Or sneak off to find my father and fight Faenwelar without my knowledge?"

"The latter of course. I can't risk you."

"I'm not yours to risk," Alique said, whirling around from the fire.

"You know what I mean."

"Yes, I think I do," she said. "You're the kind of man who makes decisions for women, thinking he knows what's best."

"In this case, I do know what's best," he said, joining Alique by the fire. He admired her courage in wanting to travel into battle, but how could he stand knowing she was in danger? "Please reconsider," he said, softly. "I won't be able to concentrate on my job, knowing you're in the firing line."

She met his gaze with her stunning blue eyes and Kain felt he could see right into her soul. She tilted her head and he leaned toward her, drawn against his will and his better judgment. He swallowed hard, trying to fight the attraction, knowing it would get him nowhere but in more trouble. He couldn't drag Alique down to where he was headed, and he certainly didn't want to witness her death.

"I'll have my own band of soldiers, Kain," she said. "I'll stay away from the fighting if there is any. The king and queen have already given me leave to go, and have arranged my escort so, you see, there's nothing you can do to change this."

He closed his eyes and took a deep breath, battling despair at this turn of events. He thought he'd been so smart, managing to extricate himself from Alique, ensuring she could remain safe and free of his taint, but now…

He opened his eyes. "If you insist on this madness, there's nothing more I can say. I'll escort you back to the castle." He walked to the door and held it open, gritting his teeth as Alique swept through and out into the public bar, drawing her hood up as she went.

CHAPTER 14

ALIQUE sat her horse in the weak light of dawn, this time riding astride. Ebony snorted as one of the soldiers allowed his horse too close. Perhaps she had picked up some of Alique's temper. Usually mornings were her favored time of day, but she couldn't get rid of the feeling of disquiet that dogged her.

They mustered outside the castle gates. At least the elite first hundred were here, the other two hundred regular troops awaiting them outside the city with the wagons. Kain was present too, of course, trotting back and forth, seeing to last minute problems and consulting with Josef Formosa. Apparently, he would accompany them. Kain didn't seem very pleased with that turn of events.

Just as he had been furious with her last night. Well, he'd have to accept he couldn't have all things his own way. Her father was missing, and a battle threatened. Where else would she be but in the field, tending to injured men, and finding her papa? And while she did her job, she could keep an eye on Kain.

He needed someone to watch his back, especially with that sister of his lurking somewhere to the east. Alique couldn't trust a dark elf, no matter how friendly she might seem. Isiloe certainly wasn't friendly. She'd stick a knife in Kain as soon as look at him.

Kain's parting words last night had been for her to stay safe and stay well away from him. Alique's eye was again drawn to him, and she wondered how she would distance herself. Perhaps it wouldn't be a problem, as it appeared he could ignore her quite thoroughly. His gaze hadn't come near her since she had ridden through the gates. He looked tired though, like he hadn't slept well for days. She knew the feeling.

Alique turned to her maid, Julli. "Are you quite sure everything is loaded on the dray? I wouldn't wish any of my medicines to be left behind."

"Quite sure, My Lady," Julli said. "I had Doctor Mosard check every package against your list, and he added more as well. I personally packed all your clothes."

Alique nodded. The girl was so serious it was difficult to believe she was only nineteen summers old. She had been assigned to Alique when she came to work for the queen and would make a good assistant when Alique's medical skills were needed.

"Move out!" Kain's voice echoed across the parade ground and, as if by magic, men and horses moved into four columns for the march. Alique's twenty soldiers formed up around herself and Julli as they joined the back of the line.

"We're coming, Papa," Alique breathed, as they ventured into the streets of Wildecoast, bound for the north.

* * *

Kain updated his notes after dismissing the latest scout. They were three days out of Wildecoast and deep into the forest. Again, the trees whispered to him. The words "forest mage" swirled around him and Kain finally had to accept that the trees had named him a magician. He found himself wishing for Gwaethe so she could explain it all. The bracelet he wore grew warm at times but usually it appeared a completely inert piece of jewelry. He knew it was linked with his heritage and with Gwaethe, but no more.

Of Gwaethe he had seen no sign. She'd be somewhere to the east, keeping an eye on them and a lookout for Faenwelar. His sister would get word to him somehow if needed, he was sure.

Formosa was a painful reminder of Kain's fall from grace. The lieutenant scrutinized every order Kain gave and was a party to each piece of information received. He couldn't even pick a flea out of his bedding without Formosa knowing about it. But it was what happened when you were under suspicion.

And then there was Alique. She had come nowhere near him but still he felt her presence. He knew where she was at any moment of the day. He had detailed one of his personal aides to keep an eye on her, to make sure her guard stayed vigilant, and that she traveled in the safest part of the column.

Formosa cantered up. "Dark elves to the north-west and heading this way, General," he said. "I suggest we angle to the west to engage with them."

Kain ground his teeth. Of course, they were going to swing toward the elves. That was what they were here for. "How large is the force?"

"Scouts were vague, Sir, but estimated around a hundred."

"Could be double that," Kain muttered. The elves had an uncanny knack for hiding the size of their forces. Some traveled through the forest itself, perhaps swinging between trees, so they could surprise their foe. But he had a solution. "Put the path blazers to work. Angle directly toward the elves but make sure the scouts stay vigilant. And Formosa? Get the path cutters to use current trails wherever they can."

He frowned but nodded and cantered off.

That last request would create gossip amongst the officers, but Kain couldn't stand the constant muttering from the trees each time branches were hacked, and saplings felled. He had learned to shut out the murmuring of the forest, but still it was a constant reminder of his new status as "forest mage". Pity he couldn't just touch his bracelet, mutter a few words and have the trees create their own path for him.

At the thought, the branches overhead shook violently, raining down leaves on the soldiers. *What the hell does that mean?* He gripped the band and imagined a path opening before the troop. The trees beside him swayed but there was no change to the path that he could see. *Another question for Gwaethe.*

Kain was running battle strategies through his mind when Formosa rode up again.

"Elven force is less than an hour's ride ahead, General," he said. "What are your orders?"

"What would you suggest, Lieutenant?" Kain asked.

"Continue our advance as is, Sir."

"Agreed but select archers to fan out through the forest on either side to guard our flanks," Kain said. "That way they can keep a lookout for dark elves in the treetops."

Formosa's eyes widened at Kain's last comment, but he merely saluted and cantered his horse away. Kain called one of his aides over.

"Ride forward and make sure archers are dispatched to guard our flanks, Corporal."

The man saluted and galloped away.

Kain shook his head. *Too many leaders here, and about to be more when Vorasava arrives from Brightcastle.* He pulled his horse around and cantered back down the line until he found Alique and her maid.

He bowed from his saddle and Alique inclined her head.

"There'll be a battle in less than an hour, My Lady. You must stay back and not race to tend the injured. They'll be brought to you when it's safe." He found Sergeant Mazesta, the leader of Alique's soldiers. "Stay vigilant, man. Nothing must happen to Lady Alique."

Kain cantered back to his position. Alique should be safe enough toward the rear of the procession. They outnumbered the elves, even if estimates were way out.

* * *

Alique crouched low on Ebony's neck as arrows flew across her party. One of her soldiers was dead and two more injured and she could do nothing but sit. She swiveled her head to find Julli crouched low over the neck of her bay mare, eyes wide and fingers clawing the reins.

"Take cover, Julli," Alique shouted. "We'll be shot here!" She slid off Ebony, careful to keep hold of the reins. The horse was battle trained and appeared unflustered by the chaos around her. Julli's mount was another matter. The bay snorted and pulled at its reins. Alique seized the leather straps from Julli and handed them to one of her mounted soldiers.

Sergeant Mazesta shouted down to her. "Stay inside the circle of our horses, My Lady. You'll be safer there."

Alique shook her head. It didn't feel safer, and she could see nothing. Horses milled around her, the soldiers alert for danger and firing off their short horse bows when they spotted an elf. Another of her men fell, an arrow through his chest. He landed at her feet, eyes staring. Julli screamed. The horse beside Alique stepped on her foot and she punched his shoulder and pushed him off. The rider looked down apologetically.

Foot throbbing, she peered between the horses, but it was no good. She couldn't see anything. She looked up into the trees and her eyes met those of a dark elf. He sneered as he raised his bow and aimed at her. Alique froze, waiting for the sharp bite of the arrow in her flesh but as she watched, the elf toppled out of the tree. His fall revealed Gwaethe in the tree behind. She grinned and leapt away.

But Alique had no time to be grateful, as her group was forced backward up the path. It had to be advancing elves. *Fight, Kain!* Or did this advance mean Kain was dead, that their force was leaderless? *I can't think like that.* Men pushed forward from behind them and suddenly Alique and her soldiers were alone on the path. Silence fell in her part of the forest. She dropped to her knees and checked the pulse of a man at her feet. *Dead.*

Alique limped from soldier to soldier, elf to elf, checking for signs of life. Those she could help, she had her soldiers lay along the path with six men to guard them. Julli trailed behind with a small medical bag, bandaging some and murmuring words of comfort to others. Sergeant Mazesta found a clearing close by and Alique decided it would suffice for her hospital. She had the injured moved there but the rest she left where they had fallen.

A half hour passed and still Alique moved further afield, finding fallen soldiers. She was running short on medicines. *Where are the supply wagons?* The cumbersome things were always hours behind the main force. Soldiers were dying as she waited for supplies.

When she had roamed as far as she was game, Alique retired to the clearing and tried to formulate plans for the injured, once she had her field hospital set up. While she waited, she cleaned and sutured small wounds, administering pain drafts to those who needed them.

There were two elves amongst the injured, one a young man, the other a seasoned veteran.

"Do not tend to us, woman," the older one said. "We do not need your primitive care."

The younger man had a serious wound to his stomach and Alique knew he would die of it.

"Allow me to give your friend something for the pain," she said. "He suffers."

The older elf shook his head. "We expect suffering and long for it. Our pain will see this land returned to our people."

"He is young and afraid," she snapped. "His mother would want me to tend him."

"His mother offered him up for this task, woman," the older elf said. "Do not speak when you have no understanding."

The elf refused to talk further, and his young companion died soon after. At least the end didn't seem painful, and for that Alique was glad.

At luncheon time, the wagons arrived, including the medical wagon.

"Thank heavens," Alique said, dragging herself to her feet and limping out to meet them. "I want food for the wounded brought to me in that clearing." She unloaded what she needed from her wagon and started work on the seriously injured, Julli at her side.

* * *

Two hours later, Kain cantered along the forest path back toward where the fighting had been most ferocious. They had routed the elves, but not without the loss of too many men. He had spent the last hour harrying the remaining elven force back toward the north, and now he needed to find Alique. She had to be safe, although it would be a miracle if she was.

Kain started to find order in the bodies he saw along the track and hoped it meant Alique was in charge here. Next he heard groans and then a female voice.

"Hold him down, soldier! How do you expect me to stitch with his arms flailing about?"

A huge wave of relief crashed down upon Kain. He threw himself off Snow and strode in the direction of the voice. Alique, sleeves rolled up, was suturing the shoulder of a soldier. Her hair stuck to her face and she had blood smears on her dress, but she was beautiful. Kain swallowed a vast wave of emotion.

"Thank the Goddess you're safe!"

Alique looked up and smiled. "Where have you been?"

He squatted beside her as she tied the last knot and then applied a bandage. "We chased the remaining elves north and managed to take a few more down."

"Enjoy your small victory," the surviving elf said.

"What shall I do with you, then?" Kain asked.

The elf raised his chin and stared at Kain with cold dark eyes. "Kill me."

"I don't kill in cold blood, elf," Kain said.

"I am your enemy. You cannot afford to let me live."

Kain could feel Alique's eyes on him. "I can't afford to kill you either, but I have another solution." He leaned closer and whispered. "I'll allow your own people to decide your fate." He stood and dragged the elf up with him then marched the enemy from the clearing.

CHAPTER 15

ALIQUE sat lost in her thoughts, grateful for the warmth of the fire. She hadn't seen Kain since he had stormed off with the *Sis Lenweri* captive. Julli, poor girl, slept beside her, having hardly touched her supper. She had shown much courage during the day and the battle had taken its toll. *As it has on all of us.*

Was this what it would be like? Alique looked around the fire at her guards. Two of them wouldn't draw breath again, and three more wore bandages on wounds that would normally see them relieved of active duty for weeks. But there would be no recuperation for them on this trip. *Unless I can send them back to Wildecoast?*

Feeling eyes upon her, Alique looked up. Kain stood at the entrance to the clearing, his dark gaze unfathomable. Where did they stand? He cared for her, that much was clear. But in this situation, with everything so tenuous, so in flux, how could she know which way to move?

"I need to speak with you, Lady," he said.

She rose and stretched, working the knots out of her back. Pain shot from her foot as she took a step toward him.

He was beside her in a flash. "Why are you limping?"

"A horse trod on my foot, but it's just bruised." She stepped off, determined to show him the truth of her words. As she walked, the pain grew a little less.

Kain kept to her slower pace along the forest path. *What does he want?*

"This was a disaster," he said, scraping his hands through his hair.

"You're tired, Kain," she said. "It will seem better in the morning."

"No, it won't. We lost too many men. Formosa obeyed my instructions only in the most basic sense and now we've lost a quarter of our force."

"Josef?" she said, guilt washing over her that this was the first time she had thought of her cousin. "He's alive?"

"Yes," Kain snapped. "Alive and uninjured, which is more than I can say for seventy- three of my men. If he was here with me right now, I don't know if I could restrain myself."

"What did he do?"

"He used his so-called scouts instead of mine, for one. Atan and Darin have been sidelined for Formosa's men, who grossly underestimated the extent of the elven forces. Damn him!" Kain smashed his palm against the nearest tree and winced. "There were close to two hundred of those bastards in that force."

He leaned his forehead against the tree and Alique came to stand beside him. "What else happened?"

"The archers he sent to guard our flanks were totally inadequate. The man is a joke." Kain turned back to her. "And that last oversight put you at risk. He exposed his own cousin because he is either too conceited or too incompetent to know better."

Alique felt the first stirrings of anger. It certainly sounded like Josef. "What will you do?"

"He and I need to talk, but it will do little good. Formosa is on special assignment from the king as sub-commander of this force, and I don't have the authority to change that."

"Surely if you're unhappy with his command—"

"No, Alique, not even then. The worst thing is, having used his inferior scouts to find your father over the last weeks… well, I wonder if Darin and Atan could have found your papa by now and returned him safely."

She turned away. "I'm scared, Kain." She felt his heat close to her shoulder.

"That's another thing we must discuss. You should return to Wildecoast. It's not safe for you here."

"No!" she said, turning to him and peering up into his face. *Damn this dark forest!* "My father needs me and so does this force." She grasped his forearm, the muscles tensing under her fingers. "*You* need me, Kain."

"Listen," he said, the strain in his voice palpable. "This is going to get ugly. The elves won't give up until they've won, or we decimate them. Either way, it'll be brutal. I can't put you at risk. As it is, I'll have to detail men, who should be fighting, to watch over your safety."

"Vorasava is bringing soldiers from Brightcastle," Alique said. "That will aid us."

"They won't arrive until the day after tomorrow at the earliest."

"Perhaps the elves won't attack on the morrow," Alique said. *Goddess, I hope they don't. We're all so tired.*

"Go home," he said. "Please."

"No," she said. "Don't ask again, for the answer will be the same. I'm here to help the soldiers and to find my father. And I'll keep Josef accountable even if you cannot."

"Don't interfere," he growled.

She raised her chin. "I'll deal with my family as I see fit and no one will stop me. Not even you."

He grunted. "I'll escort you back to your men."

The walk was taken in silence, Alique desperate to have Kain's arms around her, just to take away some of her fear. Of course, it was out of the question.

"Get some rest while you can," he said, and vanished into the dark.

* * *

The entire company rode on tenterhooks the next day as they traversed the forest heading north. Kain's nerves were wound tighter than the skin on a drum but he felt better having Darin and Atan scouting, along with two junior aides. They sent messages back to Kain and reported minimal activity within a day's ride of their position. He hoped Gwaethe and her soldiers were far enough to the east to avoid notice. So far, they had been, although yesterday he swore they had helped in the skirmish.

Formosa had been sullen when Kain announced he'd be using his own scouts. The discussion had become heated when it turned to Josef's failure to detail enough men to protect their flanks. The lieutenant had learned though. He wouldn't make that mistake again.

Kain stayed away from Alique. Better that than witness more of her bravery, her competence – both characteristics he hadn't looked for in a female. Women were supposed to be tender and soft, giving comfort and care, not barging their way through battle and saving soldiers at the risk of their own lives. He wished he could send her home; then he might be able to concentrate on winning this fight.

The fate of Yaral Zorba was another cause for concern. So far, they had picked up no information on his whereabouts. Anger gnawed at his gut. The man might have been found and returned by now if Formosa had done his job properly. The thought that the lieutenant had achieved favor with the king while he, Kain, had suspicion swirling about him made him furious. Well, he would bail the kingdom out of this difficulty and then he'd be free to decide where his future lay.

* * *

Alique drew the fletching to her ear and the arrow flew at the target, missing the bullseye by a hand span.

"Very well done, My Lady," Sergeant Mazesta said. "You learn quickly."

"Not quickly enough," she snapped, sending another arrow into the target, this one further away from her goal. She gritted her teeth.

"Perhaps it's time for a break," Mazesta said, smiling at her, a slightly crazed look in his eye.

Alique knew she tested his patience. She tilted her head to one side.

"When the elves come at us again, I must be ready," she said. "I won't be ready unless I practice."

The sergeant frowned. "Forgive me, My Lady, but you're not here to fight."

Brave man. This time only, I'll be kind to him. "I need to be able to defend myself and my knives will be small help in the forest. It's arrows that rule here."

He opened his mouth to speak but she held up her hand. "Whatever you're about to say, don't bother. What I do is my business, and you will not tell the general I was practicing with the bow."

This made the man frown even more deeply and her suspicion, that his next move would be to bring Kain into the picture, was confirmed.

"Whatever you say, My Lady. Now it's time to mount up."

Indeed, the soldiers ahead of them had doused their lunch fires and were mounting their horses to continue the trek north. Alique gathered her weapons and satchel and hung them about Ebony's saddle. She mounted and joined the rest of her men and Julli. As she rode, she reflected on all that had passed the day before: the battle and loss of life; her efforts with the injured; her discussion with Kain. Was it true that Josef was incompetent? If so, this mission might be threatened. And what of the recovery of her father? He should have been safe at home already if Kain's words were truth.

Her weapons practice helped to keep her mind off her current dilemmas. If it made her tired enough to sleep at night, that was welcome. Kain couldn't object, could he? Yesterday had shown how vulnerable she was, but her skills weren't advanced enough to be of use yet.

Alique was shaken out of her brooding when a soldier came trotting back along the line. Her heart missed a beat at the sight of the horse he rode. It was a chestnut mare. *Papa's favorite brood mare!*

"Halt, man," she cried, throwing her hand into the air.

The soldier hauled the horse to a stop. "Lady?"

"That horse! Where did you get it?"

The man's eyes widened. "Why, I took it from an elf yesterday." He grinned. "He didn't have any further use for her."

Alique drew a long steadying breath. "You must turn around right now and ride for General Jazara. Tell him you ride one of Yaral Zorba's brood mares."

The soldier's eyebrows rose. "Are you sure, My Lady?"

"Of course, I am," she snapped. "I trained her to the saddle myself. Her name is Fire."

The man nodded. "I'll tell him. Right after I deliver a message."

"Get someone else to do it, and ride back to the general, now." It was an effort for Alique to remain calm, but she thought she almost achieved it.

"Right, ah, it's just that—"

"Now!" Calm shattered, Alique's screech echoed along the track, and riders close by turned to see what the fuss was.

"Yes, My Lady." The soldier on Fire rode a little further on and gave instructions to another man, then pulled Fire around and galloped back up the track. Alique kicked Ebony out of the circle of soldiers and charged after the chestnut mare.

* * *

Kain rode toward the head of the column, his eyes everywhere at once, his senses straining to detect danger. The murmur of the trees he had managed to relegate to a compartment of its own. Most of the time it worked, especially when he was preoccupied as he was today.

He became aware of a commotion behind him and called a halt. The soldier he had sent behind with a message for the supply wagons barreled up to Kain, sawing at his horse's mouth, the chestnut mare rearing to avoid hitting Snow.

"Have a care, man!" Kain said. "You'll ruin that horse the way you're yanking on her!"

"General, this mare belongs to Lord Zorba!"

Kain stared. "You're not making sense. Start from the beginning."

Before the soldier could go on, Alique and Ebony slid to a halt beside the chestnut, the members of her guard close behind. Kain drew a long breath and counted to ten before he spoke.

"Lady Alique, you shouldn't be here."

She waved her hand at him. "Don't concern yourself with that. This mare belongs to my father. She's his favorite brood mare and I believe he rode her in search of me." Her face was flushed and her eyes bright. Kain wanted to kiss her on the spot.

"Are you sure?" he asked instead.

"Of course, I'm sure. I know this mare and she was Papa's mount when he left the estate. This soldier took her from an elf in yesterday's fight." Alique pushed some stray tendrils of hair from her eyes. "They have him, Kain!"

He frowned and looked at the mare. She certainly could have been from the Zorba stables. "Soldier, take this mare back down the column until you find the lady's maid, Julli. Give her this animal and take her mount. Go now."

The soldier on Fire turned her, more sedately this time, and rode back down the column. Alique waited until Fire had gone before turning on Kain. "Well? What will you do?"

"There's nothing to be done at this point, My Lady. We have the mare back, and we now have evidence your father has been in contact with Faenwelar's party. The closer we get to the elven high prince, the closer we are to rescuing your papa."

"Can't you mount a search party to find and rescue him? A separate force?" Alique's eyes pleaded her case more eloquently than words ever could. He hated saying "no" to her.

"Perhaps when Vorasava gets here we can do as you suggest, but for now we must be cautious. You saw what happened yesterday when we spread ourselves too thin."

"But, Kain—"

"No, Lady." Kain hardened his heart against the fear and pain in Alique's gaze. She loved her father and it was difficult for her to think of him amongst the elves, needing help and her unable to do anything for him. "I promise I'll do all I can but for now you must return to your allocated position, along with your guard." He hardened his tone as he made eye contact with Sergeant Mazesta.

The sergeant's face turned beet red. "Yes, General," he said, saluting. "Come, My Lady, we must do as the general says."

Alique cast him a last hurt look as she rode past and back along the line. Kain watched her until he was sure she would go all the way and then signaled for the column to continue its advance.

As he rode, he mulled over the latest information. If Gwaethe were here, she might be able to locate Faenwelar and Lord Zorba. Her elves would have the best chance of spying undetected. The thought of his sister made her image appear in his mind's eye and he allowed it to crystallize. If only he could talk to her, to know she was safe, and to ask her about Lord Zorba.

Kain.

He jumped and looked around for who had spoken his name. What the…?

You spoke my name, Brother.

I did not, Kain thought.

You spoke my name. What is it you would ask?

Kain looked all around him but none of the men close by were paying attention.

Is that truly you, Gwaethe? He thought.

It is I. Now tell me what you wish or get out of my head.

Kain swallowed down the strangeness of the situation and composed his mind. It wouldn't do for Gwaethe to feel his confusion, if that were even possible.

One of the elves from the attack yesterday rode Lord Zorba's mare. He must be with Faenwelar. I can't spare the men, but I wondered if you could send some of your force to locate Faenwelar and Alique's father? Kain thought.

This might be possible, Brother. I will see. Gwaethe's face faded with her voice.

Kain was left reeling at yet another surprise. He could communicate with his sister over distance just by thinking of her. Was it possible to communicate this way with all the elves? Or was it only family, or just Gwaethe and himself? He looked down at the bracelet. Perhaps that was the link? Kain's mind scrambled to understand what the future might hold. Would there not be a week go by where normality could be guaranteed? This constant shifting of the ground beneath his feet was wearying to say the least.

* * *

A stray band of sunlight woke Alique from a dream. She felt beside her, expecting to touch Kain's hard body, but instead the soft curves of a woman greeted her. Alique flopped back down on her bedroll. She slept next to Julli, not the general. It had all been some cruel trick of her mind.

She groaned as she rolled over and onto her feet. Yesterday had been almost as hard as the first day of battle, and Fire's discovery had brought up more emotions than she wanted to deal with. Having the mare beside her made her feel close to her father but it was also a constant reminder that he was still lost. If only the poor beast could talk. She had been starved by the elves and had cracks at the corners of her lips where the bit had been yanked on. Alique had longed to ride her but realized Julli might not handle Ebony.

Her patients were progressing well. The most severely injured had been transferred to a covered wagon, while the others rode at the back of the column and might be fit to fight again soon. While her professional duties were taking a turn for the better, her emotions were like a storm brewing.

Kain avoided her. He was desperately trying to shut himself away and the easiest way to do that was to stay physically remote. It wasn't difficult in a long column, but Alique wasn't going to make it easy for him. It was one of the reasons she had followed Fire yesterday. She had needed to see her general. *Her general!*

There she went again with the silly attachment to a man she could never have. Alique hoped she would have learned more from her infatuation with Nikolas Cosara. She thought she might have grown enough to never attach herself to a man who didn't want her.

The trouble was, she cared for Kain in a way she never had for Nikolas. The admiral had been a whim, a suitable marriage, a handsome distraction. Kain could never be said to be suitable for her and yet she longed for his company, worried about his troubles, and could see herself being happy with him, if only he could accept himself. He must find a place in this new world despite his mixed heritage.

Alique allowed herself to fantasize, to envision herself walking down the aisle to Kain at their marriage, the king and queen, her parents and Kain's family all smiling upon them. She frowned. There was something wrong with that picture. Her mother and father wouldn't be happy with the match. They were hoping for more than Kain could offer. And if they learned he was an elven prince it might be worse, so much worse.

She shook her head. There was too much to do today to be daydreaming. All would be well, or she would die attempting to make it so.

CHAPTER 16

PAIN sliced across Kain's temple and he ducked as a second whoosh of air passed his scalp, eloquently demonstrating how narrowly he had avoided death. Blood trickled from the wound, but he couldn't spare the time to tend to it. The elves came again and again, from the front and the sides, from between the trunks and from the branches overhead.

He sent out another silent plea for help. *Gwaethe! Where are you?*

I come, Brother. Hold!

Hurry!

There was only silence in reply but Kain thought he detected a vague disgruntlement as his attention whipped back to the battle. The fight was hottest where he was, or so it appeared. The elves had come at dawn and it was only a sixth sense the night before that made Kain double the watch. But the blighters were stealthy, even getting past whatever watch Gwaethe had set. She had possibly been camped too far east to be much help in the warning.

I have found him, Gwaethe sent.

Kain was too distracted to reply. If his sister had found Lord Zorba, there was little they could do about it until they had dealt with this latest attack. Thoughts of Alique tried to take hold but he shoved them away and parried the sword thrust of an elf who sprang up before him. The enemy died silently and fell under Snow's hoofs.

He looked left and right. All about was carnage. Men and elves snarled at each other and horses screamed their battle cries. Most of the elves were on foot but this didn't make them ineffective. The trees gave them the cover they needed, and their tactic of swinging across the Thorian soldiers and landing amid the column created chaos in the ranks. His men fought well and bravely but there were too many of the enemy. Kain longed for a huge open paddock. It would be a different story then.

He helped a soldier nearby beat off his attacker and leapt from Snow as a group of elves emerged from the forest on the left. There must have been six or seven of the enemy but Kain threw himself at them, yelling for others to help. In moments he had three more men at his back but the elves before them only grinned their feral grins, their cat-like irises sending a shiver down his spine. They were taller than any of the soldiers before them, and they were at home in the forest.

His sword in his right hand and knife in his left, Kain engaged the enemy, sending a blood-curdling cry into the tops of the trees. The elves froze for a split second in surprise and it was all Kain needed. He had the leader on his knees in a breath, cradling his stomach while guts spilled all over the leaf litter. Kain sliced the elf's head from his shoulders as he passed and engaged the elves behind.

In moments the fight was over, and seven elves were dead, while only one of his own soldiers lay dying. Kain knelt beside the injured soldier. "All will be well, man," he said, pulling a handkerchief from his pocket to mop blood from the soldier's face. "We'll win this fight and the next until all the elves are back where they belong." He gripped the man's shoulder. "You fought well."

"Aye, General," the dying soldier said. "I know you'll send them packing. It's not true what they're saying."

"What do you mean?" Kain asked.

But the soldier had breathed his last. Kain looked up into the faces of the other two men but they wouldn't meet his eyes.

"One of you tell me what he meant."

"I never heard what he said, General."

Kain's head exploded with noise and he dropped to his knees, hands over his ears. There was room for nothing else in his skull except the piercing wail that ricocheted through his head. And then it was gone. Kain breathed a ragged breath and opened his eyes to find the soldiers staring at him as if he were mad.

"General?" one of them asked.

He took another deep breath and tried to concentrate but his head still ached. He stood and looked around the column. It was in disarray, horses riderless, injured and able bodies alike slumped over their saddles or leaning against their mounts. The one thing he didn't expect to note was the absence of the enemy. Not a single elf remained, not even the dead.

Kain looked to the men with him. "What happened?"

"All of a sudden they just stopped, picked up their dead and injured and took off into the forest, General," a soldier said.

Kain was having trouble taking it all in with his skull pounding fit to burst. One thing was clear – they seemed to have been given a reprieve and it was time to regroup. He spoke to the most senior man before him.

"Sergeant, find Formosa and ask him to give me a report on the state of our force at the earliest opportunity." He turned to the other man who still eyed him warily.

"Corporal, head back down the column and check on the wagons. Take whomever you find injured to Lady Zorba and get help as you go."

The men saluted and trotted off. Kain tilted his head back and looked up into the trees.

Your other force has arrived, Gwaethe sent.

Kain groaned. But it was a good thing that Vorasava was close by. They needed the extra two hundred men desperately, even though the Brightcastle captain would complicate the leadership of the force.

A horn sounded through the forest, coming from the southwest and Kain slumped to the ground, resting against a broad tree trunk. A water carrier brought him a drink.

"Pass the word as you go, man," Kain said. "Captain Vorasava from Brightcastle approaches. He brings reinforcements."

The man smiled. "Not a moment too soon, General Jazara." He saluted and moved on. A buzz sounded along the column as news of the Brightcastle force spread.

After a half hour, Formosa approached on his horse and Kain pushed himself to his feet. The man appeared fresh as though he had washed and shaved. His shirt looked clean. *Probably has half a dozen men to look after him.*

Formosa saluted from his saddle. "I'm glad to see you well, General. I heard the fighting was fierce along here."

"It felt so, Lieutenant," Kain said. "What news?"

"Vorasava is only minutes away."

"I know that," Kain snapped. "What of our casualties?"

"One third of our force is dead and another fifty injured, nearest I can make out. I'm yet to tour the wounded. Have you heard how my cousin fares?"

"I've heard nothing from the wagons, though I sent a man to check a half hour ago," Kain said, pushing his hand through his hair.

"I'll go and find her," Formosa said, pulling his horse around.

"You do that," Kain muttered, turning his back on the lieutenant. Formosa trotted off with his cronies while Kain mounted Snow and went to find his scouts.

In the end, they found him. They had led the Brightcastle force to Kain.

Vorasava saluted after dismounting. "I'm glad to see you again, General. I had thought we might be too late for the fight."

"No chance of that, Vorasava." Kain shook his hand. "We've lost a third of our force and still they come."

"More than we thought, eh?" He pulled at his dark mustache.

"For certain," Kain said. "They fight fiercely and we're at a disadvantage in the forest."

Vorasava nodded. "I've fought the elves before in smaller skirmishes. They're good in close and incredibly sneaky. Get them out in a field and it would be a different story."

Kain eyed him. Vorasava was cocky, but if his reputation was correct, he was a canny fighter and good leader. "I'm glad to have you and your men. At least now we might succeed in pushing them back."

A high-pitched screech echoed through the forest, followed by what sounded like swearing. There was a ruckus at the back of the Brightcastle lines and then two soldiers appeared, dragging an elven woman between them. She came kicking, struggling and fighting them for dear life. Kain only just stopped himself from groaning. It was Isiloe.

"Unhand me, human dogs," she hissed, eyeing Kain warily.

"Leave her be," Kain said, not prepared to acknowledge he knew her but realizing she might expose him anyway. Vorasava nodded to his soldiers.

Isiloe shook off their hands and stood, head high, blue eyes staring defiantly at the entire army. For once she was silent.

"Who are you?" Vorasava asked.

"I do not have to answer to you, human."

"You do if you wish to live." Vorasava folded his arms across his chest. "I didn't think females fought in elven culture, but you seem to be fully equipped."

"I fight and so do my sister-elves. Take care, kingdom man, we might sneak up on you one night when you least expect it."

Kain couldn't help but admire Isiloe's courage in the face of such overwhelming odds. He had no doubt she'd go down fighting.

Vorasava's eyes narrowed and he turned to Kain. "What shall we do with the she-cat, Jazara?"

"Send her back to her people with a message?" Kain said.

Vorasava's right eyebrow rose. He stepped closer to Kain. "Of all the suggestions I thought you might make, that wasn't on the list. What do you mean?"

"This is the perfect opportunity to send a message to Faenwelar," Kain said quietly.

"I thought you might suggest a hostage swap. Isn't Lord Zorba held by the enemy?"

Kain nodded. "We've been able to confirm that somewhat. His horse was amongst the mounts taken from the elves."

"Ah, excellent news. His son is beside himself with worry."

"Why is Ramón Zorba himself not with this group?" Kain asked.

"He would have been, but someone had to stay to look after Brightcastle and the Princess. She hasn't been well."

"Not an easy choice," Kain said.

"Quite. Now, what shall we do with her?" Vorasava jerked his thumb over his shoulder.

Kain sighed. He was so damned tired. "I'll think on it. In the meantime, leave her with my force and we'll watch her."

Vorasava frowned then nodded. "I suggest you get as much information out of her as possible, not that she's likely to tell you much." He motioned for his soldiers to bring Isiloe forward and left to organize his men.

Kain dismissed the soldiers and led Isiloe away from his men. "Thanks for not giving me away."

Isiloe smiled but it was almost enough to send a shiver up Kain's spine. She very definitely had her own agenda.

"I contemplated revealing your secrets," she said, "but it is not yet time. There is too much which might go wrong for me to take such impulsive action."

"Damn right," he said. "Just remember that." He lowered his voice further. "Where is Gwaethe?"

"She was with me, but we became separated when the new soldiers came. I am hoping she made it back to safety." Isiloe cast him a cunning glance. "Will you now let me go?"

He ran his hands over his face and up through his hair. When had things become so complicated? The answer was the moment the elves had invaded his personal life. "I don't think so, not yet. Vorasava expects us to hold you for now. I'll take you to Alique, and her soldiers can guard you. Please stay with us until I decide the best course of action."

"I might do as you say," she said, "but what is in it for me if I do?"

Kain threw his head back, casting his gaze into the treetops. He breathed in a long breath, held it, and let it slowly escape. "I promise I'll take up Gwaethe's cause to see her faction rule the elves, and I'll be present in her life."

Isiloe stared. "A very vague promise indeed. How do you know it means anything to me?"

"Because I know you love Gwaethe and would do anything for her, even supporting me. Face it, Isiloe, I'm your best chance of success."

"I am not so sure, kingdom man," Isiloe said. "You still do not know which side you will choose."

"It's becoming clearer every day," he said, thinking of his link with Gwaethe. How could he turn his back on her when he couldn't even get her out of his head?

Kain turned down the track. "Walk with me. We'll find Alique."

Isiloe hissed out a breath but complied, keeping an eye on the forest as she walked. She was one of the shortest elves he had seen, but what she lacked in height she made up for in fire. He was glad Gwaethe had this woman on her side, even if she was endlessly prickly.

* * *

Alique had never been so tired. The battle that morning had been vicious, and at one point she had even brought her fighting skills into play to defend her patients. She had ridden back to the hospital wagons for emergency supplies, accompanied by Julli and some of their guards. As they approached the wagons, they surprised a small group of elves attempting to enter the wagon housing their most seriously injured.

At the time, all she thought about was saving her defenseless patients. She had pulled her knives out and hurled one without thinking, downing one of the elves as he climbed into the wagon. A second elf had fallen, her knife in this throat, and she had charged forward on Ebony. She knocked two more elves out of the way and trampled them under her mare's dancing hoofs. Her men had taken care of the rest.

Sergeant Mazesta found her later, checking on her patients. She had never seen a man so red in the face. She invited him to say what he had to say, and he didn't hold back. But no matter how irresponsible he thought Alique was, she'd do it all again if faced with the same situation.

But Mazesta's reaction would be nothing beside Kain's. Anyway, everyone was safe and Alique had rejoined the column in her usual position, with the hospital wagons now just behind her. Josef visited to check on her and objected to the wagons being further up the line, but the logistics of the previous arrangement hadn't been ideal either. At least now she could reach her patients quickly and restock supplies when needed. It would save lives.

She laid her head back against the tree behind her and closed her eyes. Just a few moments of rest and she could be up and caring for the latest batch of wounded. Julli was doing the medical rounds in the wagons with the help of a guard. The girl had been an angel sent from the Goddess. She learned quickly, and Alique knew men would have died without her. Just a few more moments of rest…

Alique woke with a start as a hand gripped her shoulder. Her eyes flew open to the concerned gaze of Kain Jazara.

"Lady Zorba," he said, "I thought you were ill."

"Ha," Isiloe said. "He thought you were dead!"

Kain glared at the elven woman.

What is she doing here? "I'm just resting," Alique said. "The battle was long and hard."

Kain nodded and helped her to her feet. She had aches in places she never knew existed.

Kain's eyes ran over her as if taking inventory. "You're still limping."

"Yes, my foot hurts like a demon," she said, "but I'm fine as long as I ride."

"Then you must keep the weight off it," Kain said, leading her over to a stump and helping her to sit.

"I'm well, General," Alique said. "I'd rather you tell me what Isiloe is doing with you?" She lowered her voice. "She's supposed to be in hiding, is she not?"

"I can speak for myself," Isiloe said. "I was captured by the soldiers from Brightcastle as I was coming with Gwaethe to reinforce your numbers. We were too late, and the enemy called the retreat but not before I was spotted."

Alique pointedly ignored Isiloe. The elven woman annoyed her more than any other living being. "What will you do with her?"

Isiloe hissed but Alique ignored that as well.

"That's why we're here," Kain said. "Isiloe will stay with you and your men until this matter is resolved."

"Until I manage to escape, you mean," Isiloe said, her pale blue eyes cold and serious.

"We had an agreement," Kain said.

Alique leaned toward Kain. "I can't have her here," she whispered. "We don't... I mean I can't..."

"Just for a couple of days until I work this out," Kain said. "She has to be seen to be a prisoner or suspicions will be aroused. Please?"

Alique frowned. Only for this man would she put up with Isiloe for even one hour. "I'll see how this arrangement works and send word if there's trouble."

Kain smiled, one of the few times he had done so in recent memory. "I knew I could depend on you. Now, Isiloe, make yourself useful with any task given to you. I'll check back later in the day." He walked off, stopping to have a word with Sergeant Mazesta on his way. Both women watched him go.

When Alique turned back to Isiloe, she found the elven woman studying her. "He will be a tough nut to crack, that one," Isiloe said. "If you ask me, I would give up on him now. He has given his word to support Gwaethe."

Alique's heart took a dive. "What do you mean?"

"Just that," Isiloe said. "His very words were that he would 'take up Gwaethe's cause and be present in her life'. Seems to mean he will choose his elven heritage over the kingdom."

Alique surged to her feet, a sharp jolt of pain rocketing from her injured foot. "Kain would never leave his family or the kingdom."

"We shall see," Isiloe said. "In the meantime, I suggest you sit down again, and I shall examine your foot."

Isiloe pushed her none too gently back down on the stump and began unlacing her left riding boot. Alique gasped with pain as Isiloe pulled the boot off.

"Roll down your stocking."

Again, Alique complied, fuming, dumfounded and shocked all in one that Isiloe had the audacity to use that tone with her. A large purple bruise had formed over the top of her foot, which began throbbing and swelling the moment the boot was removed.

"Have you done nothing with this injury?" Isiloe snapped.

Alique swallowed down a whimper at the pain. "I've been too busy. It was bearable when the boot was on."

"Who will these soldiers depend on when you are no longer able to care for them?" Isiloe said, glaring. "Where are your bandages and ointments?"

Alique pointed and held her breath as Isiloe applied ointment and a bandage then mixed a powder into some wine for Alique to drink.

When she was finished, Isiloe slipped the boot back on Alique's foot and tied the laces loosely. "That is the best I can do on the trail. If we were in the mountains, I could fetch ice and it would give you much relief."

Alique didn't know what to make of the elven woman. The last thing she expected was for Isiloe to tend her wound. Still, it would be a long time before Alique could trust her, probably never. "Thank you for your care."

"We are not the savages you think us. Now, Jazara has said I must help so what would you have me do?"

Alique buried her discomfort and set her to cutting bandages and preparing medicines and poultices.

CHAPTER 17

KAIN was awoken at midnight by Gwaethe's voice in his head. *Faenwelar's camp is a half-day's march north from you and Lord Zorba is his prisoner.*

What do you suggest? Kain sent back.

Your two forces should be able to overpower Faenwelar and we will help with the rescue of the prisoner. But you need to mobilize now and strike at dawn. He will not expect it. Isiloe?

She's with Alique, Kain said. He sensed alarm and then amusement from Gwaethe.

That would be something to see. Your lady is quite the handful.

Not my lady, Kain said.

Whatever you say, Brother.

I'll let you know when we're on the move, Kain said.

Gwaethe's presence vanished from his mind but he didn't feel completely cut off from her. It comforted him to know he had a connection with his sister; that she was linked to him in this way.

He rolled out of bed and sent his aide to wake Formosa and Vorasava. While he waited, he packed his roll and saddled Snow. He had pulled out his breakfast of stale bread and was munching on it when the two leaders arrived with their entourages.

"What's the meaning of this, Jazara?" Formosa asked, poking a flaming torch at Kain's face. "I thought we agreed on the elven position?"

"I have word they're only a half day away," Kain said. "It's an ideal time to ride now and strike at dawn when they don't expect it."

"Where does this intelligence come from?" Formosa asked. "Do you have scouts I know nothing about?"

Kain took a step away from the flame. "If your scouts had done their job properly in the first place, we wouldn't still be looking for Lord Zorba and we would've had more warning of the first attack."

Vorasava stepped in. "Answer the question, Jazara."

Kain drew a deep breath. "I do have extra scouts and they've pinpointed the elven camp, and that Lord Zorba is being held there. So, you see, we can achieve both our objectives if we strike now."

"The men are tired," Vorasava said. "Mine have marched non-stop from Brightcastle and yours have fought two battles. Do you really think they can go without sleep?"

"Ask for volunteers," Kain said. "We need half our force ready to march in twenty minutes. The rest can sleep another two hours and follow."

"Suicide," Formosa said. "I see the king was right to worry about your command."

Kain knew he shouldn't rise to the bait, but his words were too much on top of all that had occurred over the past weeks. "It's your command that should concern His Majesty, Formosa."

"Gentlemen, gentlemen!" Vorasava said. "Now isn't the time. Jazara, I can't agree to leaving half our force behind. We won't have enough men to ensure success."

"Then bring them all, but we must move now."

Vorasava struck his right fist into his left palm. "I can't allow that either. This is all terribly irregular, man. I'm also beginning to think the king was right."

"For the love of the Goddess," Kain said. "Will you just trust me?"

Formosa waved the burning brand above his head. "Trust you? Why should we? There are all kinds of rumors flying around about you. Many of them say you're half elven. How do we know you won't lead us into a trap?"

Kain knew he couldn't convince them as things stood. They were here to prevent a disaster from occurring. "If we go on as we are, the elves will win. We need to strike with the element of surprise." He paused. Dare he tell them about the other elven faction? "Also, there's something more I should reveal."

"Hah," Formosa said, "I knew it!"

"Hush, Josef." Vorasava turned his hard, dark gaze on Kain. "Go ahead."

Kain took a deep breath. "There's another elven faction, one opposed to Faenwelar."

Formosa lunged for Kain, burning brand and all. "Clap him in irons, men" he said.

Kain protested as his elbows were wrenched behind him. "You have to listen to me. This is our chance to get on top of Faenwelar and reduce the threat he poses."

"Wait," Vorasava said. "Let him speak."

"I've heard enough," Formosa snapped.

"Well, I haven't. The king didn't send us here to act in haste. We have a task to complete and I wish to have all the facts." He turned back to Kain. "Explain yourself, man."

Kain drew another deep breath. *From here, everything changes.* "When Lady Alique and I were kidnapped by Faenwelar, we didn't effect our own rescue. Faenwelar's force was attacked, and in the ruckus, we slipped away but were intercepted by more elves. They were led by Lady Gwaethe Arenil who belongs to another elven faction, one dedicated to peace between our peoples."

"A likely story," Formosa said. "I suppose these elves are the extra scouts you speak of?"

"They are," Kain said. "Gwaethe has a force very close to Faenwelar, ready to assist us."

"Why should these elves help us?" Vorasava asked.

"It's not so crazy," Kain said. "They're locked in a civil war and Gwaethe sees this as a way to gain the ascendency, with our help."

"And that's all she wants?" Vorasava asked.

"For now," Kain said. "I can't see the harm in allowing them to help us. Both parties benefit."

"And I suppose the elven female we captured is this Gwaethe?" Vorasava said.

"No, she is Isiloe, Gwaethe's cousin."

"That is right, kingdom men," Isiloe said into the silence that had fallen. "And you would be wise not to cross me." The elven woman stood in her forest garb, arms crossed over her breasts and oozing defiance. Swords slid from every scabbard within ten paces.

Kain couldn't help the groan that escaped his lips. "Silence, Isiloe," he said.

"You should know better than to think you can silence me, Kain Jazara. I have stayed quiet for long enough, and now that you have exposed me, I will speak." She stepped forward past the circle of men around the three leaders. "My cousin wishes for nothing but peace between our peoples, but Faenwelar seeks dominion over all the lands previously elven. That means all the land you know as Thorius. I think you had better decide whom you would rather have to your north, Gwaethe or Faenwelar."

Formosa snarled. "I think neither. We shall sweep all of you from the region." He waved the tip of his sword in Isiloe's face.

Vorasava grasped the hand of the fiery lieutenant. "Don't be an idiot, Josef. Now is not the time to allow your passion to run free. It's time for cool heads." He turned to Isiloe. "Speak on."

"There is no more to be said. My people stand ready to aid you. In these conditions, one elf is worth two humans. We have fifty. I do not think you can afford to leave half your men behind, though. Even tired, we might need them."

Vorasava looked back at Kain. "The freshest soldiers will lead us, and the others shall follow. Give the order, General."

Kain nodded his head and turned to his aide. "Pass the word. Any who can fight in six hours must move forward. Others behind. We engage Faenwelar at dawn. Silence is paramount and tell them we have elven friends this time." He looked at Isiloe. "We must have some way of telling your people from the enemy. Can you wear something prominent?"

"I will discuss this with Gwaethe and send word," Isiloe said.

Kain looked to Vorasava who nodded.

"You may leave, Isiloe," Kain said, "and may the Goddess protect you."

Isiloe smirked at Kain and, with a short sprint and a leap, she disappeared into the treetops.

"Rather like those monkeys you hear of," Vorasava mused as he watched her disappear. "I begin to think she may be right about one elf equaling two of us."

"Move out," Kain said, mounting Snow. Formosa scowled at him and trudged away. Alique's cousin wasn't the sort of man to let go easily.

Burning brands were lit to aid them in the first part of the journey. Kain moved down the column, checking the men who advanced to the forward ranks. They were weary but grimly determined. He nodded his approval. If they felt anything like he did, they would need all that grit by the end of this trek.

He met Alique and her men long before he expected to.

"Where's Isiloe?" she asked, her blue eyes wide in the firelight. "I awoke to find her gone."

"And that's why you are here?" Kain asked. "Looking for her?"

She blushed. "I heard we were moving out and wanted you to know she was gone."

"*And* you wished to be closer to the action."

"If my father is in that camp, I want to be there when he is found."

"He's there," Kain said.

"When were you going to tell me?"

"There hasn't been the chance."

"This is my father we're talking about. I thought if there was news, you'd pass it on."

"Regardless, I can't have you up near the front." Kain found Sergeant Mazesta amongst Alique's escort. "I expected you to keep the lady safe, man, not tag along like a faithful dog."

Mazesta's mustache twitched. "It's been more difficult than you would ever imagine keeping Her Ladyship safe, General. She insists on placing herself at risk."

"I sense a story here, Sergeant," Kain said, glaring at the man.

Mazesta shook his head, jowls jiggling. "No, General, nothing to report." His eyes slid across to Alique, who frowned at him.

Kain shook his head. "Lady Zorba, you won't advance any further. Sergeant, you may restrain the lady by any means necessary if she disregards my orders."

"You can't do this to me," she said, barely able to form the words.

"I'm still leader of this party and you'll do as I say." He sidled his horse up to Ebony, so he was leg to leg with Alique then seized her hand and gave it a squeeze. "Please look after yourself," he muttered. "It would pain me were anything to happen to you." He glared at Mazesta. "See that she is safe, man, or you'll answer to me."

He wheeled his horse about and cantered to the front of the column.

CHAPTER 18

ALIQUE'S skin burned where Kain had touched her. How could the merest contact evoke these feelings? She should be furious with him and yet her body ached with the need to be near him, skin to skin. If only she could convince him to let down his guard.

"My Lady?" Sergeant Mazesta said. "The rest of the column is on the move."

She felt her face heat and pulled her thoughts from her infuriating general. *There I go again! He's not mine and best I get used to it, especially if Isiloe is right.* She sent a quick prayer to the Goddess to keep him safe and joined the column filing past, falling in with her men and Julli.

The night rolled on with only the reflection of the dancing flames on the tree trunks to relieve the monotony. Several times Alique caught herself dozing and shook herself awake. Many of the men around her fared the same and she wondered at the wisdom of mounting an attack when they'd all had so little rest. At least come midday this might be over, and her father safe and sound.

Three hours into their trek, the brands were extinguished to prevent drawing attention to their arrival. Gwaethe's elves joined the party at that time, silver bands tied around their foreheads. There was one elf every ten rows to help guide them. The elves had superior eyesight at night, a fact which made Alique shiver. They were so foreign.

The elf stationed near her was the one who had been with Isiloe when she and Kain were rescued from Faenwelar. He nodded at her and she dipped her head in return. That was the total communication they had for the remainder of the trek.

Once the brands were extinguished, the forest plunged into a spooky, brooding blackness, the gentle squeak of harness and the grinding of wagon wheels the only sounds. Alique and Julli climbed into the moving wagons each hour to check the injured, speaking in hushed tones when they had to and reassuring those who were conscious. One man died in the hour before dawn and had to be left where he lay, in the wagon with the living. He would be buried soon enough and likely have plenty of company.

A faint glow lit the forest after the fifth check of the wounded. They must be close. She slipped back onto Ebony from the wagon, waited for Julli and they rejoined their guard. Soldiers on horseback pushed past them, anticipating the battle ahead, but one glance at Mazesta had Alique reining Ebony back instead of pushing her forward. The sergeant wouldn't allow her access to the front, not if he could help it. But there was danger everywhere along the column, not only at the front.

A half hour later, the elves sat up straight in their saddles and looked off into the forest. A whispered "alert" swept up and down the column. The *Lenweri* had heard something the humans could not.

"They've seen us, My Lady," Mazesta said. "The battle is joined."

Sounds of fighting and men screaming drifted down the column to them. A stray arrow whizzed by her right ear and Alique ducked and looked behind. The arrow had lodged in the throat of a soldier two rows behind her. She turned Ebony out of the line and rode back. Mazesta followed with another of her guard. The injured man's terrified eyes met hers as blood trickled from his lips.

Alique didn't hesitate but snapped the fletching off and pulled the arrow through, plugging the hole with bandage and then binding the man's neck all around. He sagged against her by the time she had finished.

"Sit up, soldier," she said. "There is hope for you, but I must get you to the wagons. "Julli, come with me."

Julli joined her and they managed to support the man on his horse until they reached the wagons. Mazesta and the other guard helped them get the injured man into one of the drays, and Alique gave him a draft for the pain. He was unconscious by the time they left.

"Is there truly hope for him, My Lady?" Julli asked.

"There's always hope," Alique said. "If the shaft and head haven't done any major damage he may be saved. We shall see."

Alique cantered her horse forward, stopping to bandage another arrow wound as she went. Julli stayed with her, though the girl's eyes were wide with fright. They reached their guard and drew back among the soldiers again, Mazesta heaving a great sigh, and then immediately ducking as an elven enemy swooped at him from the trees.

Alique had a knife in her hand and had thrown it at the elf before she had time to think. The knife lodged in his shoulder and he fell at the side of the path, but not for long. Before she could blink an eye, he rose, pulled the knife from his flesh and launched himself at her. Ebony's battle training saved her, for the mare swung her rump at the attacking elf, knocking him flat. She turned the horse forward again and bolted toward the front lines.

"My Lady, stop," Mazesta called from behind her but she ignored him. The front lines couldn't be any more dangerous, surely, and that was where Kain was, and beyond, her father.

She pushed her horse into a reckless gallop, squeezing through the narrow gap between the side of the column and the forest, a gap which frequently disappeared as soldiers engaged the enemy. Several times she barely avoided mowing down groups of men battling elves. She spotted Isiloe on one of these occasions, a silver band tied around her forehead. Only Gwaethe's elves wore the headgear. That must be so Thorian soldiers didn't kill the elves aiding them.

When Alique was forced to stop for battling soldiers, she helped the injured; wrapping cuts to stem the bleeding, which sapped a man's strength over time. She even removed several arrows from arms and legs. The soldiers were amazed to see her amongst them and sent Mazesta harried looks which were returned in full measure.

"The general will have my head for this," Mazesta muttered at one stop, as he slammed the butt of his sword against an elven enemy's temple. "We must turn around, My Lady."

Alique finished tying a bandage and handed the supplies back to Julli. "There is danger everywhere, Mazesta."

"The fighting just gets hotter the further up we go. I insist we turn back, collect any wounded, and tend their injuries." He laid his hand on Alique's elbow.

"If you think I will fail my father in his moment of need you're wrong, Sergeant."

"He needs you whole, not with an arrow through you!"

"I'm finished here," she said. "Come!"

A path had cleared and Alique pushed Ebony into a gap and broke into a canter once again. She had no care for whether Mazesta followed or not. If she kept on the move, she could reach Kain and her father and at least be of some help.

She dodged a pack of warring men, and then another, before she glanced up and saw the thickest patch of fighting yet. It appeared to be a clearing in the forest and a dart of excitement shot through her. This must be Faenwelar's camp. She craned her neck to peer over the backs of battling soldiers and elves, trying to locate Kain. She couldn't see him.

A pack of fighters on horseback swept against her and Ebony sidestepped bringing her up against another group battling in the opposite direction. Her eyes met those of an enemy elf, and she gasped. *Celri, Prince Gorin's aide!* Celri's eyes widened, before his mouth curved into an evil smirk.

"You will not escape me again, kingdom wench." He brought his hand up and slammed the butt of his short sword against Alique's temple.

Pain smashed through her skull and she gripped the pommel of her saddle to avoid falling off Ebony. The mare danced away from Celri, kicking out at the horses around her and nearly unseating Alique. Sickness curled in the pit of her stomach and darkness pushed in, but she wouldn't let this stinking elf win. She threw her knife at his face, but something slammed into the back of her head and the light snapped out.

* * *

Kain sank to his knees, exhausted. They had won, and he'd received word that Lord Zorba was safe; a little roughed up, but he'd live. So why did he have this terrible sense of foreboding?

Brother, you are needed at the western side of the clearing, Gwaethe sent.

There was urgency in her tone that heightened Kain's dread. *What now?*

Just come, she snapped back.

Kain jumped. That had been a private thought, not for Gwaethe. He'd have to be more careful until he worked all this out; if he wasn't clapped in irons as soon as he returned to Wildecoast. Perhaps he shouldn't return at all; just slip away one night and start a new life elsewhere.

He was musing on where he'd go and what he'd do when he became aware of shouting. He looked up to see a cluster of soldiers. Wasn't that Mazesta? What was he doing here so soon? Isiloe was standing in front of him, clearly upset.

"You were supposed to keep her safe!" she cried.

Kain broke into a run and pushed through the crowd, his heart in his mouth. Julli was on the ground, Alique's head in her lap. His heart gave one thud. His lady looked dead.

"Is she…" Kain asked.

Isiloe stopped shouting at Mazesta and turned to Kain. "She is barely with us. She has sustained two head injuries, and this woman" – Isiloe gestured to Julli – "all she can do is cry. What is the use of her?"

Kain sank to his knees beside Alique. Her face was deathly pale, and her chest scarcely moved. "She's tough, she'll be fine," he said, even though she looked as close to death as anyone he'd ever seen. Kain's world shrank to the size of her face. Nothing mattered but that she would survive. "Can anyone here help her? Julli?"

Julli looked up with tortured eyes. "I don't know, General. Perhaps some herbs might help if we could get her to take them?"

Panic battered at Kain; panic he'd never known. Mosard might save her but he was nearly a week's march away. He felt a hand on his shoulder and looked up to find Gwaethe standing there. "I have a healer with me. Let him help."

A tall, incredibly thin elf stood behind Gwaethe. He must have been very old, for he had gray hair amongst his dark curls. His eyes were wise and kind, but he didn't smile. He knelt beside Kain and placed his hand on Alique's forehead, above the bruise on her temple.

"My name is Tuthariel. I will care for your lady if you wish."

Kain nodded, not even thinking to deny Alique was his. "Please do all you can. Julli, I'd like you to stay with her." She nodded, and it was only then that Kain noticed her skirt was soaked in blood where Alique's head lay. His gut clenched. *Let her be well.*

"I too shall stay, Jazara," Isiloe said, sitting cross-legged beside Julli.

Kain nodded again though he didn't understand the elven woman's offer. There was little love lost between Alique and Isiloe.

Vorasava appeared at Kain's side. "I'm sorry she's injured, Jazara, but I need you. Formosa is badly hurt. I wonder if this elf can take on the lieutenant's care?"

Kain turned on him. "He has his hands full here at the moment, Captain!"

Gwaethe laid a hand on Kain's forearm. "I have some training in battle wounds, Kain. Let me help where I can until Tuthariel is free."

Vorasava escorted Gwaethe to Formosa and Kain stood gazing down at Alique. He knew he should be doing a hundred things, but he couldn't move. *Alique!* He realized her father would want to see her. Perhaps it would make a difference if she could hear his voice.

Kain grabbed the arm of a soldier trotting past. "Take me to Lord Zorba, Corporal."

They found the old lord in a shabby tent at the back of the elven camp, a soldier with him. He was slumped in the corner on the floor, his face sporting several welts and bruises. He was clad only in a shirt and breeches and had lost weight since Kain had last seen him.

Kain knelt beside him. "Yaral?" he said. "I need to take you to see Alique."

The older man sat up straighter and a burning light came into his eyes. "She is here?"

Kain's heart broke at raising his hope but he couldn't give into his fear or it would finish him. "She's here, but was injured trying to rescue you. I'll take you to her."

He helped Yaral rise and noticed the lord's bare feet. "Find a pair of boots for Lord Zorba, Corporal." The man who had been guarding Yaral dashed off and soon returned with the footwear. The going was slow on the cold, bloody ground but soon they stood over Alique. She looked even paler, if that were possible.

Yaral's wail echoed around the clearing and speared Kain through his heart. The older man collapsed to the ground beside his daughter.

"Alique! Daughter!" His tears fell on her bloodied sleeve. Tuthariel moved to the opposite side and continued his ministrations. He looked up at Kain and gave a small shake of his head.

Kain's heart lay like a stone in his chest as he walked away.

Kain sat in a meeting with Vorasava, by Josef Formosa's bedside, but he only heard one word in two. His heart was with Alique as she battled to stay alive. He wanted to be there with her even if she were to pass from this life. His mind would still not accept it was a virtual certainty he would lose her.

"Jazara?" Vorasava said.

Kain looked up. "I'm sorry, I didn't hear."

"I said," Vorasava started again, his whole frame oozing impatience, "I think we've done enough damage for now. The enemy is on the run and we need to take our men back for some much-needed rest and recovery. Many have wounds, and others we need to bury."

"We've achieved our objectives," Kain said, "but it gripes me that Faenwelar and Gorin have slipped away yet again. They *will* regroup."

"We always knew this was just the beginning of a long campaign."

Formosa stirred, his eyes fluttering open. "How is Alique?"

Vorasava looked to Kain. "She's gravely ill, Josef. The elven healer doesn't hold out much hope."

Josef's face turned red and then purple. "That scum shouldn't be allowed to touch my cousin. We must get her back to Wildecoast where the doctor can see to her care."

"The elves here are our allies, Josef," Vorasava said, "and Tuthariel is doing his best."

"I still don't understand how we came to have such allies."

"Lucky we did," Vorasava said, "or we might not have been the victors this day."

"Doesn't feel like much of a victory," Josef said.

Kain had to agree with Formosa for once. It certainly didn't feel like a victory, more like a truce where each side crawled away to lick their wounds. "We've made a dent in their numbers and learned a thing or two. It'll be several months before they're back at us."

"And in the meantime, we need to make plans," Vorasava said. "We can't allow them to catch us on their favored ground next time. In future, our battles must be in open land where our long bows can inflict maximum damage."

Personally, Kain looked forward to getting back to Wildecoast and normality, but it would only be possible if all the revelations of the past weeks turned out to be a bad dream, including Alique's injury. "We'll return to Wildecoast with Alique and the injured. What will you do, Vorasava?"

"I'll travel to Wildecoast and report to the king. Then I'll carry on to Brightcastle. I hope I'll have good news for Sir Ramón."

Kain shook his head. "Then let's prepare to leave as soon as our injured can be moved."

They stayed the night in the clearing. Tuthariel had flatly refused to allow Alique to be moved, and watching the elven healer during the afternoon, Kain had formed a deep respect for his opinion. He was Alique's only hope at the present time.

Formosa too needed a night's rest before being trundled out. Several of the injured had died during the afternoon, making more room for the dozens who needed wagon transport. Kain winced at the thought. Alique would chastise him for having it. She hated losing anyone, taking it as a personal insult if they died on her watch.

By dusk, Alique had stabilized enough to be moved into a wagon and now rested with her cousin Josef to watch over her. It was still a close-run thing whether she would survive, but Kain had allowed a small chink of hope to slide into his otherwise black mood. He glanced across the fire at Vorasava, who chatted to Gwaethe in low tones. Occasionally, one or the other of them laughed.

When Gwaethe got up to return to her people, Kain followed and caught up with her outside the light of the fire.

"What will you do now the battle is ended?" Kain asked.

"I just discussed that with Vorasava," she said. "He thinks it a good idea I travel to Wildecoast for talks with the king."

Kain swallowed hard. His two worlds colliding was one of the most uncomfortable feelings he had experienced. "But there's risk in that."

"Risk for you," she snapped. He thought she just caught herself from adding "brother". "I am sick of sneaking around, watching every word, every look. I wish to celebrate that I have found my brother and have him be happy he has found me."

"Hush," Kain said, trying to lead Gwaethe further away from the others.

"I wish to gain the support of the kingdom in ensuring *my* people are the future, not Faenwelar's." Gwaethe paused. "You are key to that and yet you are reluctant to allow me into your world."

"Yes, I'm reluctant," he said, walking a little away to think on what he wanted to say. He turned back to her. "*My* world has been flipped upside down and I don't know what's right anymore. I think you're being unfair. You've known about me for months, had time to come to terms with it. And what *really* changes for *you*, Gwaethe? You gain a brother but everything else is much the same. Have you looked at this from my point of view?"

She considered. "I see I have been somewhat unfair."

"Somewhat?"

"Very well, quite unfair. This is a big upheaval; however, it should not change what is the right thing to do."

"Well, obviously you've already made up your mind that I should throw over my people and take up with you and yours," he snapped, raking his hands through his hair.

"They are your people too, and when you meet them, you will see what is right."

"We'll see, Gwaethe. In the meantime, I have other things on my mind."

"Alique," she said.

"Yes, I thank the Goddess she's still with us. If I lose her…"

"You love her."

Kain drew in a breath to deny it but it was no use. He nodded. "Much good it does me. She and I come from different walks of society, not to mention different races."

"You resent this, don't you?" Gwaethe said. "You hate the fact you are half elven."

"Honestly? Yes, I do. I hate that my life has been a lie, that I never met my father, that the man who raised me is hurt by my anger. I asked for none of this!"

"And Alique?"

"She hasn't really thought it through, what my parentage means. She thinks we can overcome anything, but that's the voice of youth speaking. I've seen a little more of the world than she has. And she hates the elves for what they did to her family, her father."

"She is right to hate," Gwaethe said, with more than a little heat in her words.

"Even if the hate extends to your people?"

Gwaethe's eyes widened. "Is it so?"

"Ask Isiloe, she'll tell you. Alique doesn't discriminate between you. She wouldn't want to be tarnished with an elven husband." Kain stopped at telling Gwaethe that Alique wanted all elves driven from the kingdom.

"This too shall pass, Kain."

"I wish I believed that," he said. "Your counsel would be to reveal all to the king, wouldn't it?"

Gwaethe nodded. "It is the only way forward for both our people." She clutched Kain's forearm where the band lay. "You are the key to this. You span both worlds. Why can you not see you could be the one who brings humans and elves together?"

He frowned, not able to see the king embracing him after he learned the truth. And he didn't want to leave Wildecoast unless it was to set up a farm with Alique. But that would never happen. "I'll think on it as we travel. Good night."

He crossed the camp to the wagon in which Alique lay and climbed in. Formosa glared as he knelt beside Alique. "How is she?"

"There has been no change since she was moved," Josef said, raising himself on one elbow. "That elf says she is stable."

"And you?"

"I'll live," Josef said, "long enough to see you pay for your sins."

Kain grunted. "What are you talking about?"

"Consorting with the elven scum," Josef said. "You might have Vorasava fooled but I know what I see and hear. There were rumors of your elven heritage before we left on this mission. It was no surprise to me that you admitted to a liaison with them."

"Do what you have to," Kain said, "but understand that Gwaethe's people aren't linked to Faenwelar. She wants peace as much as we do."

"Until she defeats Faenwelar," Formosa snapped. "Then we shall see her turn her eyes toward the kingdom. Oh yes, it would suit her very well to be rid of Faenwelar, and it appears the kingdom has already helped to this end. Wouldn't you feel stupid if she were to turn on you?"

"She won't."

"How can you be so sure?" Formosa asked.

"I trust her."

Josef snorted. "You really are pathetic."

"Look, Formosa," he said, "I didn't come here to talk with you but to visit with Alique. Would you mind being quiet?"

Josef shook his head. "She's miles too good for you."

Kain ignored Josef and turned to Alique, reaching for her hand. It was cold, her skin pale. She seemed to hover between life and death, and he was desperately afraid moving her would kill her. There had to be something more they could do but getting her back to Wildecoast was all he could think of.

He raised her hand to his lips, uncaring what Formosa thought. He closed his eyes, sending a prayer to the Goddess. *Please lady, send your healing upon this woman whom I love and bring her back to her family and to me.*

"She was injured fighting, you know," Formosa said. "She should never have been anywhere near that clearing."

"Alique wanted to see her father," Kain said. "I told her to stay back but she never listens to me. Was she always like that?"

Josef chuckled. "I remember her almost drowning in a dam because she wouldn't stay away." His face grew serious. "I saved her then, but there's nothing I can do this time."

Kain squeezed her fingers. "Come back to us, Lady. We all need you. Your family needs you."

He left the wagon and sought his bed.

CHAPTER 19

THE column was on the move at sunrise the next morning. Vorasava led the men while Kain brought up the rear with the wagons. There was no way he'd be separated from Alique until he knew if she'd survive.

He had tried to convince Yaral Zorba to travel in one of the wagons, but he insisted he was well enough to ride. He spotted Fire and looked at the mare with such longing that Kain asked Julli to give her back. Yaral Zorba was a proud man, and yet some of his resilience had been destroyed by his recent experiences.

Tuthariel rode with the wagons. At Kain's request, he had taken on the care of all the wounded – elven and human. They had left a burial detail at the campsite. Kain hoped the hundred men and twenty elven prisoners would be safe from enemy attack. He'd wanted to burn the enemy dead but Gwaethe had flatly refused to be associated with that, saying it was disrespectful to the elves and the forest. He'd had to talk fast to get Vorasava to agree to the burial detail. Kain winced when he thought about the funeral pyre he'd made of the last group of elven dead after the attack on Ramón Zorba's party.

They made good time, Sergeant Mazesta's men forming a guard of honor around Alique's wagon. He was a broken man since Alique's injury and wouldn't meet Kain's eyes. Shame was a terrible thing.

Day two rolled around and Formosa declared he was fit to ride. He hardly looked able to sit a horse but Kain privately cheered at the empty space the lieutenant left. Julli would travel with Alique much of the time, but when he was free, Kain intended to spend as much time with Alique as possible.

He got his first chance just after lunch that day and made himself comfortable beside her. It was difficult to tell in the dim light, but she didn't look much changed. At least it meant she hadn't slipped backward with the travel. Kain wet a small towel and bathed her forehead. She mumbled something and rocked her head from side to side. She hadn't done that before.

"Alique?" he said, leaning closer. "Can you hear me?"

If he could've made her well by sheer force of will she'd be up and tending the other victims by now, so much had he concentrated on her recovery, so many prayers had he said. So far not a one had been answered. She drifted back under, and though Kain kept bathing her face and hands, not another murmur did he hear.

"Your father is well," he said, replacing the cloth in the basin. "He longs to hold you and speak to you as he once did; probably scold you for putting yourself in danger as well. He'll have to wait in line for that. I think Mazesta and I will have rights over him."

Kain paused, remembering his first sight of Alique lifeless on the ground of the clearing. "You've given us all a fright," he said, lifting a small cup of water to her lips and trickling some into her mouth. She swallowed twice and Kain put the cup back down. "Myself especially, as there is much I need to say to you. Now I fear my words will fall on deaf ears. Still I must speak them."

He swallowed hard and blinked tears away. "I've become attached to you in the time we've spent together." He straightened the bed covers and laid Alique's hands beside her body. "More than attached. You've shown me so much care and I've thrown it back in your face. But it wasn't because I felt nothing. I avoided and rejected you because I wished to protect you. Being associated with me is something I wouldn't wish on anyone; let alone someone I care for… someone I love." He swallowed again. It was difficult to admit his feelings for this woman, even if she could hear nothing.

"I've dreamed of a life with you and I wanted to share what I think it would look like." He drew a deep breath and settled himself more comfortably. "We would be married, naturally, and escape to the country, perhaps on a small estate – not too far from the city, as you must practice your medicine. You're so good at caring for others." His voice broke and he cleared his throat. "I'd raise horses. It's something I've never told you but it's my fondest wish, or was until I fell in love with you."

Now Kain wept, overcome by a dream he could never realize. *Why am I torturing myself?* But somehow it seemed right to tell her. "Eventually children would come, and we'd raise them in a world where elven heritage was an honor, not a curse. I think four an ideal number – two girls with golden hair, and two boys who will love and respect their mother just as I do." He collapsed across Alique, drawing strength from her fragile body and trying to conquer the sadness and regret that kept welling up. Her arm crept around his shoulders and he froze.

Kain levered himself up so he could look upon her face but there was no change. He sat up and her arm flopped away. He gripped her hand and squeezed. "Alique! If you can hear me, open your eyes. Give me a sign, anything."

His moment of hope died as the frail body before him lay unmoving. There wasn't a flutter of the eyelids nor a twitch of a fingertip, only the slow rise and fall of her chest beneath the blankets. Kain stared at her, trying to convince himself she might have heard at least some of his words, that his voice might bring her back to them. But it was crazy to believe such things. He was getting very good at self-torture.

He tidied the blankets, drew a deep breath, and left the wagon. He had to stay strong for Alique's sake and for the kingdom. He had a role to play, or at least he hoped he still did.

The remaining days passed in much the same fashion: Kain spending what time he had with Alique, talking to her and even reading to her.

It was just passages out of her medical journals, but he hoped she might hear the familiar terms and latch on to them. There was no repeat of the moment when she had touched him, nothing to indicate she heard anything he said. Kain's spirits sank so low he couldn't think of anything but getting to the end of this journey and handing Alique over to Doctor Mosard. He had tried his best and been found wanting. The waiting and hoping had worn him down to the point where he'd all but lost his appetite.

On the last day of travel, Vorasava approached him. "There's no point in starving yourself, man. The lady will live, or she will die."

Kain glared at him. "She's special, Vorasava. I don't appreciate you being flippant."

"They're all special, Kain. There isn't a man here who wishes to see a woman die in battle, especially one who is so brave and beautiful. But there's nothing you can do to change this."

"Don't you think that's part of the problem?" Kain asked. "That I can't help her?"

"You love her."

"That's irrelevant. Lady Alique and I can never be together. I accepted that long ago. It's the waste of a young and productive life that eats at me. She was so good. Gah!" He threw his hands in the air. "Listen to me! I already speak of her in the past tense."

"You're merely preparing yourself for the inevitable," Vorasava said. "There has been no improvement."

"I'll never give up on her," Kain said, running his hands through his hair. "Not until she's gone from this world, and I'm praying that will be when she's an old woman."

Vorasava shook his head. "Then I can't help you."

"I'm not the one who needs help." Kain stormed away to sit with Alique for the last time before they reached Wildecoast.

Kain knew desperation as he made himself comfortable beside Alique in her wagon. Soon they'd enter Wildecoast and all would change. It would be difficult to visit with her. The Zorbas would close in around Alique as would the monarchs and Doctor Mosard. Kain would lose her, perhaps permanently. He had allowed himself to hope on this journey, especially after she held him that day, but with no further change, his faith had started to wane.

The only way Kain had survived these last days was to lock himself away, concentrating on Alique and remembering her in her health. He'd relived the days with her on the road, when they were taken hostage, and the intimate moments when he'd dropped his guard and taken her lips and her body. The regret he had felt at taking her virginity was one burden he no longer carried. Kain had been her first and only; he had that to hold tight to.

He seized Alique's hand and raised it to his lips, kissing each of her fingers, inhaling the essence of her. "We'll soon enter the city, my sleeping beauty," Kain said. "I'm glad the good doctor will care for you as you should be cared for, but I'll miss you. Please know I love you and will always hold you in my heart." He choked on the words, finally allowing reality to sink in. Alique might die, and he wouldn't be with her. The next time he saw her might be as she lay in a coffin at her funeral. He slammed the door shut on the vision.

"I've treasured my time with you and wish for your speedy recovery. I pray for it every day, even though I'm not sure the Goddess will listen to such as me."

A shout came from outside – the city had been sighted.

"I must go." He pressed his lips to hers. "Goddess protect you, my love."

Kain left the wagon, mounted Snow and galloped to the head of the column to join Vorasava.

The column entered Wildecoast amid cheers from the city's residents. The bulk of Vorasava's force camped on the cliff tops outside the gates and hawkers moved out amongst the soldiers to trade their wares. After two weeks on the road, many of the men seemed glad to see the merchants.

Gwaethe's elves camped with the Brightcastle force, furthest away from the city, but Gwaethe, Isiloe, Tuthariel and three elven guards entered with the wagons.

Kain continued to ride at the head of the column, determined to meet whatever waited head on. Lord Zorba rode beside his daughter's wagon.

The force entered through the gates and continued up the main thoroughfare toward the inner keep gates. The sergeant on duty saluted respectfully enough, but Kain swore the man looked a little harder at him than usual. It was Grif Tyne, who had looked after him the night he got drunk. It appeared word had spread of his elven links.

Kain shook off the pointless musing and focused on their passage through the city. Archers stood on many rooftops, and Kain pointed out the security and any notable buildings to Vorasava as they passed.

"It's quite a splendid city compared to Brightcastle," Vorasava said. "I've visited from time to time with official functions but riding in as part of an army gives a different perspective. The news of our victory over the elves has obviously come before us."

"The people do seem excited, though it doesn't take much," Kain said. "Wait until we get to the castle. The nobles really know how to make a fuss."

Vorasava frowned. "Mind what you say, man. I'm from a noble family, albeit one to the west."

Kain allowed himself a small chuckle. "I'd never have known!"

Vorasava frowned again and Kain slapped him lightly on the shoulder. He could be friends with this man given the right conditions. "Ah, the gates lie ahead, and I for one can't wait for a good stiff drink."

He saw Vorasava frown out of the corner of his eye but didn't care what his companion made of the remark. He trotted Snow forward and led the force to the gates, directing his soldiers to their barracks, outside the castle compound. As the riders dispersed, they made way for the wagons, Alique's in the lead. They had arranged the order so the seriously injured were in the first wagons. They'd be moved into the castle to be close to Doctor Mosard. The less seriously injured were taken from the wagons to the barrack's infirmary.

Kain stood off to the side with Vorasava, Snow having been taken to his stable. He watched as Mosard descended the steps and greeted Lord Zorba, before tending to Alique. She was whisked into the castle in seconds. Kain yearned to follow. He was already bereft knowing she was locked away in that place.

"Kain!"

Nikolas enveloped him in a bear hug, and he had to blink tears away. *What's happening to me?*

His friend held him at arm's length. "It's good to see you again, especially after such a successful mission." He turned to Vorasava. "Captain, we meet again." The two shook hands.

"Congratulations on your appointment, Admiral," Vorasava said.

Nikolas laughed. "Thanks. I don't know if congratulations or commiserations are in order. My cousin has been after me for months to return to the sea. I don't like to let her win too often."

"The queen is a very persuasive woman," Vorasava said.

"That she is. You'll want your quarters so you can freshen up, Captain?"

"That would be kind."

"I've had a suite prepared in the castle and your closest aides have accommodation nearby," Nikolas said. "The steward is ready to show you to your rooms."

Vorasava nodded and left with his aides.

Nikolas stared over Kain's shoulder. "I see Lady Gwaethe and her cousin are back, and this time game enough to enter the castle precinct. What does that mean?"

Kain glanced at the elven women. Isiloe looked anything but relaxed, but Gwaethe had cloaked herself in composure fit for a queen. She'd need every shred. "I had to reveal Gwaethe's elven faction. She now insists on meeting their majesties."

Nikolas frowned. "Putting pressure on you, is she? Don't let yourself be railroaded, Kain. You must make your own decisions."

"But that's just it, Niko. I can't act on my own behalf. This kingdom needs leadership and so do the elves. I'm the common factor."

Nikolas shook his head. "I don't like it. You can't possibly predict how Beniel and Adriana will react to the elves, let alone your other news."

"I've more important things on my mind at the moment," Kain said. "I have to know how Alique is. Promise me you'll keep me updated, no matter where I end up."

Nikolas ran a hand along the stubble of his jaw. "I'm sorry, man. I hope the lady makes a full recovery. Of course, I'll let you know of her progress when I can."

Kain nodded. "I'd kill for a drink."

"General Jazara," the queen said, joining them. "I am glad you have returned safely."

Kain bowed low, his gut clenching into several large knots. "Your Majesty." He turned to King Beniel who stood beside Adriana. "Your Majesty." He bowed again.

Nikolas merely nodded.

"General," King Beniel said, "I suggest you tidy yourself and meet us in half an hour in the small audience hall. The admiral will accompany you." The king stared at Gwaethe and Isiloe then turned to the queen. "My dear, perhaps you could see that our elven guests have chambers prepared."

"Why of course, husband," Adriana said. "General, Admiral." She swept over to the elven women and their guards, herding them into the castle. Gwaethe threw a last panicked look over her shoulder as she disappeared.

Brother! What shall I do? Gwaethe sent.

Just act with your usual royal decorum and keep Isiloe under control, Kain replied. *This is what you wanted, remember?* He couldn't suppress the sarcasm of the last remark and was rewarded with a burst of anger from Gwaethe.

Come, Niko," Kain said, "looks like you've been appointed my guard. Let's use the cavern baths. It could be my last time."

CHAPTER 20

IT was closer to an hour by the time Nikolas and Kain presented themselves outside the small audience hall. Gwaethe and Isiloe were already seated in the waiting room. Isiloe looked daggers at Kain but Gwaethe appeared at ease.

"You will pay for putting her in this position," Isiloe snapped, standing and shoving her face in Kain's.

"Isiloe!" Gwaethe said. "Be seated and remember what I said."

Kain gritted his teeth. "Gwaethe insisted on this. I'd rather she not be here."

"Oh, that would suit you, wouldn't it?" Isiloe said. "You could pretend she did not exist then."

"Do you hear yourself?" Kain asked. "I can't win no matter what I do." He turned to Gwaethe. *Get her under control, or she'll spoil everything.*

I will try, Brother, Gwaethe replied.

You'll have to do better than that.

Nikolas guided Kain over to two chairs against the opposite wall. "A little spitfire, isn't she?" he said.

"Feisty as all hell," Kain said. "I think she hates me."

Nikolas's eyes widened. "You think?"

The door opened and Formosa stepped from the audience chamber. He cast Kain a smug look. "I'd like to see you worm your way out of this, Jazara." He looked at Nikolas. "Be careful whom you associate with, Admiral. I'd hate to see your career suffer further."

Nikolas started to rise but Kain pulled him back into his seat. Formosa smiled and left the room, his boots clicking on the tiled surface.

Kain could feel the tension in his friend's body.

"That bastard has been after me for years," Nikolas said. "I hate to see him elevated at your expense."

"Don't worry, Niko. He'll get his reward eventually. Men like him always do. In the meantime, you can't possibly be implicated in any of this."

"I don't care about that."

"Well, I do," Kain said. "If I go down, I want it to be just me. Not you, and not Alique."

Nikolas slouched back into his chair, arms crossed. "It's not right."

Vorasava was next to enter the waiting room from the audience chamber. "Lady Gwaethe," he said, bowing low. "I trust you're well."

Gwaethe nodded, and only a slight widening of her eyes told Kain she was shocked that Vorasava should speak to her here. He studied his sister. She was beautiful, with a presence that was hard to ignore. Had Vorasava been smitten? Poor bastard if he had. It could never lead anywhere.

Vorasava seemed to shake himself out of his study of Gwaethe, nodded to Nikolas, and turned to Kain. "General, I gave my report which was factual. Of course, I had to mention your alliance with Lady Gwaethe's elven faction. I think you should know that Formosa has raised questions of your parentage and your loyalty to the kingdom."

"Only what I expected of him, but thanks for the warning."

"I can't gauge the mood of the monarchs," Vorasava said, "but I wish you well. You're a decent man."

Kain smiled. "Thank you."

Vorasava glanced at Gwaethe, bowed again, and left the waiting room.

"Wish I'd had three ales instead of two in the baths now," Kain said, straightening his uniform.

The door opened and the steward summoned Kain.

"Call if you need me," Nikolas said.

Kain nodded and entered the audience hall.

King Beniel and Queen Adriana sat on thrones on the dais. A senior page took notes beside them. The steward guided Kain to a chair placed before the monarchs.

Kain stood in front of the chair, awaiting instructions.

"You may sit if you please, General," the king said. He had lost weight since his brother's death but some of the spark had returned to his eyes.

Nothing like a crisis to bring you out of melancholy.

"I'll stand for now, Your Majesty," Kain said.

King Beniel nodded. "First, congratulations on your successful mission. Our objectives have been achieved and the dark elves pushed as far north as we could have hoped. They also must have sustained a blow to their confidence. One would imagine their campaign is in tatters."

"The loss of life was higher on our side than I had hoped, Your Majesty," Kain said, meeting the king's eye. "As for our enemy, they also had a high casualty count. However, we don't know what the total elven numbers are."

"Still, a good result, and the rescue of Lord Zorba will be a boost to the men. Was it ascertained why he was taken?"

"He may just have been in the wrong place at the wrong time, but I believe he was being held as bait and because he would be useful to their cause. The elves have a plan to breed better war horses and Zorba's are the best in the kingdom. Lord Zorba also rode one of his best brood mares, and it's well known that the elves took four stallions in their earlier raid."

"Vorasava reports you have an alliance with an elven faction, and they were helpful in securing victory," King Beniel said, leaning forward on the throne. "How did the alliance come about?"

Kain paused, knowing his next words would decimate his credibility. "I've not told you the truth of my escape from the dark elves when the Zorba estate was originally taken hostage."

"Oh?" the king said. "Then I would hear the truth now."

"Lady Alique and I didn't escape by ourselves, we were rescued by another elven party." Kain closed his eyes, head down, wondering how much of the truth he should reveal. He wasn't ready to divulge his blood links to Gwaethe yet.

"Why would this faction rescue you?" the queen asked.

"Apart from the fact that they seek to disrupt Faenwelar's faction, they wish for the kingdom's help in gaining ascendency. Their leader aims to defeat Faenwelar and unite the elves."

"And why would the kingdom assist this elven leader?" King Beniel asked.

"Because these elves want peace," Kain said. "They're content to live in their northern mountains and leave us be, except for the occasional trading excursion."

"And the women who reside in this palace, who are seated outside this room, represent this faction?" Queen Adriana asked.

Kain nodded. "They do."

King Beniel's eyes widened. "You trust these leaders?"

"I do," Kain said, realizing it was true.

The queen stood. "Why did you feel the need to lie about your rescue from this Faenwelar? I am afraid I do not understand."

Kain's hopes took a dive. The queen had seized on the very issue Kain couldn't explain away. Not without revealing the truth.

The queen continued over Kain's silence. "I cannot understand unless there is much more to this story than you have revealed. Unless there is some truth to the speculation which Lieutenant Formosa brought us?"

The room tilted and Kain sat down heavily in his chair. He couldn't protect anyone, not his parents, Alique, Niko or Gwaethe. Well, Gwaethe wouldn't care. She'd wanted all this out in the open since they first met.

"General?" King Beniel said. "Your silence damns you."

"Gwaethe searched for me as did Faenwelar," Kain said. "They were in a race to see who could find me first. It was why the Zorba estate was taken hostage, to draw me out."

"And why are you so important, General?" Queen Adriana asked.

"Because I have elven blood. It's alleged I'm the son of past elven king, Orionkael Arenil." He was glad he was seated for his legs shook and his stomach wanted to hurl its contents at the feet of the monarchs.

When Kain finally met King Beniel's eyes, the man appeared fit to explode. "General, I chose you to lead my army because I believed you had integrity. Now I find you lied about your rescue from the elves and even about why you were taken in the first place. You are a pawn in an elven power war, and you did not think it important to inform me?"

"I was wrong, Your Majesty," he said quietly.

"How long have you known?" the king asked.

"I discovered my parentage from Faenwelar," Kain said. "At first, I didn't believe it was true, but as time went on, more evidence mounted. When I returned, I confronted my mother."

"She confirmed it?" The queen's eyes were as hard as Beniel's. Neither were pleased he had lied.

Kain nodded. "Orionkael was my father."

"Let me get this straight, General," the king said. "You are heir apparent to the elven throne? Who is Lady Gwaethe? Your lover?"

"She's my half-sister, Your Majesty. We share a father, whom I will never meet." Kain stood and stepped forward. "You must understand, Sire, when the revelations broke, I was under extreme pressure. Lady Alique and I were fighting for our survival. I couldn't believe that everything I had ever known was a lie. Do you think I welcome this news? I'd rather be just plain General Kain Jazara, son of a master craftsman, not a missing elven prince."

"So, you kept the information hidden because you could not accept it?" the queen asked. "When were you going to reveal this to us?"

"Honestly, I wasn't sure I would," he said. "I'm still not sure this will change anything for me."

"Well, General," King Beniel said, "let me make this clear – your elven heritage, and the fact you kept it secret, changes *everything* for me. I cannot have a man I don't trust leading my army. As of now, you are relieved of your position. I will have further decisions to make as to your status in the kingdom, but for now you should remain in the city. Pack your things and move out of your rooms. Formosa will take your place until I make a final decision regarding the leadership of the army."

There was plenty Kain could've said but nothing that would help, nothing that would ease the shame that threatened to cripple him. He saluted the king, bowed low to the queen, and left.

Nikolas leapt to his feet as Kain emerged and Gwaethe sent a strangled plea.

Tell me what has occurred, Brother. You are distressed!

Kain ignored her. "Let's get out of here," he said, glancing at Nikolas. "I'm going to collect my things and then I need a drink."

Kain stared into his ale as he sat with Nikolas at The Soldier's Arms. It wasn't the best tavern in the city, not what he was used to as general, but it suited his new status. The clientele was a mix of enlisted men, mercenaries and shady businessmen. Nikolas looked decidedly uncomfortable there.

"I still don't get why you chose this place," he whispered across the table. "If these men get wind of the reason for your disgrace, they'll kill you."

Kain shook his head. "It's close to the castle. I have to be near her."

"I told you I'd keep you posted," Nikolas said, rubbing his hand through the stubble on his chin and casting his eye across the patrons at the bar. "I'll check on her every day and let you know, only please don't make me come here."

"Don't you see, Niko," Kain said. "It doesn't matter where I am. *I* don't matter."

"This will blow over and you'll be reinstated," he said. "Go and stay with your folks."

"You didn't see the king's face. I've made a fool of him and broken his trust. He'll not have me back. I'll be lucky if he doesn't try me for treason."

"Then perhaps you should lie low for now?"

"I'm not going anywhere until Alique..." The thought of her snatched the breath from his lungs. Her condition was unchanged. He suddenly felt totally devoid of hope. "I have to know how she fares. When I do, then I can make some decisions."

"Gwaethe will want to see you."

"Perhaps," Kain said. "Don't tell her where I am. I need to sort through things without her pressuring me."

Already Gwaethe's messages were a buzz he couldn't quite shut out. She'd completed her audience with Beniel and Adriana. They were polite but it was clear they didn't trust her. Kain hadn't replied and his sister's pleas had become ever more desperate. She was terrified her people would lose their next king, but Kain didn't care. He'd lost almost everything that had been important to him. Right down to his identity.

He shut his eyes and tried his soldier's trick of packing unwelcome thoughts away and shutting the door on them. Gwaethe wouldn't be shut away. She kept forcing her way back at him.

I know what you are trying to do, Brother. It will not work!

Leave me alone! His tone must have been savage for Gwaethe's presence in his mind vanished as though he had clicked his fingers.

Nikolas looked at him strangely. "Are you sure you're all right?"

Kain almost laughed. "I'm very certain I'm not, but don't concern yourself. Once I hear Alique is recovered, I hope I'll know what to do."

"If you're right, you don't have too many options. I don't wish to see you hung for treason."

"I must know Alique's fate. Besides, the king has commanded I stay in the city and, despite what he might think, I'm a man of my word. I'm going to see this through, and no one will push me one way or the other."

Nikolas shook his head. "How did it get this complicated?"

"No point in going down that track. I just have to take one day at a time. You'll let me know of Alique's condition, won't you?"

"I can for the next few days, but after that I'm back to my estate. Merielle is waiting for me."

Kain drew in a breath. "Then I'll get my information some other way. Gwaethe perhaps."

Nikolas nodded. "Listen, I must get to the docks and check on my ship. How about we meet later for some sword practice; take your mind off all of this for a while?"

Kain smiled. "I'll meet you at the barracks."

Kain stalked back and forth across the private dining room in The Soldier's Arms. He felt like a caged lion. He'd received no word of Alique for two whole days and he'd go crazy if he had to wait any longer. Nikolas had returned to his estates and Gwaethe wasn't responding to his messages. That meant either she couldn't hear him, or she was ignoring him. Perhaps she was holding out, to make him desperate. Well, he wasn't going to beg, not yet anyway.

No, he wouldn't ever beg. Gwaethe had to understand that anything he agreed to was on his own terms. If he allowed her to manipulate him it would set a dangerous precedent for the future. But how to get information on Alique? Could he somehow get into the castle and see her? His heart leapt at the thought of being able to touch her again. He could do this if he planned carefully.

CHAPTER 21

ALIQUE wandered through a wasteland seemingly devoid of any living thing, though voices came and went through the fog. One voice was constant or had been in the beginning. She hadn't heard it for some time now and found herself slipping deeper into the mists. It was a deep voice, a loving voice, one full of regret. She knew she should remember to whom the voice belonged, but her thoughts wouldn't order themselves.

Sometimes there was pain, shooting agony that rocketed through her skull and made her wish for release. Then would come the cool moisture on her brow and soft soothing sounds that allowed her to drift back into the mists. Alique lived in a state of permanent thirst. Could the voices not see she needed water? So little water came to her and any offered was greedily consumed, but then she would slip away again.

She had been searching before this happened, that she remembered. Searching for her papa. Had she found him? She seemed to remember his voice, low and sad and hopeless. Why did he despair so? It was frustrating hovering here in this nothingness. Alique was a woman of action, she knew for a fact. She should be up and caring for others.

Was she dead? Was this the place between heaven and hell where you went to be judged? It certainly wasn't heaven, for she would've seen the Goddess by now. It felt more like hell – being unable to communicate with anyone and having voices drop away one by one. What she feared most was the moment when the last voice was silenced and replaced by the void. Yes, it was far closer to hell than anything else.

Goddess, what have I done to deserve this? She hadn't always been virtuous – not ever really – but lately she had tried very hard to be a person her family could be proud of. She had tossed away her girlhood and embraced a career of service. She had stood by her family. She thought she might even have been a little brave, though she couldn't remember specifics. Perhaps it was all a dream.

The man with the deep voice wasn't a dream though. He had been real, and she had loved him. He might even have been part of the reason for her transformation. What was his name? If only she could remember, perhaps she might claw her way out of this place.

"Rest, Alique," a man's voice said. "Don't fight this. You must rest."

No, I can't rest! I must fight! You don't understand. Alique instinctively knew if she didn't fight, this would be the sum of her existence. The pain struck her, and she curled her toes. Someone shoved something in her mouth, something hard, but she pushed it away and screamed. She had to scream, to make a sound, and this time she heard herself, felt herself draw closer to the surface of the wasteland. Perhaps if she continued to scream, she could pull herself out of this?

But a cup was raised to her mouth and a bitter liquid trickled past her lips, just a few sips, which she swallowed obediently, as she had always taken her medicine. Slowly the pain ebbed and Alique slipped away into the gray mists.

* * *

Kain was up before the dawn and washed his face with cold water from the basin in his room. The shock drove the last vestiges of sleep from his brain, not that he'd been getting much sleep. The thought of seeing Alique kept him awake at night, planning how he could visit her. Finally, last night, Gwaethe had sent him one sentence. Alique was unchanged, and all thought she wouldn't recover.

Which only made him more frantic to get to her. Late yesterday, he sent a note to the queen asking for permission to see Alique. His request had been denied. Common sense told him to drop the matter, that he could do nothing for her, and he should be content to remember her as she was – vibrant and quarrelsome. *To hell with common sense!* As long as she was alive, he'd hope, and remember, and long for her.

He crossed to the chest at the end of his bed and opened the lid. He drew out the priest's cassock and held it up. It was dark blue with a hood and should disguise him well enough. He had paid men, still loyal to him, to start a ruckus at the castle gates, so he'd be under less scrutiny when he sought to gain admission. Priests were welcome, and at this time when so many were injured, there were more about.

This had to work because if it didn't, castle security would be tightened, and it would be even more difficult to gain admission. He pulled his breeches and tunic on and slipped the cassock over his head. He wouldn't take weapons into the castle, instead relying on his bare hands for defense if required. There was no point going in armed.

He slipped down the back steps of the tavern and out into the stable yard, exiting through a rear gate into the alley behind the inn. All was quiet, with just enough light to see by. He strode up the alley, heading in the direction of the palace.

Kain soon came within sight of the palace gate and found the group of men who had agreed to create the diversion. He nodded at them and they walked toward the gate, engaging the two guards on duty.

Kain tightened the rope at his waist and lit the incense in the holder that hung from it. *May as well look the part*. He walked slowly toward the increasingly loud ruckus. As he drew level, one of the guards spotted him.

"Good morning, Father."

"Good morning, my son," Kain said, his voice low and husky. "I have been called to prayers for the Lady Alique Zorba. Dawn prayers," he added, to heighten the urgency. All knew that prayers at dawn and dusk were more often answered.

"Yes, Father," the guard said. "A terrible business. So young, she was."

Kain's jaw tightened at the past tense. "We still hope for recovery," he said, working hard to keep the anger from his voice.

"Of course, I meant no disrespect to you or the lady. I'm sure your prayers will be answered."

At that point, the men started pushing and shoving each other and the soldier with Kain ushered him through the gate. "Go in peace, Father," he said before turning back to the mob.

Kain didn't need more urging and rushed through, remembering to slow his strides to a more sedate pace once he was inside the castle grounds. He'd never seen a priest hurry about his business. Avoiding the front entry, he walked around to the servant's door. Another two guards stopped him as he reached for the handle.

"Wait a moment!" the burly one said. "What's your business?"

Kain's heart thudded but he turned to the men and smiled. Not that it was light enough to see the smile, but they would hear it in his voice. "Glad I am you're on duty, my sons," he said. "I would not wish for the good people inside to be unprotected with things as they are."

The men frowned in unison and Kain was suddenly certain he had failed.

"Speak your business, priest," the burly guard snapped. His companion pulled at his sleeve and whispered into his ear. "I'm waiting," he said, tugging his sleeve from the other man's grasp.

"I've been called to dawn prayers for the Lady Zorba," Kain said. "You might have heard she is gravely ill."

"I've heard," the burly man said. "What do you want?"

"I seek admission to the castle," Kain said. "Allow me to pass and I'll be about my task."

The guard's companion spoke up. "We don't want to invite the ire of the Goddess, Enry! Leave the man be."

Enry glared and Kain held his breath. *Don't pick this moment to do your job properly, Enry!*

Enry reached past Kain and opened the servant's entry door. "Go, priest, and make sure you put in a good word for me with the Goddess. I could use some luck."

Kain slipped through the door and closed it behind him, pausing to recall the layout of the palace. Certain chambers were reserved for the care of sick nobility. The Chamber of the Sky was the premiere chamber and Kain would bet that was where Alique was. It was at the front of the castle on the third floor.

He waited a moment longer, mapping out the route in his mind so he could avoid most people. Adjusting his hood, he set off for the upper reaches of the castle.

The halls were almost completely devoid of guests and residents at this hour, with a smattering of servants beginning their day. The smell of baking bread coming from the kitchens was quickly lost as Kain climbed higher. He kept his head down and swung the incense pot, wafting the sickly scent around the hallways. Any servants he did meet stepped out of his way with a muttered "go in peace".

Even the odd noble he encountered avoided him. Priests were mysterious people and while folks respected them, few felt comfortable around them. Kain had long ago decided the clergy reminded the populace of their failings and no one wanted to think about that for too long. He might as well have been invisible to most folk in the castle. If he didn't come across the monarchs or the good doctor, he might just get to see Alique.

He paused outside a door like any other along the hall. This was it. *I think. No point waiting in the hall.* He turned the handle and entered, finding sky blue walls and white drapes that mimicked fluffy clouds. *The Chamber of the Sky.* A faint noise came from the bedchamber adjacent and Kain crouched behind a chair that sat by the fireplace. The murmur of a male voice floated from the room. Doctor Mosard?

Kain settled in to wait until the doctor left. His ears strained to pick up sounds from the adjacent room. Was Alique awake? But there was no feminine voice, and Kain would've heard hers instantly. *Goddess, please send him out so I can see her! I need to touch her, feel the soft skin of her fingers against mine.* He yearned to be in that room. It was torture beyond anything he had experienced in the five days since he had seen her. Tension mounted, his body thrumming with it. He swallowed the moan that rose as the minutes ticked by. They seemed like hours. His body protested the cramped space, but he barely noticed.

And then the good doctor entered the sitting room from the bed chamber, but instead of leaving the rooms, he sat in the very chair behind which Kain hid.

"Goddess, help me," Doctor Mosard said, "I've done all I can and still she doesn't respond."

Kain's heart bled at the despair in Mosard's voice. *You can't give up! You must try everything! Everything!* Kain was helpless, trapped behind the chair, not able to expose himself, even to give the doctor a piece of his mind. If the man was this close to giving up, no wonder Alique still lay in her bed.

While Kain silently railed at the doctor, Mosard rose, squared his shoulders and left the room. Kain stood and hurried to the bedroom door. He froze, not able to believe the sight before him.

Alique was thinner than she'd been five days ago, the skin stretched tight over her cheekbones, her lips cracked and dry. Had everyone given up? Were they all just waiting for the inevitable? Gwaethe had said there was no change. She'd lied or was completely unaware. Alique hovered on the brink of death, her body under-nourished. And Kain had thought Mosard was the answer to her recovery. *I'll kill him!*

All the days he had longed for Alique and wondered how she was, he'd never imagined this. This shell of a woman wasn't the feisty, beautiful, daunting Alique Zorba. He fought down the sob that rushed to his throat. It wouldn't help! But what *would* help?

He forced himself to place one foot in front of the next as he covered the six paces to the bedside. Close up, she looked far worse. *What keeps her alive?* He drew a deep breath and reached for her hand. *Skin and bones!* Her skin was so dry it felt like it might tear if he didn't handle it gently.

"Alique," he said, barely recognizing his own voice. This would never do. "Alique." That was stronger, more like the man she was used to fighting with. "Come back to me."

There was no response, indeed her chest barely rose and fell. He had no medical training, but was certain she was moments away from death. Surely no one could last long in this condition?

He dropped her hand and fetched the water jug. He poured a glass and lifted the cup to her lips, dribbling the liquid into her mouth. *She swallowed!* Goddess, she swallowed it. *Careful now, Jazara, don't overdo it.* He offered her three more sips and placed the cup on the bedside table. She whimpered and his heart leapt with joy.

"Darling," he said, "I'm here and I won't leave you." No matter how difficult, he would see her through this. He wasn't leaving her side.

A pot of honey rested on the bedside table. He placed a scoop in the water and mixed it in, then offered her several sips. When he had finished, she sighed and appeared to relax against the pillows. *At least I've made her comfortable.* Was it his imagination or did her face have more color than when he'd first entered?

But then she seemed to lapse into a deeper sleep where he couldn't reach her. As he bathed her arms and face, Kain pondered how he could stay with her. Was there room under the bed? He ducked down and found just enough clearance underneath for a body to lie. *Yes!* He could do it. He could stay with his love until her fight was over, one way or another. It was obvious she needed him.

After the bathing, Kain applied cream to Alique's skin, rubbing it in until she regained some of the suppleness she'd once had. But though he talked to her throughout the process, she gave no indication of hearing him. He was almost finished when he heard the door to the sitting room open. Replacing the cream pot on the table, he slipped under the bed.

A maid entered the room. She crossed to the larger table and placed something upon it. Light flooded the room as the curtains were swept back. She snuffed the candles, refilled the water jug and left the room.

Kain slipped out from under the bed. A breakfast tray lay upon the table, complete with goat's milk, crusty rolls, butter and creamy porridge. He buttered the rolls and wolfed them down. After a gulp of the milk, he carried the tray over to Alique and placed it on the bed beside her. He trickled honey over the porridge and held the bowl under her nose, allowing the steam to waft across her face. She stirred and moaned.

"Alique, you need to eat something," he said, taking a spoonful of the porridge and offering it to her. She took several mouthfuls before turning her face away.

"You've done well, my love." A small ray of light crept into the darkness in Kain's heart.

All day, he followed this pattern: offering honeyed water and whatever invalid food was brought; bathing her and applying cream to her skin; hiding when the servants or Doctor Mosard came. He ate a little from each tray, always careful to leave the bulk of the food to avoid suspicion. Not once did he hear Doctor Mosard offer Alique anything except for the medication he religiously forced down her throat. Alique had had so much faith in Mosard, but Kain was beginning to wonder if her trust was misplaced.

Alique's parents visited late in the day and almost caught Kain dozing in the chair by her bedside. They said prayers to the Goddess and Lady Zorba senior cried as she bathed her daughter. At least Alique might know her parents prayed for her recovery.

The Zorbas left when the evening meal was brought and Kain slipped from under the bed, hoping for a sign that Alique had been improved by the visit. There was none. He spooned a little soup between her lips and washed it down with goat's milk.

The strain of the day had brought Kain almost to breaking point and he had new respect for Alique. She cared for people day in and day out, watching them get better or die and not showing the pressure of it all. But Kain had never felt this on edge – not when awaiting a battle, when fighting, or even when he was called up to explain his actions to the King. He began to wonder if he could endure the hours and days ahead, and as he wondered, he finally fell asleep.

A nagging pressure in his bladder woke Kain and he lay under the bed, watching the dawn light creep through the curtains. There was nothing for it. He'd have to use the chamber pot, then place it where it would be emptied. Hopefully the servants would think a visitor had relieved themselves. He lay still for another ten minutes, to be sure no one else was in the room, then rolled from under the bed, pulling the empty pot with him. He stood and gazed upon the face of his beloved, still lost in a sleep from which she might never awake.

The day ahead crashed in upon him and he fell to his knees, his face in his hands. Another day like yesterday: tending and feeding her, watching for the slightest sign of improvement or deterioration; trying to push his fears to the back so he could be the man she needed. A crouching sick dread swamped him.

"What are you doing here?" The hissed words were like ice water over his body.

He turned to find Gwaethe glaring and fury replaced the fear. How could she walk these halls freely when he had to skulk around like a criminal? "I could ask you the same thing," he said, not bothering to climb to his feet. He must look a sight, kneeling before this furious elven woman.

"You risk everything," she said.

"Oh," he said, rising slowly, "that again. The whole elven civil war thing. Do you think I care? It's so far down on my list of priorities it doesn't even register."

Gwaethe's eyes widened in shock. He'd probably done irreparable damage to their relationship, but he really didn't care.

"So, this woman is more important than your people?"

"She *is* my people, so yes. Go back to your family and to your life. I have my own concerns."

"You are not the man I thought you were," she said, her body trembling and hands bunched into fists.

"That's not my fault," Kain said. "I've tried to tell you so many times I've lost count. You're focused on what needs to happen in your world and you expect I'll just fall in with you." He softened his voice. "It's not that simple, Gwaethe. I have my own needs and plans and until very recently, they had nothing to do with you."

"And your plans are?"

"I need to support Alique, right now. She was near death when I found her yesterday." He pointed to his love. "I have to try to help."

She offered him a sad smile. "After all this time you still believe she can be saved?"

"I don't know but she sure as hell won't be saved if she starves to death."

"Tuthariel would not allow that to occur," Gwaethe said.

"He hasn't been here, at least not yesterday. I've only seen Mosard and the servants."

Gwaethe frowned. "That is strange."

"Not if Mosard is so conceited he thinks only he knows how to care for Alique," Kain said. "What of the other injured?"

"Most are well now. Tuthariel has been helping with their care."

"Why haven't I seen Julli?" Kain asked.

"Julli has been helping Tuthariel."

This is wrong, so wrong!

"You need to go now, Gwaethe." Kain turned back to the bed and began dribbling honeyed water in Alique's mouth. She looked a little better this morning; her skin had more give and her cheeks had picked up color. He wasn't imagining it.

"I have to know what you intend," Gwaethe said. He couldn't mistake the desperation in her voice.

"I can't give you what you want right now," he said. "I have to see this through, whatever the outcome. Then I'll be able to move forward."

"If you are caught here, you will be thrown in the dungeon," she snapped.

He didn't turn to her. "Don't worry. I don't intend to be locked away. Alique can't afford to lose me yet." There was no noise but Kain knew the exact moment when Gwaethe left because he felt her absence.

She wouldn't give him away, he knew that much, but her continued presence nagged at him, reminded him he had unfinished business with the elves and the kingdom.

When Alique had taken as much water as he could administer, he relieved himself and pushed the pot back under the bed. At a noise from the outer door, he shuffled into his hiding place.

A maid and Mosard entered. The maid went about her duties while the doctor prepared his medications. Kain lay unmoving, anger gripping his gut.

"She looks a little better today, Doctor," the maid said.

"Do you think so?" Mosard asked. "I suppose there's more color in her cheeks. Perhaps the medicine is working."

"I'm sure it is, My Lord," the maid said, "you're a gifted healer."

Gifted healer, my ass!

Seconds later they both left and Kain rolled from under the bed. This was killing him! If he had to listen to much more Mosard-worship... He pushed the anger aside and prepared the porridge the maid had brought. Alique took the food more readily than yesterday. She really was stronger; he wasn't deluding himself. All he had to do was get through another day like yesterday, another day where he didn't know if there would be a tomorrow for Alique.

The candles were lit. Night had fallen and the evening meal had been delivered. Alique ate much of the soup but otherwise there was no change. What was the use of this if her body improved but her mind withered? Gwaethe had sent him several mind messages which he ignored. He could tell she wasn't a patient woman. She'd have to learn forbearance.

All that remained was to turn in, spending another uncomfortable night on the floor under the bed, but that thought wasn't the only thing keeping Kain awake. In this light he could almost forget she was ill, could almost believe she was merely asleep. She was in a way, her brain resting from the rigors of the injuries she'd sustained.

How did she feel in there? He had talked to her all day, telling her about the weather and the small things he could see from her window. He had ranted about Doctor Mosard and the lack of care. He had told her that when she recovered, she could no longer train under the man. He had told her she was so superior to Mosard it didn't matter. There was no response.

She felt pain from time to time because she cried or grimaced. Did she hear him? Was she lying trapped in her body, yearning to communicate? Did he just have to find some way of breaking through to her? But how?

Kain remembered the last time he truly had connected with Alique – the night before he shut himself away to save her. It was the night he had confronted his mother, and he had been drunk. She probably believed he'd forgotten.

"Remember the night in my rooms, beloved?" he asked. "You came to see me because Grif couldn't think of anyone else who could help. You came even though you had no real reason to. I loved you from then. Remember how our bodies felt? We fit together like two halves of a whole and ever since I've been running away. It scared me a little, I think. Did it scare you?"

Kain leaned toward Alique; raised her hand to his lips. He kissed each finger from the tip of her nail down to her palm. "This connection with you is special to me, even if you can't feel or hear. I need to say this, I need to do this, to connect with you." He pushed back her sleeve and kissed the velvety skin of her inner forearm up to her elbow. She whimpered. Was this a response to his kisses?

He stared at her face. Her eyes moved beneath the lids, as though she had forgotten how to open them. He leaned over and kissed her restless eyes through the lids until they stilled, and she sighed. Now he knew she responded to his attentions. If he never had anything else from her, at least he'd know he had reached her in the end; had given her solace.

Kain kissed Alique all down the bridge of her nose. She murmured something and fell silent. He had to chance this, had to give her one last kiss. It had been so long. He allowed his lips to drift over the top of her nose and planted a chaste kiss on her mouth. But the feel of her lips against his undid him and the pressure of his mouth increased, deepening until he felt her lips open. He drew back but Alique's eyes were still closed.

"Don't stop," she whispered, so quietly Kain wondered if he had imagined it.

His mouth fell upon hers, his tongue forcing its way past her lips of its own accord, and then a miracle happened. Alique's arms enfolded his body then slid up so her fingers could trail through his hair.

"You need a trim, General," she said, and Kain wept.

"I knew you'd come for me," Alique said, when Kain had pulled back, frightened he was too heavy for her. "I waited for you. It's the only thing that kept me alive."

He drew her fingers to his lips, the tears still fresh on his cheeks. "You were near death yesterday when I arrived. If I had waited another day…"

"You didn't, beloved," she said, grimacing.

"What's amiss?" he asked.

"I still have frightful headaches."

"You should rest," Kain said.

"Will you be here?"

"I'll be here," he said.

CHAPTER 22

THE next morning, Kain awoke from his best night's sleep in weeks. He lay under the bed in the near dark, trying to come to terms with the events of last evening. Had it all been a dream? Casting caution aside, he rolled from under the bed and stood to find Alique's glorious blue eyes upon him.

"It's not a dream, beloved," she said, smiling.

He took her hand and kissed her longingly on the lips. "I thought I had lost you."

"You never gave up on me, not for one moment," she said, tears in her eyes.

"When you were hurt, a part of me died," he said. "I realized then that our lives are inextricably linked. Even if we're from different worlds, and despite the fact I don't deserve you... Alique, I can't live without you."

"Oh, Kain, I know all of that. I heard your words of love; I think that's what kept me going. And then you went away."

"Not by my own choice, my love. I've been banished from the castle, stripped of my position."

"And yet here you are."

"I had to see you and I'm so glad I did."

She raised her palm to his face and the love in her eyes sent a fire burning through his chest. Hope for their future nearly overwhelmed him, after the bleak days he had endured.

"We'll face whatever the future holds together," she said.

"But first you must heal."

"What's the meaning of this intrusion?" Doctor Mosard said, from the doorway.

Kain, still in his priest's cassock, stood and turned to face him.

"You!" Mosard's voice rang in the chamber. A maid who appeared behind him scurried away.

Kain walked toward the doctor, his fists bunched at his sides. He had waited two whole days for his chance to make the man pay. He held up his right fist and the doctor stepped back. "I should smash this into your sad old face, Mosard," he snarled.

The doctor drew himself up to his full height, which was a little taller than Kain. "I don't know why you would. What have I ever done to you?"

"Your handling of this lady's illness has been nothing short of neglectful. If I have my way, you'll never practice again."

The doctor looked smug. "I hardly think you're in a position to make that threat, General. Or have you had the title stripped from you?"

"I don't care," Kain said. "All I care about is this woman. When I arrived here two days ago, she was near death from starvation and thirst. Her people trusted you. I trusted you! And you almost allowed her to die."

A commanding voice issued from the sitting room and Kain stifled a groan. "Is this true, Mosard?" King Beniel appeared in the doorway to the bedchamber.

"Look, Your Majesty," Mosard said. "Lady Alique has regained her senses and appears to be on the road to recovery."

King Beniel smiled at Alique. "Glad I am to see you back with us, Lady Alique." He glared at the doctor. "Mosard, answer my question! Is what Jazara said true?"

"I gave Lady Alique the best of my care, allowing none other to touch her. I only did what I thought best, what I was trained to do. How could a common soldier possibly understand medical matters?"

Mosard drew himself up as he spoke, wrapping assurance around him like a cloak.

The king frowned. "Very well. Wait for me outside, Doctor."

Mosard, for all his haughtiness, paled several shades before leaving the room.

King Beniel waited until the door clicked shut, then turned to Kain.

"Jazara, what in hell are you doing here?"

Kain drew a deep breath, totally unprepared for this impromptu audience. "I've developed an attachment for this lady, Your Majesty, and was concerned for her. I admit I disguised myself in order to see her one last time. What I found here disturbed me so much, I secreted myself in her room to look after her."

"Extraordinary!" Beniel said. "You mean you've been playing nursemaid under the doctor's nose?"

"I have, My Liege. I could think of no other way to help her."

"And you say Mosard's care was suspect?"

"I believe it was, Your Majesty," Kain said.

The king stepped further into the room toward Alique. "And what do you say to all this, My Lady?"

"I was thirsty, Your Majesty, but what I really missed was Kain's voice. I believe I had given up and it was his care that drew me back. Perhaps Doctor Mosard lost faith in my recovery as well." She smiled. "I can't blame him for that."

"You are most forgiving, My Lady," King Beniel said.

"How can I not forgive when I'm so lucky, Your Majesty," Alique said. "Kain's love gave me strength when I was injured, and he brought me back from a darkness I thought I'd never escape."

"This is most irregular," Beniel said, turning to Kain. "People banished from the castle do not usually sneak back in and hide themselves away. In this case, I find myself glad you defied me." He reached out and shook Kain's hand, then hurried from the room, his eyes suspiciously moist.

Alique smiled at Kain. "I think that went rather well."

Kain shook his head. "He'll be back, probably with the guard."

"I won't let them throw the man I love in prison. Whatever it takes, I'll see you restored if it's what you want."

He didn't care about his career. "You really love me?"

Alique smiled and gripped his hand. "I love you more than life itself and I've come back from death to you. I promise to love and protect you all of our days."

Kain's heart did a tumble at her words. Could this really happen? Could he, a disgraced army general, make this magnificent woman happy? Could he be everything she needed? "I love you, Alique, and I'll spend the rest of my days showing you how much."

He pulled her into his arms and despite her frail form, she gripped his body as though she'd never let him go.

"Make love to me," she said. "I yearn to be one with you."

"Not yet, my darling," he said, against her lips, "but soon, very soon." He crushed her against him, breathing in the scent that was Alique. From the depths of despair had come this moment of hope and love. Kain vowed to nurture it until death parted them.

EPILOGUE

THREE months had passed and Alique was happier than she'd been her whole life. As her twenty-second birthday approached, she looked forward to starting a new life with Kain. The first stage of her recuperation had been spent at the castle, but after a week Kain had moved her to the Zorba estate and the care of her parents.

He had stayed in the city in his temporary digs and traveled out to the farm every second day to visit with her. His ban on entering the castle had been lifted by the king, but His Majesty was yet to make a final decision regarding Kain's future in the army. And so, while they reveled in each other's company, there had been only brief moments of intimacy.

Today, Alique accompanied Kain to a farm on the southern outskirts of Wildecoast city. Julli had come along as chaperone. The maid was a vital part of Alique's new life, supporting her when her healing body failed to respond to her many demands. It was frustrating when she couldn't tie a ribbon or put on her shoes, but Julli was always there to help, with a calm voice and an open heart.

The estate they traveled to had belonged to a disgraced earl, and then been passed to Nikolas by the queen. He, in turn, had gifted the land to Kain. Alique hoped it would enable Kain to begin again, to salvage some pride and take his mind off the kingdom and his elven heritage.

Gwaethe and Kain rode up front while Alique and Julli traveled in the carriage with Kain's things. She still couldn't come to terms with Kain's elven sister, but had begun the long road to accepting the woman. Gwaethe, in turn, had tried hard to befriend Alique – she had to admit. It did seem Gwaethe's people wanted peace within the kingdom, desiring only to unite the elves and then live quietly in the northern reaches of Thorius.

Over the preceding three months, Alique had watched Kain grow closer to his sister. She had learned they spoke to each other over distance with the aid of the amulet and the ring. It made her a little jealous. She had also been distressed to discover that trees talked to Kain and had named him a forest mage – an elven magician not known amongst the *Lenweri* for centuries.

It appeared Kain wasn't walking away from his heritage any time soon. Alique had to admit the future scared her, promising changes she wouldn't welcome. But with Kain by her side, she'd face the changes and forge a life together. It just remained to be seen how that life would look.

Just then, a wooden gate appeared. They veered off the road and entered a shady lane overhung by willows. The drooping leaves brushed the coach and she laughed with delight. "This is wonderful!"

"I thought you'd like these trees." Kain had dropped back beside the coach and wore a big grin.

Alique felt she was in a magical fairy tale and anticipation built at what the manor might look like. She didn't have long to wait. At the end of the lane was a large open space with the house as backdrop. It had two stories and two wings. The family wing lay to the left and the servant wing to the right.

The white stone walls beckoned her, and she left the carriage and entered via the golden oak doors. Immediately, she veered to the right entering a broad hallway with spacious rooms to either side. Excitement bubbled inside as she retraced her steps to the entry and took the central staircase to the upper level. The layout was much the same as the lower floor.

Kain trailed along behind her, watching her reaction. "Is it suitable, darling?" he asked.

"Suitable?" Alique said. "It's magnificent! I can see us here, raising our family and serving the kingdom."

He frowned. "I can see that too, but I want you to establish a hospital here. I thought the servant wing would be ideal."

Alique's breath caught. *My own hospital?* She threw her arms around Kain, inhaling his scent and desperate to show him how much she loved his suggestion. Loved him. "I couldn't think of anything better."

He took her hand and led her across to the other wing. The first door they came to on the right opened on a huge chamber with ceiling to floor views of the property. Alique gasped as she took in the rolling hills and the tree-lined banks of a stream. She turned to Kain. "This is your suite?"

He nodded. "*Our* suite."

Alique squeezed his hand. "I love it, and it's so close to the hospital wing." She raised an eyebrow. "Do you have any other surprises I should know about?"

Kain's pupils dilated and Alique smiled at him. "Show me."

He led her through the sitting room of their chamber and across to the door into the bedroom. It hosted a huge four-poster bed draped in ivory satin.

Alique squealed and clutched at Kain, drawing him closer to the bed. "Let's christen it now, beloved. We've waited so long," she said, pushing him down on the covers and laying herself over the top of him. He was ready for her, if that bulge was anything to go by. She kissed him with all the love in her heart. His lips parted and Alique needed no more invitation to enter and explore his mouth. She moved her kisses to his ears and neck and Kain groaned.

"Not yet, my love," he said, breathing hard.

"But we've waited so long, darling," she said between kisses. "There's no more reason to delay."

"There's one reason," he said, grasping her shoulders and rolling her to the side.

"No reason I can think of, love." She reached for his face, intent on dragging him back to her mouth. Then she froze, her heart thudding a dull stony beat. "Unless you've had second thoughts?"

Kain shook his head. "How could you ask? I love you."

She heaved a huge sigh. "Then kiss me!"

He broke free and stood up, the bulge in his breeches evidence of his desire. *Thank the Goddess! He's behaving most curiously! I believed he'd be hot for me after these months of deprivation and still he delays.*

Kain cleared his throat. "I've another surprise for you and after that, perhaps we can return to this moment."

She shook her head. "I want you now."

"Come with me, my darling," he said. "One more detail needs addressing and we can start our life together."

Despite her mood fast turning cranky, Alique decided to humor him. She rose from the bed, straightened her gown and her hair and allowed Kain to take her hand. He led her out of the chamber and back down the central staircase to the entry. Julli and Gwaethe awaited them, huge smiles on their faces, and with them was a priest.

Alique let go of Kain's hand and went to greet the cleric. "Hello, Father, can I help you?"

The priest bowed. "My Lady, I am Father Edestino and I am here to celebrate your marriage to Kain Jazara."

Alique's hands flew to her mouth and she turned to find Kain with an uncertain smile on his face. "A wedding? Today?" she asked.

Kain took her hands. "If you'll have me, Alique. I'd very much like to marry you. I know you'll want a proper wedding with our family, but I hoped that in the meantime this would suffice."

"Are you certain?"

"More certain than I've been about anything," he said.

He still looked unsure of her answer. After all they'd been through, all he had done for her, he still doubted his value in her life. Perhaps he always would, but there was one way to show him today how much she loved him. Well, perhaps there would be other ways later.

Alique smiled up at him. "I love you, Kain, and it would make me happier than you can ever imagine accepting you as my husband." She placed a chaste kiss on his lips, a promise of things to come, and turned back to Father Edestino. "Come along, Father, you will marry us right here, right now, with Julli and Lady Gwaethe to witness."

Julli clapped her hands, clearly delighted at the sudden nuptials. Gwaethe stepped closer, giving Alique a bouquet of flowers from the garden and placing a single rose in Kain's buttonhole.

Moments later, Kain and Alique were husband and wife, ready to begin life in their new home. As she looked up at her husband, Alique truly knew it wasn't possible to be any happier than she was, in this moment, with this man. She couldn't wait for tomorrow.

THE END

GLOSSARY

Places

Kingdom of Thorius (Thor- ee- us) -the kingdom of men which encompasses the King's seat of Wildecoast and the Prince's seat of Brightcastle, along with other smaller towns

Wildecoast (Will – dee – coast) -the capital city perched on the top of a cliff overlooking the sea on the east coast of Thorius; climate is mild but windy

Brightcastle - large inland town surrounded by forests and farms, three to four days ride west of Wildecoast

Amitania (Am – it – ay – nia) or *Elvandang* (Elle – van – dang) in elvish - the deserted city north of the Usetar Mountain Range in northern Thorius; once a thriving city; disputed ownership between elves and man

Usetar Range (You – set – ar) -the mountain range running across the northern parts of Thorius

People

Lenweri (Len – weir – ee) -the elven people who are tall and elegant with black skin and pointed ears and mainly dark hair; live in mountainous forests north and west of Thorius, in places encroaching onto Kingdom lands; also known as dark elves

Sis Lenweri - the faction of dark elves that wishes to take the kingdom of Thorius back from men

Defender - a race of shapeshifters who are created to defend those in danger; they sense those in need of their help; a Defender can shift into animal form and the ability is inherited through family lines

Characters

General Kain Jazara (Cane Jazz-arra) – general of the King's Army and hero of The Elf King's Lady

Lady Alique Zorba (Al-eek Zor-bah) – heroine of The Elf King's Lady; Ramón Zorba's younger sister and one of the queen's ladies-in-waiting

Lord Nikolas Cosara (Nikolas Cos-arra) – admiral in the King's Navy; he is cousin to Queen Adriana and best friend of Kain Jazara

Lady Merielle Cosara – wife of Nikolas Cosara; was once a mermaid

Princess Gwaethe Arenil (Gway-eth-a Ar-en-ille) – half-sister to Kain Jazara

Isiloe (Iz-ill-oh) Gwaethe's cousin and second-in-command of Lenweri forces

Princess Alecia Zialni (Al – ee – sha Zee – al – nee)) – of Brightcastle; the king's niece and daughter of Prince Jiseve Zialni.

Vard Anton - a shapeshifting Defender; once army captain of Brightcastle; absconded from Brightcastle with Princess Alecia

Prince Jiseve Zialni (Jiss – eve Zee – al – nee) – was next in line to the throne of Thorius, younger brother of the King; father of Alecia Zialni

Lady Benae Branasar (Ben-ay Bran-a-sar) – married to Ramón Zorba and joint steward of Brightcastle

Ramón Zorba (Rah – mon Zor – bah) - Lord of Wildecoast and steward of Brightcastle; his family have an estate south of Wildecoast; brother of Alique Zorba

King Beniel Zialni (Ben – ee – elle Zee – al – nee) - King of Thorius; lives in Wildecoast; older brother of Jiseve Zialni and uncle of Alecia Zialni; married to Adriana

Queen Adriana - wife of the King; lives in Wildecoast; Alecia's aunt; Nik's cousin

Doctor Achan Mosard (Uck - ahn Mow - sard) – court physician in Wildecoast

Lady Diseta (Diss-etta) – oldest of the Queen's Ladies-in-Waiting and their trainer

Lady Krina (Kreena) – youngest of the ladies-in-waiting

Lady Emmella - one of the ladies-in-waiting and Alique's friend

Yaral Zorba – Alique's father; landholder, forester and horse-breeder

Nyon (Nie-on) – Alique's older sister, married to a ship builder in Wildecoast

Guile (Geel) and Astelle Jazara – Kain's parents; Guile is a Master timber craftsman

Jans Jazara – Kain's younger brother; works with his father

Jer Blas – sergeant in the Wildecoast army

Mazesta – sergeant in the Wildecoast army and head of Alique's bodyguard

Darin and *Atan* – scouts in the Wildecoast army

Sergeant Grif Tyne – gate sergeant at Wildecoast and Nik's friend

Elven Characters

King Orionkael Arenil (Or-ee-on-kale) – once king over all the Lenweri; Gwaethe and Kain's father

High Prince Elvor Faenwelar (Fen-well-ahr) – leader of the Sis Lenweri

Prince Niel Gorin (Ny-elle Gore-in) – son of Faenwelar

Celri – aide to Prince Gorin

Failora (Fay-laura) – attendant to Faenwelar

Tuthariel (Too-thar-ee-elle) – elven healer

About the Author

Bernadette Rowley is a lover of epic fantasy who is a veterinarian by day and an author by night. She is currently published in the genre of high fantasy romance with eight books, all set in her fantasy world of Thorius.

When she was a young teenager, an aunt gave her a copy of The Sword of Shannara by Terry Brooks and Bernadette has lived in various fantasy worlds ever since. It's no surprise that her chosen genre when writing romance is fantasy.

"I can see these settings so vibrantly in my mind and hope my readers can too."

But Bernadette has no desire to spoon-feed her readers by laboriously describing her fantasy settings. She would rather the reader use their own imagination.

Along with sword and sorcery, dashing heroes and stunning heroines, this author includes strong healing themes in many of her books- an element central to her everyday job.

"When I started writing the Queenmakers Saga, I never imagined my day job would force its way into my stories as it has."

And of course, there are animals, especially Bernadette's beloved horses.

Bernadette lives in Brisbane, Australia, with the four heroes in her life- her husband Michael and three grown sons.

Connect with the Author

Website: www.bernadetterowley.com
Facebook: www.facebook.com/bernadetterowleyfantasy
Twitter: www.twitter.com/bt_rowley

www.ingramcontent.com/pod-product-compliance
Lightning Source LLC
Chambersburg PA
CBHW071517110726
47908CB00003B/868